THE
BURNING

THE BURNING

S. O. ESPOSITO

misterio press

For Sadie, may you find both the fire & the love.

*"To every crime, there should be a witness.
Someone to care, to cry, to choke on their outrage.
Someone who will then rise up and use that fire
like an alchemist to make the world a safer place.
I'm hoping that witness will be you."*

-Alice

ONE

The irony alone could make a mad woman out of me. When I think about how Jake believed he was saving me—he liked the idea of being my knight in shining armor, rescuing me from the rusty trailer park full of meth addicts and sex offenders and tucking me safely up in a tower like a fairy princess—while all along I'd carried her, harbored her within me like a virus, brought her into our home. Neither of us was aware of her, waiting in the shadows to burn our new fairytale life to the ground. Neither of us saw the darkness coming.

Our "tower" is a five-million-dollar condo in Sarasota, Florida, on a twenty-two acre peninsula called Golden Gate Point. The peninsula is a coveted waterfront community, once owned by the circus magnate, John Ringling. I find this ironic now, too, as my life has quickly spiraled into its own miniature version of a media circus. I've been reduced to gossip and speculation, the thing splashed over the internet which people pass back and forth over roasted chicken, fodder for armchair detectives. I am *the* news.

So where to begin? That's always the hard part, isn't it? You have to pick an appropriate moment, like

1

finding the frayed end in a tangled ball of yarn, and let it lead the way. I guess I'll start with this: My name is Alice Brown-Leininger. I'm a thirty-year-old mother of two, and I'm in deep, deep trouble.

They say there are two sides to every story and then there's the truth. I can only give you my side and hope that it's the truth. But who knows. I haven't been present for large chunks of my life. How is that possible, you ask? Asking that question led me to the place where I am now … the forensic wing of Bayside Psychiatric Hospital.

Being committed and separated from my children has always been the thing I've feared most. When it came to pass, it was almost a relief. Like an exhale, a letting go. Knowing the worst has happened, the monster in my rearview mirror has me in its jaws and my only choice is surrender. Pretty freeing.

Of course, that relief has faded quickly. Now that I must inhale each new painful, bleach- and-urine-scented moment here at Bayside, enduring a lonely month-long evaluation. One that will tell the courts whether I'm fit to stand trial on charges of first degree murder and arson.

Either way, I must warn you, this story won't have a happy ending. I will either be deemed incompetent to proceed to trial and spend the rest of my days within these walls, or I'll be found competent and spend them behind bars.

I haven't decided which fate would be worse. As it is now, I'm surrounded by electric barbed wire fencing and am housed in a unit with twenty other beds and group showers. I may have more privacy in prison. Maybe even coffee.

Either way, being there to tuck in my kids at night, pressing my face to their silky hair, hearing them laugh, watching them discover the world, this is all just a memory for me now. Moments blown away like dandelion seeds, a breath and a wish. My sweet, sweet fairytale life has dissolved into the darkness. All that's left for me is grief. Of course, it's probably what I deserve. Now that I've learned I was the monster all along.

TWO

Two Months Ago...

Rena Flores lay in a donated coffin under a bright blue Florida sky, the name of her pimp tattooed on the back of her neck. Her final resting place was a crude, unstained pine box. Floating above her were thin wispy clouds, delicately spun ... like angels gently falling apart.

As I stood beneath the same azure sky, there were two injustices I couldn't let go of: That it should be possible to bury a seventeen-year-old girl on such a flawless day and that she'd been sent from this world branded like livestock.

The rage sparked and swelled. I watched it inwardly even as outwardly my attention was fixed on my friend, Angeline. Eyes hidden behind dark glasses, she tossed a wilted, white rose onto Reyna's coffin. The others followed her lead.

It wasn't my own rage, this I was sure of. I was still numb. Still unable to process the death. This rage felt foreign and primal—like it was born from the same infinitely hot, dense furnace that birthed time and space. Only whatever burned within me didn't want to create anything but instead destroy everything. It was an inferno that, if allowed to be expressed, would scorch the world, turn it to ash. I could taste the ashes of the world on the back of my tongue.

Sometimes when this rage flared, I blacked out. But mercifully I was still present. By anchoring myself to the coffin, the sky, concentrating hard on the faces around me and the pain from the thorn on the rose I was clutching, I was able to press myself flat against the page of my story and not disappear.

I moved my hand to rest on the hot core, the womb of this rage, burning beneath my red sleeveless Armani dress, between the thin silver belt and my ribcage. I actually hadn't realized I'd worn the red dress until I happened to glance down in the car. I'd been startled by my inappropriate choice. Actually I couldn't remember getting dressed at all. These memory lapses were happening more frequently, but I had more important things to worry about today.

Jake shifted his hand to my lower back and rubbed lightly. This had been our dance for almost a decade, though I'm not sure he was even aware of what he was doing. He may've been reaching out from instinct. We'd never spoken of it. Either way, he felt the disturbance within me on some level. I was sure of it.

I was concentrating on the Project Freedom director's clear voice. Veora was reading a Henry Wordsworth Longfellow poem aloud: *The Reaper and the Flowers*. It was nice, her voice. It held the kind of strength these situations called for.

The cemetery was bordered by heavy traffic on Route 41, so car exhaust mingled with the sickly sweet smell of funeral roses. The sun was already blazing. Outwardly I was calm and in control, but a trickle of sweat rebelled and rolled between my shoulder blades.

Absentmindedly, I fingered the hammered-gold bracelet on my wrist and frowned. Another thing I hadn't remembered buying. I pushed away that thought as my mind drifted to the first time I'd met Reyna nine months ago. I'd been playing chauffeur that day, driving her to a dentist appointment and then to check in with her case manager. She was all lanky limbs, shiny eyes, full of newborn hope, battered but not broken.

I want kids someday. Two girls. Eve and Sunday. I'll raise 'em with a firm hand, but they'll for sure know they're loved. Kids should know they're loved no matter what.

It had touched me deeply, that after everything she'd been through, and the addiction she was fighting, she still had hope. She had a vision of something good for herself. I wished so hard she could hold those two babies in her arms someday, but she'd been robbed of her *someday*.

A different kind of disturbance rose up. One outside of myself. Black birds took off in flight. Carmen had been Reyna's best friend, and her choking sobs finally broke free, rising into one long, haunting wail. She collapsed on the sparse, sandy ground beside the grave.

Angeline and I rushed to lift the grief-stricken young woman from her bare knees.

"Oh, Carmen. We've got you, babe." Angeline wrapped one arm around the grieving twenty-two-year-old's waist, another cradled her elbow. I mirrored her on Carmen's right. Three other women from Project Freedom converged, whispering their support and rubbing her back. One of the women picked up Carmen's discarded flip-flop and slipped it back onto her bare foot. Carmen was too drunk with sorrow to resist or notice.

The three men present—Jake, my best friend, Rhys, and Angeline's husband Tai—knew Carmen wasn't comfortable around men, so they hung back.

"Rey Rey," Carmen wailed in that way humans do when their heart's been turned inside out. "Rey Rey, you didn't deserve this."

It hit me as I tightened my arm around Carmen's waist that she was the only person here who'd truly known the girl in the coffin. A small group of women from Project Freedom were here to pay their respects, women who'd worked hard the last four months to get Reyna out of the life of prostitution and who'd failed. Their faces all bore the pain of that failure.

My friends and I, who'd all worked with Project Freedom in some capacity had grown fond of Reyna, but we hadn't really known her. Not like Carmen—the one person on earth who'd been in the trenches with her and truly loved her.

I moved my attention back to Carmen. Her grief churned with sour-milk-guilt and rolled off her in hiccupping waves.

Do not despair, Alice. She is the eternal I Am.

I bristled at the thought. *She was robbed of her life!* Great. Now I was arguing with myself. My gaze caught on a white rose lying crushed on the ground. I tried to anchor myself. My heartbeat doubled, grew wings and threatened to burst through my chest. Things were starting to move away. *No. No. No.*

"I'll kill him!" Carmen suddenly screamed at the top of her lungs. The birds fell silent. "You bastard, you bastard, I'll kill you!" she screamed again.

"The police will find him, Carmen. He'll pay for this," one of the women from Project Freedom offered, an edge of panic to her voice.

A harsh laugh tore itself from Carmen's throat, ripping skin and exposing bone from the sound of it. Her voice raw, she whispered through a veil of hatred and certainty. "Men like him don't pay for anything. 'Cept their high price dope and us."

And then it happened. Carmen collapsed forward, the weight of her grief and rage too heavy for one to bear and I saw it. A greenish-gray slug against the dark skin on Carmen's neck, a symbol of ownership: DRAC

A tidal wave of rage rushed through me. The wings opened and carried me away.

❦

That night, the scream of a siren startled me awake. I stared at the scene in front of me, blinking and disorientated. *Am I dreaming?* The smell of burning plastic, paint and rubber filled my car. Coughing, I flipped the vents closed. Nope, definitely real smoke.

I stared in disbelief at the car engulfed in flames in a driveway three houses down from where I was parked. Red and orange flames danced higher and higher above the car, licking the air. Black, angry smoke crept over the yards. I glanced behind me at the unfamiliar road, the block houses.

"Where am I?" The digital clock said 1:16 a.m.

What am I doing here in the middle of the night?

The shriek of the siren rose in volume. I could now see the flashing red lights bouncing through yards of the adjacent street. People who were clustered in the street, some in bathrobes, scurried to the side as the firetruck turned the corner and roared toward us. With a shaky hand, and without flipping on the headlights, I shoved my SUV into drive and made a U-turn, pulling away slowly to keep from attracting attention. I drove until I hit a familiar street, my breath coming in short gasps. I kept the panic at bay with the mantra, "You're almost home. You're almost home."

Still trembling, I drove into the garage beneath our condos and shut off the engine.

THREE

From as far back as I could remember—which was my thirteenth birthday—all I'd ever wanted was to be a mother. It had been my one wish as I'd blown out the used stub of a candle my foster mother had jammed into a Little Debbie chocolate cupcake. No one tells you how much heartache the job comes with.

"Good morning. Who's ready for the big day?" Jake placed his briefcase on the marble kitchen counter and held out his arms.

"Me!" Adelyn, our five-year-old, squealed and ran into them as he knelt down. "Mommy made us magic pancakes to give us bravery today." Her eyes—the same gold-flecked, glass-bottle green as mine—looked up at me as she grinned and tried to whisper. "Her secret ingredient is chocolate chips but don't tell."

Jake chuckled, gave his daughter a squeeze and kissed her forehead. "Don't worry, princess. Daddies are good at keeping secrets."

The hair on my arms prickled. I glanced sharply at my husband. *Is Jake keeping secrets from me?* No. I shook off the suspicion. I was projecting my own guilt. The one keeping secrets was me. *Like what was I doing in that strange neighborhood last night?* Jake hadn't even stirred when I'd slipped back into bed.

Jake held Addie out in front of him and eyed her cartoon, fish-print tights and pink tulle skirt, which clashed monumentally with her red hair and red t-shirt with the embroidered Montessori school logo. "Did Mommy let you dress yourself for your first day of kindergarten?"

"Yep. I'm a big girl now."

"Addie, will you please go tell your brother it's time to go." I finished zipping up the lunchbox I'd packed and avoided eye contact with Jake. He'd be able to tell something was wrong, and I wasn't ready to have that conversation.

After Addie skipped out of the room, Jake strolled around the kitchen counter. Slipping his arms around me from behind, he draped my mass of dark hair to one side and kissed me on the neck. A tiny jolt zipped up my spine. "You know Aurora can pack their lunches. It's kind of in the nanny job description to feed the children."

A shimmer of resentment surfaced, but I pushed it aside because it was silly. Jake's motivation has always been to make sure we were all taken care of. Not just the children, but me, too. I had no right to resent him for hiring a nanny to take the pressure off me.

I'd lost that right seven years ago after Charlie had been born and I'd suffered horrible postpartum depression. That's what the doctors told me I'd had, anyway. I couldn't tell them what was really going on inside of me. Though, maybe it was time for me to be brave, too.

"I don't mind." I twisted in his arms and fingered his perfectly knotted burgundy tie, keeping my eyes cast down. "One day they'll realize the cool kids don't bring packed lunches, and it'll just be one more thing I can't do for them."

"Hey." Jake lifted my chin with his index finger and pressed a light kiss on my lips. "Yes, they are growing up fast, but I'll always need you." He kissed me deeper and then rested his forehead against mine. "And if you really want to pack me a lunch for the office, I won't stop you."

A small puff of laughter—of concession—escaped my lips. I blinked back the tears threatening to spill over. "Not quite the point, Mr. Leininger."

"Daddy!" Charlie came barreling into the kitchen wearing a backpack that was almost the size of him and trailing his little sister. "Are you driving us to school?"

Jake released me and squeezed Charlie's shoulder. "Can't, buddy, have an early meeting today. But I can't wait to hear all about your first day as a second grader at dinner, all right?"

I smiled down at my son, who—unlike my daughter—had insisted I pick out his shorts this morning to make sure they matched his collared school shirt. For better or worse, he'd inherited his dad's desire for perfection. "All right, time to go."

———

My mind felt crowded as I made the short drive to Rhys's house in the Laurel Park Historic district. Crowded with the goodbyes I'd exchanged with the kids, as I'd fought back the irrational panic of letting go and walked them to their classrooms at Garden Montessori. Crowded with anxiety over my blackouts and whether it was time to bring them up to Jake. Crowded with fleeting thoughts of death and funerals, wondering how Carmen was holding up and how many girls would show up today, and how many who showed up would make it out or end up in a box in the ground like Reyna.

With a headache blooming, I parked my white Range Rover Sport against the curb in front of Rhys's house so I wouldn't block the unfamiliar, black sports car in his driveway. I juggled a paper bag of bagels in one arm as I pushed open the fence gate and crossed the patio.

At the front door, I took a deep breath and tried to ignore the thumping behind my eyes. I needed to be strong for the women today. None of them had attended Reyna's funeral. Not that I blamed them. They would've imagined themselves in that pine box all too easily.

"Hello?" I called into the quiet first floor. "Rhys? You up?" I glanced around the empty studio and heard a scraping coming from the kitchen. Slipping off my flip-flops, I crossed the teak wood floor.

Rhys lived in a live-work zone of the arts district so the bottom floor was set up as a spacious photography studio, with a seating area in the back and a kitchen and half-bath sectioned off to the left. A spiral metal staircase led upstairs to two bedrooms, a large living room area and a full bath. His house always smelled lightly of motor oil and leather, which made me wonder if he rolled his beloved Harley into the studio at night for safekeeping.

"Oh, hello. Sorry, thought you were Rhys in here." I dropped the bag of bagels on the kitchen counter and held out a hand to the lanky, blond twenty-something, who was stirring creamer into a travel mug of coffee. "Hi, I'm Alice."

As he took my offered hand, ice-blue eyes swept over me curiously. He looked like something out of a Renaissance painting. "Lucas. He's in the shower. Should be down soon. I've gotta run actually." He tucked his black t-shirt halfway into belted jeans and grabbed the travel mug. "It was nice to meet you, Alice."

"You too." I watched him leave. It didn't go unnoticed that he didn't say, "See you around," or any other indication he had future plans with Rhys. I shook my head, poured myself a cup of coffee.

I was resting a hip against the black marble counter, sipping strong dark roast, when Rhys appeared on the staircase. He paused to slip his arms into a salmon-colored button-down shirt, his inky head of curls damp from the shower.

"Good morning," he said, dropping a kiss on my forehead. He smelled of the sandalwood cologne I'd bought him for Christmas, and his dark eyes were dancing with humor. The corner of his mouth ticked up. "I know that look. You must've crossed paths with Lucas."

"Yes, he seems very nice." I grabbed another white ceramic mug from the cupboard and poured him coffee. He retrieved a jar of homemade almond milk from the frig. I crossed my arms, watching the swirl of white milk lighten his coffee.

"I can feel you judging me," he said without malice.

I sighed. "I'm not. You know I'm not. I'm worried about you."

Nodding, he let his head drop and thoughtfully began buttoning up his shirt. "I know, Alice." As he rolled up the sleeves, he met my gaze. His eyes were full of old pain, old ghosts. "But, not all of us can have the fairytale. Not all of us are meant to be swept up into a five-million-dollar tower on Golden Gate Point to live happily ever after."

I ignored his effort to deflect the conversation back to me. This was serious. "Self-imposed loneliness is not fate ... it's punishment, self-flogging."

Turning away, his shoulders stiffened. He took a sip of coffee. "Don't worry about me. I'm rarely alone."

"Alone and lonely are two different things and you know it." I was too full of my own anxiety to be gentle right now. Watching my best friend forego an actual relationship for a parade of one-night stands was getting unbearable.

He shot me a dazzling smile. "That's why I have you." Then his smile faded and his eyes narrowed as he really looked at me. "You okay?" He sat his mug down and stepped closer. "You left the funeral yesterday without saying goodbye."

"Did I?" I choked out before I could stop myself. My question startled Rhys and I knew I'd made a mistake.

He pulled back in surprise. "You don't remember?"

I opened my mouth. This felt like a fork in the road. I could lie, or I could lean into him and be honest. My hesitation was stretching into the kind of silence which can no longer hide a lie. The choice was made for me.

He nodded. "You don't remember." He grabbed my hand and led me around the counter to sit on a bar stool. Perched on the edge of the stool in front of me, he held both my hands. "Spill it. What's going on?"

My bottom lip trembled. If I said it out loud, a whole life of half-truths and carefully constructed cover-ups would fall on me like an avalanche. Would probably crush me. My world would definitely never be the same. I found myself curling protectively inward, turning from the image of the car on fire. "Nothing really. Sometimes I just don't remember things. I guess I block them out when they're too painful."

"Sometimes? This has happened before?"

Damn he's too perceptive. Panic clawed at my mind. My breathing grew ragged, like an animal caught in a trap. "No. Yes ... I mean, I'm not crazy or anything."

And there it is.

I began to tremble as I realized this is what I was afraid of. This was the monster I've refused to make eye contact with. The fact that I might be crazy. That they would find out, lock me up and take my kids away.

"Well, of course you're not crazy." Rhys rubbed his thumbs over the tops of my hands. "Hey, look at me." I lifted my teary eyes. My breathing slowed as I anchored myself in his caring gaze. "But, if you're having blackouts, you should probably talk to the doctor about that. You could be having mini seizures brought on by stress or something scarier like a brain tumor. You can't mess around with stuff like this, Alice."

I found myself nodding with relief. Of course. It could just be something physically wrong. Why did I immediately jump to being crazy?

You know why.

"You're right. I will. I'll make an appointment this week." I shivered as the air conditioning kicked on. My whole body had broken out in a sweat, soaking my thin cotton dress.

"I'm holding you to that."

My comeback was interrupted by Angeline's arrival.

"Hellooo!" Angeline's voice rang out from the front of the house.

"Back here." Rhys released my hands after a final squeeze.

Angeline appeared. A large, brown cloth bag embroidered with a bright orange elephant was slung over one shoulder, and she was cradling a crock pot in her arms. "Take this bloody thing, will you," she growled. "I don't know what I was thinking."

Rhys slipped the ceramic pot out of her arms with a chuckle. "Smells delicious. Is that ginger?"

"Yeah, ginger, garlic, coconut milk. My mum's rice and peas recipe." Angeline hugged me, her gold bangles sliding down her arm and tinkling in my ear. "Hello, sweets." Then she dropped her cloth bag on the counter with a thud. "Mum considered it a traditional Afro-Caribbean food and made us eat it every Sunday. If you ask me, I think it was just cheap. Anyway," she lifted a Tupperware container from the bag, "I've made some jerk chicken to go with it. Thought the girls might enjoy something different today. And if not," she peered into the bag I'd brought with a dimpled grin. "They have bagels and lox." Cocking her head, she stared at me with inquisitive, whiskey-colored eyes. "You left the funeral suddenly yesterday."

I nodded, shooting a guilty look at Rhys. "I wasn't feeling well."

Angeline followed my glance. "That what she told you, too?"

Popping a piece of jerk chicken he'd snuck from the container into his mouth, he grinned back at her. "What makes you think I got up in her business like you do?"

Angeline shook her head with mock offense. Her shoulder-length corkscrew curls—which were newly tipped with bright purple dye—swayed. "Why Rhys Ellis, are you saying I'm nosy?"

I watched my two friends banter back and forth with warmth swelling up inside me. Despite the headache, I was smiling by the time Angeline came around the bar and plopped on the stool next to me.

It was like the sun itself coming to sit beside me. I basked in her presence.

"So, did the kids get off to school all right this morning?"

"They did," I said around a sudden lump in my throat. *What is wrong with me? I've been so emotional lately. Is that also a symptom of a brain tumor?* "They were very excited. Me not so much. Addie wore the fish print tights you gave her ... with the ridiculously expensive pink tulle skirt Jake's mom bought."

Angeline pressed her lips together, causing a bloodless ring to form around her mouth. The dark freckles scattered along her cheeks and nose popped as she held her breath and stared at me. Then, we both exploded with laughter.

Rhys shook his head at us.

"I'm so sorry," Angeline groaned when we calmed down. "Bet Jake was chuffed about that."

We heard the front door open and shut.

"I'm here," Vivi called in a sing-song tone.

"Speaking of spending ridiculous amounts of money on clothes." Angeline shot me a conspiratorial grin and then slipped her arm through mine. "Let's go see what goodies she's brought the girls."

Rhys was right behind us as we walked out to the studio.

Vivi was practically vibrating in her Manolo Blanik suede sandals as she greeted us with cheek kisses. She slid a plastic-covered dress from the pile of clothes she'd draped over the chaise lounge by the door.

"Tada! Check out this plum wrap dress." Expertly peeling the plastic off with one hand, she held up the dress against her sculpted five-foot-six frame. "Perfect for Danna's skin tone and build, am I right?"

We all nodded with a mixture of amusement and support.

Satisfied, she slipped the plastic back over the dress and draped it carefully back onto the pile. "Gretchen, over at Fashion First, has been saving these for us. And the best part is, she's donating them to Project Freedom's boutique, so I'll drop them off there after the photo session. I just may give that one to Danna though, if she likes it."

"Very generous of you both," Angeline said, glancing at her watch. "Well, the ladies should be here soon." A dark cloud passed over her expression as she wrapped her arms around herself.

"What's wrong?" I asked.

"I'm just hoping Carmen shows up. She told me last week she was coming to support the other girls, but Veora called me early this morning hoping I'd seen her. After the funeral, Carmen told her she wanted to walk a bit, said she'd take a bus back to the safe house, but she never showed up."

Vivi twirled around, eyes wide, her long hair sliding over one shoulder. "That's worrisome."

"Agreed. Veora said she'd ask their liaison at the Sarasota P.D. to look for her in all the usual places. No news is good news right?"

"Good news is good news," Rhys said. Then held up his hands as we turned on him. "But no news isn't bad news." He squeezed Angeline's shoulder. "I'm sure she's fine. She probably just needed some time alone." With a half-hearted smile, he moved into the studio to get ready for the photo session.

A chill crept up my spine as I remembered the words Carmen had screamed at the funeral. *I'll kill him*. Surely she wouldn't go looking for Drac? The other alternative—looking for a high to take away the pain—would probably end just as badly.

Carmen and I had bonded over our shared history in foster homes. Only, she'd fled an abusive one at thirteen and landed in the arms of her first pimp, something I'd managed to avoid.

An image suddenly rose up unbidden: a bearded man grabbing my arm, a hotel sign flickering behind him, spit glistening on his lip. I searched my mind frantically. My legs turned to jelly and my skin flushed. *Is he part of a memory? Or just a bad dream?*

I rubbed the space between my eyes and forced the man's face back into the darkness, where hopefully it would stay.

FOUR

Six women, smelling of soap and vanilla hand lotion, arrived at our doorstep via a volunteer from the safe house. The oldest was twenty-four, the youngest sixteen. They were in various stages of extricating themselves from "the life." None of them were good at eye contact and none of them were Carmen.

The girls were mostly silent as Vivi and Angeline kept them busy trying on outfits. I brought them cups of hot tea and lemon and bagels and lox laid out on a starfish-shaped tray.

The bubbliness that should've been present with so many young women in one room together was noticeably absent. Instead, darker, pent-up emotions had followed them in like poisonous vapor and hung heavy in the air, a reminder these women had been stripped of joy long ago.

Vivi plugged in a hot iron and brought out the lighted mirror and makeup box Rhys kept for photo shoots. She owned a fashion consulting business, ran a popular fashion blog and, unlike me, was completely in her element on photo-shoot day.

While Angeline worked on Jo-Jo—the quiet, heavyset sixteen-year-old—expertly sculpting, shading and concealing her pockmarked complexion, she tried to make casual conversation. This was always the tricky part. Most sixteen-year-olds weren't holding down traumatic thoughts like bile in their throat, or fighting a cocaine addiction induced to control them by a monster who saw them as cash flow instead of a human being.

"Have you ever tried yoga?" Angeline asked. This was her go-to connection with the girls.

"No," Jo-Jo said, while trying to keep her face still for the lip liner.

"I own Open Heart Studio on Fourth Street. You should come. I have a class on Saturday mornings I think you'd like. It's a beginner class, I have extra mats and it's free for Freedom girls. No risk."

"I'm comin' Wednesday night to the Women's Empowerment class. I'll bring her," Danna said, stepping out of the bathroom and adjusting the plum wrap dress. It did look luxurious against her rich, dark skin tone and curvy figure. Her shoulders were pulled back confidently. A nice change. I saw why Vivi had been so excited about the dress.

"What did I tell you?" Vivi twirled her around with a grin. "Like it was made for you."

Danna was one of the lucky girls who'd made it to the "relaunch phase" at Project Freedom. If she could find work, she was ready for living independently. We'd watched her fight hard to get her life back over this past year, committing to rehab and counseling. Her background was a real-life horror story, so her resilient spirit impressed us all.

"We have the perfect shade lipstick to go with that dress." Angeline dug through the makeup box and handed me a silver tube to give to Danna.

Rhys began shooting Tina, the twenty-four-year-old. Ang had tried her best to cover up the thick, amoeba-shaped burn-scar that covered Tina's cheek. The high-pitch whine of the flash charging, followed by white bursts of light, filled the room. Gentle conversation was interspersed with the flashes. He was good with the women, gently coaxing their soft inner bodies out of their hard outer shells.

Sparkle had folded inward and wedged herself on the floor between the loveseat and metal camera equipment shelving. Her eyes were cast down, and she was picking at a scab on her arm next to a tattoo of the word "Loyalty."

I went to her, kneeled down beside her. "Would you like to go next? I think Jo-Jo's about finished."

She moved her gaze slowly upward, but never let it get past my mouth. I could see the war being fought behind haunted brown eyes, a war for her sanity, her soul, her dignity. A war she looked like she was losing.

She shrugged. A gesture so inadequate and defeated, I had to fight not to reach out and gather her up in my arms. Instead I stood and held out a hand to her.

Sparkle ignored it and pushed herself off the ground. She then lowered herself onto the edge of the black leather sofa as if she were an arthritic eighty-year-old, which made me wonder if she was hiding an injury.

Sparkle stared at Vivi, who'd taken over for the hair-curling phase of Jo-Jo's makeover.

I watched Sparkle carefully. *Poised to run.*

Vivi caught Sparkle's eye over the curl she'd just created and offered her a smile.

This seemed to bring her rage to the surface. Sparkle narrowed her eyes at Vivi, looked her up and down. "Can I ask you a question?"

"Sure," Vivi said, separating a section of Jo-Jo's hair to curl.

"What'do you do this for? Help like this? Are we just a checkbox so you can go back to your privileged life with your fancy shoes, pattin' yourself on the back for doin' your good deed for the day?"

All the girls fell silent. Rage did this when it managed to seep out between the cracks of a person. Took up all the oxygen in a room. Caused everyone to hold their breath and wait for the fallout.

I could tell by Vivi's smooth, slow motion as she continued to curl Jo-Jo's hair that she wasn't offended, but she did have something to say. I wondered if she was going to open up and tell Sparkle about being raped at a high school party when she was fifteen. It was the main reason she feels compelled to help these women, according to her confession after a four-bottle-of-wine girls-night-out a few years back.

Vivi held the curling iron off to the side. "You think I'm judging you? That I look down on you girls from my ivory tower and this is my charity? That you mean nothing more to me than dropping off a load of clothes at Goodwill for a tax break?"

Sparkle shrugged her bony shoulders again, but she was making eye contact with Vivi as she waited. Rage gives you courage, too.

"Well, I can assure you I'm not judging you. I see the difference between you and me as a matter of degree, not category." She picked up another section of Jo-Jo's hair. Jo-Jo had become still as a statue, probably a learned reaction to conflict.

"When I was thirteen I got a job working under the table for a guy named Bern Mathers selling pastries in his small gluten-free shop. There was this handbag I really wanted that my mother refused to buy for me, so I thought I'd show her and earn the money on my own. It took me awhile to realize I hadn't beaten out the other applicants because of my perceived work ethic or witty sense of humor, but because he simply wanted to look at me every Tuesday and Thursday evening and Saturday morning.

"See, I didn't just learn the difference between a Danish puff pastry and a donut ... I learned about the power I suddenly possessed because of some silly budding breasts I didn't even want. I also learned about the danger that came with that power. Eventually, looking wasn't enough for good ole Bern Mathers. Eventually he started brushing up against me, touching my waist, leaning in close to my ear if he wanted to show me something. It was uncomfortable, but never obvious enough for me to say anything without feeling stupid."

Not about the rape, then. I glanced around at the women. She had their attention so it was enough anyway. Some of them were nodding. Some were held quietly spellbound. It was a spell of solidarity, tiny flies in a universal web, recognizing their own experience within the sticky parts.

"But I finally got the courage to speak up. I remember it was Saturday just before we were to open. I bent over to unlock the front case and I felt Bern Mather's press his man parts against me from behind. It was just a moment. The pressure of his body was there and gone in less time than it took me to suck in a breath. But, I knew it was purposeful. And with a shaking voice I finally got up the nerve and asked him to please not do that ever again. Can you guess what happened?" She raised an eyebrow, paused mid-roll, glanced around at the silent women. "Yeah, I know you can. Of course, I was the crazy one, right? How dare I accuse him—a man old enough to be my grandfather with grown children, an upstanding businessman loved by the community—how dare I, a spoiled little rich girl, accuse him of something so inappropriate? Of course, he fired me on the spot."

My heart ached. I could see how even reliving this small moment was costing Vivi something precious. She was struggling to keep her composure. She acted tough, but she was as sensitive as they come beneath all that practiced control.

Vivi straightened her spine and took a deep breath, allowing herself a smile. "I never did get that handbag." Then her smile faded. "What I did get was a lesson in how the world works. I learned at the next job to just keep my mouth shut, deal with the innuendos, the hungry looks, the sly touching ... just ignore it and collect my paycheck." Her intense gaze met Sparkle's once again. "I know my experience doesn't even come close to what you have endured, but at the core of it, it's still accepting the abuse in exchange for security. Only my life wasn't at stake, and I kept my mouth shut anyway. So who am I to judge you?"

I watched the anger drain out of Sparkle. Her shoulders slumped under the borrowed green dress shirt. Her mouth twitched. It wasn't quite a smile, but it was good enough for Vivi.

"You can't really say your life wasn't at stake, though," Danna chimed in. "Y'all hear about that girl waitressin' at Todd's Seafood last month? Stabbed twelve times and thrown in a dumpster 'cause she threatened to go to police about the sexual harassment she'd been puttin' up with from the chef there."

My insides stirred. I could relate, though my harassment had come from the customers. I'd had a kind boss at American Pie Diner, the place Jake had found me, and rescued me from the daily request for cherry pie with a snicker, a wink and too often a squeeze or pat. I'd fight not to roll my eyes or stab someone with a fork. It was mind-numbing.

Gilly, the nineteen-year-old petite redhead, who could've passed for thirteen, had smiled then, though it was one of solidarity through pain and not a gesture of happiness. "First lesson most of us learn is to try to stay invisible 'cause all spaces belong to men. Don't matter if you come from money or not."

"Men with money are the worst, though," Ana Paulina said around a mouthful of bagel. "Once their bank balance gets above a certain number, it's like bonus ... 'Here's your sense of entitlement, sir.'"

"Don't get too jaded, girls. There are good ones out there," Angeline said. "The trick to finding a good man is believing you deserve one."

"She's right. That and being okay with being alone so you don't settle." Rhys threw a purposeful glance my way.

I squinted my eyes at him. We both knew he wasn't just being picky.

"All right Sparkle, your turn." Vivi squeezed Jo-Jo's shoulder. "You're beautiful and ready for Rhys. Go on."

Vivi's confession seemed to have transformed the group. The rest of the morning was lighter, there were more words spoken, more stories shared, less pain to block out. Lunchtime had rolled around by the time we'd finished. Angeline served up her mother's rice and peas and jerk chicken while Rhys showed the women their photos on the computer. They *oooed* and *aaahed* and helped each other pick out favorites for Rhys to print.

I nudged Angeline's shoulder. She was staring at her phone, her brows pressed together. "What's up?"

She shook her head and blew out a long sigh. "No word from Carmen yet."

Danna held up half a bagel in our direction. "Y'all hear about Drac's car being set on fire last night? Maybe that was Carmen who did it. She was pretty tore up about Reyna. Maybe she's in hiding now."

I froze. *Oh my God, was that Drac's car I saw burning last night? Did Carmen do that? If so, did I follow her there?* My temples pulsed as my blood pressure rose. These blackouts were getting dangerous. Time to get help.

FIVE

Dr. Bertinelli's office hadn't changed in the eight years I'd been going there and probably the thirty years before that. It was a squat brown stucco building in danger of being squeezed out by one of the multi-story glass and steel upgrades surrounding it. Florida builders hated to waste vertical space. An ornamental cherry blossom tree, with a rich, fragrant scent, grew in the parking lot. When change came—as it inevitably would—I'd miss the tree the most.

Inside the exam room hung a large watercolor painting of the Sarasota skyline from the seventies, also framed photos of Dr. Bertinelli (taller with more hair) on a fishing boat, holding up various sized, milky-eyed fish. A plastic skeleton stood in the corner wearing a pirate's hat and a wooden chair sat next to his desk, where the nurse had just finished taking my blood pressure.

My blood pressure was up but I knew why. I was terrified. I'd finally gotten up the nerve last night to tell Jake about the black outs and the conversation hadn't gone well. He was worried, which made me wonder if I should be more worried, especially because I hadn't even told him the half of it. And then the nurse had given me an appointment right away this morning when I'd mentioned blackouts, which made me even more nervous. *Is this more serious than I thought?* Maybe it was a brain tumor.

I startled, whipping my head around as laughter echoed beside my right ear. No one was there. Pressing a palm against my chest, I forced a deep breath. My hands and feet began to sweat.

"Alice." Dr. Bertinelli held out his hands as he entered the room. Kind, brown eyes shone from deep in the folds of fatty, mole-laden eyelids as he smiled. "How are you, my dear?" He wrapped warm, dry hands around my damp one and squeezed. "I hear you're having some troubles."

"Yes, a bit," I answered, still breathless from the scare. I waited for him to get situated in his chair and scroll through my chart.

He slipped on glasses and squinted at the computer screen. "No changes in medications?"

"No." I twisted my wedding rings around my finger.

Dr. Bertinelli removed his reading glasses and turned in his chair. "How are the kids?"

I smiled despite my mounting fear. "Growing like weeds. Addie just started kindergarten and Charlie's in second grade."

He chuckled and nodded knowingly. "Don't blink or you'll be dropping them off at college. Okay, dear, so tell me what's happening."

I opened my mouth. *How far back should I go? And how to even describe the surge of emotion, the feeling of floating away that precedes the blackouts?* It was impossible. I decided to stick with the physical symptoms. "I've been having headaches. And once in a while I seem to have these spells where I sort of blackout and can't remember something that happened."

Dr. Bertinelli pursed his lips and studied me. "I assume there is no illegal substance or alcohol abuse." I shook my head. "No vision or hearing loss?" I again shook my head. "And when you have these spells, they are at times of stress?"

"Stress, yes." I nodded gratefully. Maybe he knew what was wrong with me. "This last time it happened at a funeral. Is this normal?" I pushed away the image of waking up to a burning car.

"Not normal, no, but not totally rare either. One explanation is you could be experiencing complex partial seizures." He rubbed the gray stubble on his chin. It made a scratchy sound. "How are you sleeping?"

"Sporadically. I can't seem to stay asleep." *I'm not ready to talk about finding myself in a strange neighborhood in the middle of the night, but should I mention the violent nightmares?*

He nodded. "A good night's sleep is the foundation of health. I'll give you a prescription, and let's see if we can't get you a solid eight hours rest. Also, let's get your blood sugar tested and get you to a neurologist to rule out anything serious. Dr. Peters is very good. I'll have my nurse set you up an appointment with him. Fast in the morning for your labs, you can have water."

I shifted in the chair. "A neurologist? So you think this could be something physical, like a brain tumor?"

Dr. Bertinelli pushed himself up with effort and then squeezed my shoulder. "Don't stress yourself over this, Alice, okay? This is what we'll find out. No good will come from fantasizing about the cause." He raised a wiry gray eyebrow. "*Capisce*?"

I was still twisting my wedding rings, but I let my mouth soften into a smile. "No stress. Got it."

–◆◆◆–

I watched from the bathroom doorway for a moment as our nanny, Aurora, gently scrubbed Addie's pile of sudsy red hair. She was humming some upbeat song I didn't recognize. Addie was blowing bubbles from her palms and watching their rise and descent. The room held the scent of tropical fruit shampoo. It was a sliver of stillness, of contentment in the chaos. My children both safe and happy. I lived for these moments. I wanted to stop time and stay in them forever. But time waits for no man. *Who said that?* I couldn't remember.

I stepped inside and knelt down in front of the spa tub, balancing myself on the black Prada pumps Vivi had given me for my thirtieth birthday in July.

Aurora's humming grew quiet as we exchanged a smile.

Aurora had two daughters of her own back in the Philippines. Working here and sending money back to them was her way of making sure they had a better life. She always had a smile for us, but I'd heard her crying in private. I knew it was tough for her to be separated from them.

I'd been both horrified and admiring of her sacrifice when Aurora first came to us after Charlie's birth. Now I just admired the hell out of the woman ... now that love for my own children had reshaped my heart and mind, reshaped me into a mother who understood sacrificing anything for your children, even being with them. (I couldn't forgive my own mother for this, and I wondered if that made me a hypocrite.)

"The bubbles are magic, Mommy." Addie's wide green eyes studied the pile of suds in her small cupped palms. "They have colors."

I reached over and popped a bubble. My daughter giggled. "I like that you see magic in everything, Addie. Don't ever stop doing that, okay?"

"Okay, Mommy." Addie dumped the bubbles and smacked the water surface, sending a spray of warm water over my forearm.

"Oh, Adelyn, your mother's dress." Aurora made a clicking noise with her tongue as she grabbed a towel and wiped at the spots on my damp bell sleeve.

"It's okay." I took the towel from her and chuckled at my daughter's orneriness. "Sometimes there is magic and sometimes there is chaos."

This was life. Magic and Chaos. Light and dark. Love and fear. War and peace.

Aurora was eyeing my dress. "You and Mr. Jake go to another funeral?"

"No," I laughed. "Just a boring fundraiser." I knew she wasn't used to seeing me in black. It didn't complement my olive complexion like the brighter colors, so I never wore it outside of funerals.

I reached over and ran a hand over the soft skin of Addie's cheek. "I want you to be good for Aurora and go to sleep right after books. I'll come in and sneak a kiss when Daddy and I get home, okay?"

Addie nodded and blew me a kiss with a dramatic lip smack, all tiny-toothed smile and mischievous, sparkling eyes. She was joy incarnate. This is what had been stolen from the girls at Project Freedom. This joy. My heart ached and I wanted to put a bubble around my daughter.

I watched stray suds float toward me and scooped them up mid-air. "Thank you, I'll take your kiss with me." I pushed myself upright and then rested a hand on Aurora's shoulder. "Please make sure Charlie's off the computer by seven-thirty."

⬤⬤⬤

"So, what did Dr. Bertinelli say?" Jake asked as we inched forward in the Ringling bridge traffic. He had the top down on his 1964 Jaguar XKE convertible so a balmy breeze played with the loose waves around my face. The bulk of my hair had been swept up and tamed into a stylish twist.

I gazed at the sky. There was something magical about this time of day. The light had mellowed into a silky glow. Billowing clouds, outlined in silver, floated above the sparkling blue Gulf waters. I sighed. People who didn't believe in magic must've never seen a sky like this.

Reluctantly, I moved my attention from the sky and met Jake's worried gaze. "He's given me something to help me sleep. And he wants me to have my blood sugar tested in the morning and to see a neurologist to rule out anything serious. A Dr. Peters."

Jake reached over. His hand was warm and familiar as it covered mine. "I'm sure it's nothing serious." But his tightening jaw and the flash of panic in his pale blue eyes said otherwise. He was worried.

His father had died from lung cancer that had spread to his brain. Jake didn't deal well with anything he had no control over. He'd chosen at that time to lose himself in work, leaving me—his new bride—to deal with his mother's grief. His mother's grief had been raw, and she'd lashed out at everyone and everything around her, so she and I had never grown close. There were too many wounds, too many words said.

Will Jake avoid me, too, if I have cancer? Is it even possible to have a brain tumor for this long and not know it? I've been experiencing blackouts and missing time ever since I can remember... though, not nearly as frequently as now. What's changed? It has seemed to escalate since I've started working with the girls at Project Freedom. Why would that make it worse?

I shifted the conversation into a new territory, one with its own perils. "So, Oliver's really going to do it? Run for a City Commissioner's seat?"

"Yeah, guess he got the necessary petition signatures to run. Wouldn't have figured him for political motivations, but I'm sure there's some advantage there for Brooks Development. Graham

Brooks wouldn't have it any other way. I'll find out tonight what it is."

I heard the admiration in Jake's tone and turned away. Graham Brooks was the creator of one of the largest privately-owned real estate companies in the U.S. and held the largest commercial property portfolio on the Gulf Coast. In Sarasota alone he'd acquired three golf courses, nine hotels, two shopping centers, dozens of business parks in prime Sarasota real estate areas and a multi-million dollar piece of property where a condo high-rise was currently going up, amid much furor from residents already feeling crushed between high-rises. He was also Jake's biggest client and the main source of our income, which made criticism of him off limits.

The house we pulled up to had also been acquired by Graham Brooks in a short sale during the real estate crash of 2008—for a fraction of its worth—and handed over to his only son, Oliver. It was a magnificent piece of property on Siesta Key facing Roberts Bay, over a third of an acre with a seven-thousand-square-foot Mediterranean-style mansion. We'd been here a dozen times over the years for various parties, but still the place never failed to awe me.

We were led through the front doors and then through the living room—which boasted high ceilings framed in cyprus beams, cherrywood and tumbled Italian stone floors, hand-painted wall murals, heavy wood and iron furniture and a massive brick fireplace—to the backyard, which was just as impressive with a spacious tiled seating area under wide, lazy palm fans; an infinity-edged swimming pool against the bay and a private, sixty-foot dock and lift where Oliver's 51' SeaRay yacht was parked. Or as he liked to refer to it—his "floating orgasm."

I scanned the crowd. Graham Brooks made his way toward us and gave Jake a hearty handshake. "There you are. I was beginning to think you weren't showing up." He signaled to a young girl balancing a tray of champagne glasses on one palm. She wore a scrap of black skirt, gold sequined top and a forced smile as she offered up the tray. Graham's thick fingers landed on her waist as he bent down, whispering in her ear before removing a glass from the tray.

I tried to make eye contact with the girl, who looked about sixteen if I had to guess, but she dropped her gaze.

"Wouldn't miss it for the world." Jake plucked two glasses from the tray and handed one to me, seemingly oblivious to the way Graham had touched the young girl. I began to doubt myself. Ever since I'd gotten involved with the women at Project Freedom I'd become hyper-sensitive to the way young women were treated in public. Graham had always been a touchy-feely guy and there were always young girls working this group's events, nothing new there. I forced myself to relax.

Graham leaned forward and kissed my cheek, the scent of pricey cologne and cigars lingering after he pulled away. I smiled rigidly as he ran his appraising gaze down my body. "You're looking lovely this evening, as usual." But his smile faltered, seemed unsure.

Was it disappointment or disapproval of my dress? A mixture of irritation and satisfaction moved through me at the thought of either.

"Thank you." I sipped the bitter champagne and waited to be dismissed now that I'd been acknowledged. Three two one ...

I walked away to find Vivi, hoping to avoid Graham's son, Oliver, for as long as possible. The fundraiser had been going on for a few hours already, so he was probably on his fifth rum and coke. A dangerous number for any unaccompanied woman in his presence.

Scanning the crowd, I noticed a half dozen other young girls dressed the same way, some carrying trays, some talking to the guests. A small waif of a girl in gold was walking toward the yacht with Jim Masters, a county court judge. He was in his sixties but dyed his hair black and walked with a limp because of an artificial leg from his right knee down. He was part of Graham's inner circle and another person I tried to avoid at these get-togethers. He had a large hand planted on the girl's lower back. My stomach filled with acid, and I had to turn away.

Finally, I spotted Vivi standing beside her husband, Rolf, talking to a well-dressed couple in their sixties. Rolf's posture was that of a considerate listener as he nodded his head earnestly. Vivi looked bored. I waved, catching her attention. She quickly extracted herself from the conversation.

"About time you got here." She hugged me. Her bare arms were warm, and I caught a whiff of lavender body lotion. "Lord have mercy, these people are killing me." She stepped back, rested a fist on her hip and eyed my ankle-length black dress. "What in the world are you wearing?"

My face warmed but I grinned. "Armor?"

Vivi's sharp laughter cut through the muggy air. "Armor's right. You're going to have heat stroke in all that dress. You look like a nun. Well played." She glanced down at my feet and grinned. "At least you have good taste in shoes." She hooked her arm in mine. "Come on, let's find the bar. You'd think Oliver would've sprung for the good champagne while digging in these people's pockets. I need a real drink."

We spent the next hour mingling, making mindless small talk and smiling until my cheeks began to ache. I scanned the crowd, noting only two of the young female servers were still around. Oliver was standing by the pool, his hand motioning wildly as he told some story to a knot of gray-haired men. I'd managed to avoid him so far.

I touched Vivi's arm to get her attention. "Going to the ladies' room. Be right back."

Meandering through the house toward the guest bathroom in the east wing, I noted how good the air conditioning felt on the damp parts of my body. A door opened at the end of the hall, and I was surprised to see one of the young servers stumble out. She was pulling her bleached hair back in a ponytail. I stopped and watched her wipe at her nose with the back of her hand and then struggled to straighten her cleavage in the snug gold top.

"Hey," I said, holding out a palm to keep her from running into me.

She stopped short, her mouth forming an "o" as she tried to focus on me. Her eyes were dilated and swollen. An angry red mark burned on her pale cheek. She swayed a bit on her heels, definitely high on something.

"Hey." She tucked her chin and tried to slide past me.

Recognition hit. I whirled around. "You work at the country club right?" She paused. "You've waited on our table. Gillian, right?"

She turned. Her profile was fairy-like, small turned up nose, long black lashes. "Yeah."

"Are you all right, Gillian?"

I watched her swallow, her long neck muscles contracting. Slowly, she lifted her gaze and made eye contact with me. She opened her mouth and tears sprang to her eyes, but then her attention caught on something behind me. "Sure. All good here." She made an exaggerated salute then stumbled down the hall on colt-like legs.

I crossed my arms and looked behind me. Two men were slipping on their suit jackets and talking as they walked down the hall. *Did they just come from the same room as Gillian?* I recognized the short, bald one as a real estate developer, though I couldn't remember his name. He winked as they passed.

I took my time in the large gold and black marble bathroom, enjoying the solitude, poking at my suspicions about these young servers. *Was Oliver giving them drugs? Did Gillian have sex with those men? Was I just being over-sensitive? Could I even trust myself anymore?* I sighed. Lifting a washcloth from the stack by the sink, I ran cold water over it, then pressed the damp cloth against the back of my neck and closed my eyes. Sounds of laughter and conversation were faint against the outside wall. The scent of the vanilla oil Reed diffuser on the sink was stronger with my eyes closed. My mind drifted to thoughts of the kids. I smiled to myself as I wondered how long it would take Aurora to get Charlie off the computer. He was really getting addicted. They were growing up in such a different world then I had, which was a good thing. Taking a deep breath, I sighed. Time to get back.

I opened the door and my pulse jumped. My hand fluttered protectively to my throat.

Oliver Brooks stood there, his six-four, two-hundred pound body between me and the hallway.

"Weren't you going to come say hi, Alice?" His close-set gray eyes were glassy, predatory. Definitely past his fifth rum and coke.

I tried to force a smile. It felt more like a twitch. "Of course. I was just waiting until you were free."

He lurched closer to me and leaned one meaty hand on either side of the doorframe. "I'm free now." His tongue darted out and wet his bottom lip as he let his gaze drop to my chest. I cringed inwardly. "Not my favorite look of yours. That red dress you wore at Baker's. Now, that was sexy." His hand moved from the door and landed on my rib cage, his thumb roughly stroking beneath my right breast. "Not that you could ever look ugly."

My breath got stuck in my throat. I wanted to take a step back, away from the pungent rum on his breath, away from his leer, his touch, his next move. But I was frozen. Prey caught out in the open.

Then a voice from behind saved me. "There you are, Alice. Jake's been looking for you."

Oliver's eyes darkened. Blood pooled in his bloated face at the interruption. "I'm done being patient," he spat in my ear. Then whirling around, he pushed past Vivi and disappeared.

I let my shoulder fall against the wall. Drained and sick to my stomach, my eyes met Vivi's. "Thank you."

She shook her head. "Guess the armor didn't work, huh? What an asshole." She looped her arm through mine, and I was grateful for the support. "Come on. It's almost over."

Yes it is. We will end it.

I whipped my head toward Vivi. "What was that? End what?"

She patted my arm, tilting her head curiously. "I said it's almost over."

SIX

The next morning, I sat in my SUV, faint from just having blood drawn at the lab and from lack of sleep—the nightmares were getting more violent. My phone buzzed in the console. I didn't recognize the number.

"Hello?"

"Can I speak to Miss Alice Leininger, please?"

"Speaking."

"Hi, this is Melanie from Dr. Peter's office. Dr. Bertinelli's office has asked us to set you up an appointment. We have a cancellation at two o'clock this afternoon if you're able to come in then? Otherwise I have an opening in two weeks I can schedule you for."

I watched a white Ibis strut across the sun-dappled parking lot, its legs like thin orange bendy straws. *Two o'clock?* I preferred to pick up the kids from school, but Aurora could do it. And this was important. "Sure, I can be there at two today."

After I got directions to their office at the Neurology Center inside Sarasota Memorial Hospital, I hung up and wondered if I should call Jake. Plucking off the cotton taped to my inner elbow, I decided against it. No reason for him to be there. I'd probably just be filling out paperwork today, anyway.

—◆◆◆—

I sat on the paper-covered exam table, in a blue cotton dressing gown, waiting for Dr. Peters. To kill time, I eyed the posters tacked up to the walls—brains sliced and labeled, color coded, lines pointing to different sections with words too small for me to read. Despite the cold air blowing hard from the air-conditioning vent above me, sweat rolled down my sides.

I closed my eyes and forced myself to take a deep breath. By the third time, I heard a light knock on the door. Dr. Peters—a tall, African-American man with short-cropped gray hair—strolled in. He must've been six-foot-six at least, though he had the stooped demeanor of a man used to ducking under things or leaning down to other people's level.

The young nurse who'd entered my information into the computer stepped back into the room behind him.

"Hi, Alice. I'm Dr. Peters." He had a deep, kind voice, tinged with a touch of the south.

His large hand swallowed mine. A nervous smile played on my lips. "Nice to meet you."

"Let's see how we can help you out today." He rolled a chair up in front of me, and, taking a seat, he read through the paperwork I'd filled out.

I glanced at the nurse, who was standing quietly by some black computer-looking machine on wheels. We exchanged a smile.

"Headaches ... blackouts." He looked up, his brown eyes meeting mine. "How long have you been experiencing these blackouts?"

"A few years," I hedged.

"Two? Five? Ten?"

As far back as I can remember.

"My son is seven. It happened when I was in labor with him." *Both children, actually. And way before that.* I don't know why I'm holding back this information. I'm here for help, after all.

"You don't lose consciousness, though?"

"No, I'm just missing a period of time afterwards." *And no one ever notices I've been gone, so I must not do anything out of the ordinary like pass out.*

"Do you have visual disturbances with these episodes?"

"No."

"What about phantom smells? Smoke or sweet scents that aren't there?"

I blinked and thought back. *Do I?* "I don't think so."

Dr. Peters continued. "And this happens with stress?"

"Yes." I'd made a point to write that down.

"I see you left your family history blank." His tone was quizzical but kind.

My hands gripped the sides of the table. "I don't know my family history. I was orphaned at birth."

He nodded once then moved on. I was grateful that he didn't seem to feel sorry for me.

We went through ten more minutes of questioning and then Dr. Peters pushed himself up. "Okay. We're going to start with a basic muscle and reflex exam."

The nurse handed him a thin, silver reflex hammer, which he used to tap below my knees a few times. A few sharp pokes to my body and scrapes to the bottoms of my bare feet later, he seemed satisfied but thoughtful.

"All right, young lady. Go ahead and get dressed. I'm going to send you down to radiology for an MRI scan."

I tugged at the edge of my gown, my pulse racing. "Do you think I could have a brain tumor?"

He shrugged a rounded shoulder beneath the white coat. "There are many possibilities for your symptoms. Some of them more serious than others ... MS, tumor, stroke, complex partial seizure disorder. Or it could be nothing physical. That's what we need to find out." He offered me a reassuring smile. "We'll figure it out. Don't worry."

❖❖❖

I lay in the plastic MRI tube after removing all my clothes and jewelry and once again donning a cotton gown. I listened to the whirling, clicking noises and the occasional instructions to hold my breath. Even though a blanket had been draped over me, it was chilly and I had to will myself not to shiver.

Dr. Peters's words "*it could be nothing physical*" should've been a comfort to me. Instead, they were needle pricks in my mind. If not physical, then what? Mental?

I blinked back hot tears. *No. I'm not crazy.*

Purple nurses' uniforms. A tall, stuffed giraffe. Wooden mural wall art, pink flowers, yellow bees. Starched, stiff sheets. The smell of bleach and mildew. Leather straps chaffing my wrists and ankles.

I pushed away the memories. They were old, unimportant to my current life.

"Please hold your breath one last time, Alice. Almost finished."

————

Angeline's yoga studio had become a refuge for me. I'd arrived early for the Women's Empowerment class this evening, but after the stressful day I'd had, I needed the shelter.

Slipping off my flip-flops at the door, I was surprised to see a dozen women, from all walks of life, already standing around talking or stretched out on their mats. Guess I wasn't the only one who looked forward to this monthly event. Attendance had tripled since she'd started it six months ago.

I added the bag of clothes I'd brought to the others behind Ang's desk and moved deeper into the room with my mat. Danna, Jo-Jo and Anna Paulina were there.

"You couldn't get Sparkle here, huh?" I asked Danna.

She shook her head slowly. "She's not ready. We're workin' on her though."

I thought of her eyes, full of anger and mistrust. "Each in their own time."

I rolled my mat out on the maple wood floor beside Danna's then glanced around, looking for Angeline.

The small studio gave off a boho vibe—colorful tapestries covered the walls, lanterns hung from the bamboo ceiling and large silk pillows had been stacked in the corners. The front wall was red brick with a large green painted lotus. Against the left wall stood a shelf stacked with yoga blankets, straps and blocks; a basket piled with extra mats sat beside that; and a large gold, goddess statue stood against the right wall. Candles burned soft and warm around the room and two essential oil diffusers filled the air with sandalwood-scented mist. Soothing music played in the background. It was a spiritual refuge.

"Alice!" Angeline appeared from the back room and headed toward me. The light scent of tea tree oil accompanied her embrace and her thick curls tickled my cheek. "Did you get my message earlier? You missed lunch today."

"Yeah, sorry. I had an appointment I forgot about." No use in worrying her until I knew something for sure. I'd texted Rhys and told him about the neurologist appointment, but only because I'd promised him I'd go. Rhys had been at lunch with Angeline, so apparently he'd kept his promise not to tell the others where I was. I was grateful for that.

"Well, I'm glad you're here tonight. Can you give me a hand passing out the foot bowls when it's time?"

"Foot bowls? Intriguing."

She glanced at the door as a group of chatty women came through. "I hope I have enough." She sounded worried but her eyes glittered with excitement as she turned back to me. "That'd be a nice problem to have, yeah?"

We shared a smile, and then she squeezed my hand and was off to welcome the new arrivals.

After everyone settled in on their mats, Angeline stood at the front of the room in mountain pose, her hands pressed together and held in front of her heart. Jade mala beads hung down the front of her black tank top.

"I'm chuffed to bits to see so many new faces tonight. Welcome, everyone, to *Women Empowering Women.*

"Just to give you an idea what to expect, we're going to start out with some light yoga to get our blood flowing and get our minds off the day ... jobs, kids, spouses, money problems, whatever is consuming your attention. Time to let it go.

"Then we're going to do some physical exercises in support of each other. While we do that, I'll be talking about the lesson for this month." She moved to the front of her mat. "Please stand at the front of your mats." She waited while everyone got in position. "We'll end with a short meditation and then the fun part, going through the clothes you guys brought to exchange." Happy murmuring buzzed in the room. "All right, let's begin then."

She led us through fifteen minutes of *Vinyasa* flow, reminding us when to inhale and exhale with the movements.

I felt muscles loosening, stress dissipating. I pressed my heels into my mat, stretching my calves in downward dog with an audible exhale. By the time we were finished with the sequence, my breathing was no longer constricted and the weight on my mind had been lifted.

"All right, I want you each to find a partner." Angeline counted the women. "There are twenty-four of you. Fantastic. Each pair please grab a silk pillow and towel from the stack over there." She nodded at me.

I weaved my way through the women and followed her to the bathroom. We filled up twelve metal bowls with warm water, added rose petals and drops of peppermint, then carefully carried them out one by one to the paired-up women. When we finished, I sat cross-legged in front of Jo-Jo, who was sitting awkwardly without a partner. Her fleeting, nervous smile greeted me.

As Angeline passed out wash clothes, she began, "I know we women can be cruel to each other, see each other as competition instead of sisters. My goal here is to change that. To help you see that your power lies within you, yes, but also around you. If we're going survive ... no, not just survive but thrive in today's society, we have to have each other's backs. We have to support each other, empower each other. And tonight we're going to do that by treating each other like the goddesses we are with a simple exercise. We're going to wash each other's feet."

Some nervous laughter bubbled up around the room.

Angeline held up a hand. "I know, touching a stranger's feet is uncomfortable ... a bit too intimate, maybe. But, it's time for us to get intimate with each other. We care about the people we know. We support the people we care about. This is how communities are built and Lord knows we need a supportive community. And we women, we're real good at giving, yeah? Time to get used to receiving, too. Accept some TLC for yourselves."

I dipped my washcloth in the warm water and squeezed it out into the bowl. The scent of peppermint bloomed in the air. Jo-Jo blushed as I lifted up her pink-rose-tattooed foot with chipped red polish, and ran the warm cloth over it.

"You guys are lookin' like you don't think you deserve this." Angeline walked around, smiling down at our discomfort. "Remember, each of you is a manifestation of Shakti, the divine feminine creative power of the universe. You deserve this. Say it with me, 'I deserve this.'"

A smattering of unsure voices repeated, "I deserve this."

"What? I didn't catch that," Angeline teased us. She held a cupped hand to her ear.

"I deserve this!" We all said louder, our words mingling with released laughter.

Angeline grinned and nodded. "That's bleedin' right. You said it. Now believe it." She leaned down and whispered something in Jo-Jo's ear, squeezing her shoulder and then moving on.

I shifted to her other foot, keeping my head bowed to give Jo-Jo some privacy as she wiped at a tear on her cheek.

"We live in a patriarchal society. One that only idolizes women in the caretaker role or for our physical beauty. I know you all feel it. That pressure to live up to society's idealized version of a woman. You're either trying to become the sacrificial nurturing archetype or the perfect physical female form. Or both is more likely, yeah?"

The sounds of washcloths being wrung out and quiet murmurs of agreement filled the room.

"Because we are worthless beyond this in the eyes of the world, yeah? Well, I'm here to tell you that the world is wrong. That what you're actually doing is sacrificing yourself and your potential for a lie. Don't buy into it, ladies.

"Society does not benefit from us playing the small, unimportant role. The supporting role in other people's lives. The role of being just a caretaker or entertainment or eye candy. You each have a gift. A purpose. It's your job to figure out what that gift is and give it to the world.

"And my job? My job is to fill you up until you're overflowing with so much love that it spills out into your relationships. And to help you realize your own worth and power." She rang a bell. "Okay, time to switch."

I patted Jo-Jo's feet dry and then we switched places.

As Jo-Jo covered my foot with the now lukewarm, wet cloth, I was surprised at how uncomfortable I felt on the receiving end of this small act of kindness. An energy stirred within me that burned like shame. I watched this inner turmoil as it grew hotter, nudging the rage out of its slumber. I forced a smile, hoping this would trick my body into calming down. But the rage began to take a shape within me, grew, pulsed like an expanding star.

Yes, enough! It hissed, whispering something else I couldn't quite make out.

I glanced up to see if Jo-Jo heard the voice, too.

She was busy squeezing water over my foot, lost in her own thoughts. My pulse quickened in my throat as the warmth traveled up my calf, along with the discomfort, feeding whatever was growing stronger inside me. *Was I losing my mind?* I turned my attention away from the whispers in my head and concentrated on Angeline's voice.

"We must first recognize our own worth if others are going to see it as well." Angeline stood by the Goddess statue, her loving gaze taking us in. "I am so proud of each one of you. Coming here to take care of yourselves, to grow, to support each other. Do you see the power you have? You have the power to heal the world. No one ... not society, not your families and certainly not you, benefits from you being a martyr. What everyone benefits from is you using your unique gift to make the world a better place. And believe me, each of you has a unique gift."

My eyes met Jo-Jo's. Her face was tilted up, the unmistakable flicker of hope there. Her crooked smile was contagious. A lightening sensation fluttered in my chest. I sucked in a jagged breath and felt the hot energy disperse, the whispers subside.

———

"Has anyone heard from Carmen yet?" I asked afterwards.

Angeline's shoulders sagged. "No. Not a word."

We watched the various women sorting through the clothes in the middle of the studio—women with deep physical and psychological scars kneeling beside trust-fund babies, stay-at-home moms, a lawyer and a reiki healer, all laughing and chatting like they were best friends.

I was impressed with the unity. "You're doing something powerful here."

Angeline shifted on her bare feet. "It's a start." She smiled warmly, giving a thumb's up to Anna Paulina as the woman held up a cornflower blue sundress against her rail-thin body.

"That'll bring out your eyes. Try it on," she called, then turned back to me. "The problem is we're focusing on getting these girls out of the sex trade business, but where are the programs teaching men to view women as more than objects to be bought? Where are the school programs teaching boys this from the beginning? Before they learn how to treat women by watching porn."

"Project number two-hundred and one?" I teased.

She snorted. "Maybe."

"So, the police are still looking for Carmen, right?"

Angeline rubbed the back of her neck. "Supposedly. They've got more important things to do than look for a missing ex-hooker junkie though. Me and Tai drove around last night to see if we could spot her. We searched left, right and center with no luck. Probably go again tonight. I just feel so helpless. The odds aren't in her favor."

I crossed my arms against the tightness in my belly. I had to do something. "Can you text me a list of places to help look? I can go after the kids are in bed."

Angeline bit her lip and bumped my shoulder with her own. "I could use some help checking out a few hotels she used to frequent. Not alone though. Make sure Jake goes with you and be careful. I'm not sending you off to Disneyland." She squeezed my arm. "I have an extra photo of Carmen you can use, too. Hang on."

She went to her desk and came back with a photo that had been folded in half. I recognized the front porch of the half-way house where Carmen was standing in a black mini-skirt and orange, flowered tank top. Carmen had her arm around someone. I unfolded the photo. A tiny jolt of sorrow hit my heart as I recognized the dead girl in the second half—Reyna Flores. Reyna's skin was sallow and shadowed beneath her eyes, but her smile was genuine. It was like looking at a ghost. I hoped I wasn't looking at two.

SEVEN

"**M**ommy, can you shut my closet doors? There's a monster in there."

I pushed Charlie's hair off his forehead and gazed into his fear-filled eyes. They were the same green as mine and Addie's. Had they come from my own mother or father? I would never know.

I tucked the blanket around the worn bear he was clutching to his chest. "Why do you think there's a monster in there?"

"It's where the portal is. For them to come through when it gets dark," he whispered.

I suppressed a smile. He was such a unique mixture of serious and creative. "I see. Okay. I tell you what." I kissed his nose and then slid the hairband from my ponytail. "I'll do one better." I crossed his room and pulled the shuttered wooden doors closed, then wrapped my hairband around both knobs. Whirling around, I smiled and held up my hands. "What do you think? Portal secure?"

Charlie snuggled deeper into his covers and giggled. "Yes, Mom."

"Good." One more child to tuck in and then it was time to head out into the real world. Where there were real monsters.

—◆◆◆—

I moved through the front doors of the Grand Riviera condos to meet Rhys, the photo of Carmen tucked into my back jean's pocket. Jake had to work tonight so Rhys agreed to go with me.

The rumble of his Harley reached me before I spotted it. Shaking my head, I made my way to him. "You couldn't bring the truck?"

"Too nice of an evening. What seedy part of town are we off to first?" He handed me his spare helmet.

"Ang gave us a few motels to check out around the 4900 block." I slipped the helmet on and tightened the strap, then swung a leg over the bike and wrapped my arms around Rhys. The smell of his leather jacket mingled with the motorcycle exhaust. Not an unpleasant combination. It whispered of adventure. "Head north," I called over the noise as he revved the engine.

Traffic was moderate as we made our way back over the Ringling Causeway and then hung a left on Tamiami Trail. I made sure to lean into the turn like Rhys had taught me.

Once on the Trail we hit stop and go traffic. More and more people every year were abandoning the cold northern winters and becoming permanent Florida residents, so even off-season traffic jams had become the norm. Tonight, I didn't mind the delay so much. Even though I'd given Rhys a hard time, I did like the freedom of being on his bike, and it was a beautiful evening. My gaze lingered on the fading patch of fluorescent orange sky and a sigh escaped me. I'd grown to love this city, which would be postcard-worthy after dark, too, with its glittering high-rises and the moon glowing on the water. Though the route we were on—with old strip malls, gas stations, and repurposed buildings lining both sides of the busy four-lane road—wasn't its best side.

When Jake had moved me here from Orlando eight years ago, I'd felt an instant kinship with Sarasota. Like me, it had simple roots, starting out as a small fishing village and then morphing into a tourist destination when investors built Lido Beach Casino in the twenties. That casino, along with the warm, balmy weather, was like a giant, shiny fishing lure that tourists couldn't resist.

The changes over the years came with a sense of loss, or maybe it was nostalgia, as the land morphed from large swaths of citrus groves and cattle farms to gated neighborhoods and commercial developments. Either way—like a beautiful woman thrust in the spotlight—Sarasota had been stripped of her citrus-perfumed, barefoot-farm-girl innocence and dressed up in glittering baubles and expectations by all the money thrown at her by wealthy foreigners and retirees. Entertain us, feed us, dance for us. Though, I had to admit, all the demand to be entertained did make for a flourishing art community.

"Up there on the right," I shouted, pointing at the cracked *Sleep Inn* sign when we stopped at another light.

Rhys drove up in front of the mustard yellow building. Parking in front of the sliding doors, he shut off the bike. "You want me to go in with you?"

I slipped off the helmet and handed it to him. The slight breeze felt good on my sweat-dampened scalp.

"You can wait here." I glanced around nervously. Four Hispanic men in their teens or early twenties were smoking and eyeing us from their perch in front of the tall ashtray can a few feet away.

A skinny, sun-wrinkled redhead in high heels, cut-off jean-shorts and a silver bikini top pushed out the front door, her voice cutting through the muggy evening air. She was arguing with someone on her cell phone.

"You sure?" Rhys's dark eyes squinted up at me.

Taking a breath, I nodded.

"Be careful then."

"You be careful, too." I felt silly saying it. Rhys was six-four and had a black belt in Brazilian Jujitsu. I'd watched him take down a two-hundred-pound knife-wielding man in a bar fight last year, but guns could kill from a distance and drive-bys in this area weren't unheard of. I'd make it a point to hurry.

Moths and mosquitos swarmed the outside lamp, some drifting in with me as the doors slid open. The inside of the hotel lobby was dark and musty. A dirty, worn red runner stretched in front of a faux-wood paneled front desk.

"Can I help you?" A bored-looking, middle-aged man with greasy hair asked.

I held up the photo of Carmen. "I'm looking for a friend of mine and was wondering if you've seen her around here lately."

Not bothering to lean forward, his gaze flicked to—and then quickly slid from—the photo. "Nope, sorry. Don't recognize her."

Was he lying? Or just not willing to help me? I propped my wrist on the edge of the counter to steady my shaking hand. "Her name is Carmen Castiel. She's twenty-two and ... she's in trouble. Please, if you've seen her—"

"She's a hooker, yeah?"

Heat prickled my skin. I wanted to yank this man by the shirt, make him understand that Carmen was a human being ... a woman ... a victim.

A sudden sharp pain behind my eyes made me grip the counter. I bit my lip to keep from crying out. The laughter I'd heard before rose up and echoed around me as I felt myself shrink down to a pinpoint. I glanced down. My knuckles were bleached white by the force of my grip. *Are these even my hands?* They didn't feel attached to my body. An intense energy filled me like helium in a balloon, only it pulsed with heat. My vision blurred, obscured by some kind of red mist, and in that mist I watched one of those hands grab the man's shirt, jerk him forward. The other curled into a fist, lashed out and connected with his nose. Blood splattered, merged with the mist, wet and bright as rubies. It ran down his lips, his chin, his neck.

I gasped and squeezed my eyes shut.

From somewhere far away I heard a voice. "Are you okay?"

It was the man's voice. *How can he talk through all that blood?*

When the last echo of laughter died down, I opened my eyes. The man's own eyes were narrowed suspiciously behind black-rimmed glasses. "You're not going to be sick or something are you?"

No blood. I glanced down at my hands. They still had a death grip on the counter. I lifted them, rubbing the stiffness out. *What the hell was that?*

I cleared my throat and took a deep breath, tamped down the rage and elbowed the violent vision away with effort. "Have you seen her or not?"

He relaxed, leaned back, rolled a piece of fluorescent green gum around with his front teeth and let his gaze travel down my neck to my chest. I felt it like physical slime. "We don't allow prostitutes to do business here, sorry."

I'd had enough. I pushed away from the counter, my temple thumping and my legs trembling. I turned as a woman's laughter echoed behind me. This time it was a real woman. The redhead I'd seen before had strolled back in on the arm of a heavy-set man in a business suit.

I glared at the man behind the counter. "Thank you for your time."

"Asshole," I added as I pushed back out the door.

I stopped, caught off guard by the sight of the four young Hispanic men standing around Rhys. Still feeling disorientated, it took me a few seconds to assess the situation. They seemed to be checking out the Harley, and Rhys looked relaxed.

"Show these gentlemen Carmen's photo," Rhys said as I approached.

I handed the photo to the man closest to me. He was intimidating, with tattoos running up his arms and neck and an angry scar curling from the corner of his right eye down to the corner of his mouth. Also, he smelled like dollar-store cologne and stale cigarettes, but he seemed friendly enough.

He was shaking his head as the other three crowded him to have a look at the photo. "Nah. Sorry. I haven't seen her around in a few months." He unfolded the photo and after a second, tapped Reyna's face. "Her, though. She was 'round maybe two weeks ago. She had some Roxy she was sellin' that she'd ripped off from some rich guy."

"Roxy?" Rhys repeated.

"Roxycodone. Shit will fuck you up. Easy to OD on. I don't mess with it personally."

The other two mumbled their agreement.

Reyna had OD'ed on heroin, not this roxycodone. But the bruises around her neck and mouth when she'd been found made for "suspicious circumstances." The police were looking for her pimp, Drac, to question.

Rhys handed me the helmet. I slipped it on and then took back the photo. "Thanks for your help."

Three hotels later, we hadn't had any luck. It was like Carmen had disappeared off the face of the earth.

"Good morning, Alice. Sorry to keep you waiting." The next morning, Dr. Peters held out his hand to Jake and introduced himself. Then he slid into the rolling chair behind the desk and opened a folder in front of him. His office was stark: desk, chair, window, commercial sailboat paintings, no personal photos, nothing that gave away a sense of the man behind the profession.

Is the news good or bad? I tried to read his expression, but it was a practiced neutral.

Jake reached across the empty space between us and took my hand, squeezing it. I was grateful for the anchor.

"Well, the good news is your lab work and MRI scan came back normal."

"No tumor?" I pushed out on a short breath. I realized I'd been expecting that word—cancer—and I needed to hear him specifically say no tumor.

He shook his head. "No tumor. No sign of a stroke."

Jake and I shared a relieved smile.

"That's the good news," Jake said cautiously, turning back to the doctor. "What's the bad news?"

Dr. Peters closed the file and folded his hands on the desk. They were nice hands, large with buffed, manicured nails. "The bad news is we don't know what's causing the headaches and blackouts. There are a few more physical tests we can perform, but for now I'm going to refer you to Dr. Evelyn. She's a psychologist who specializes in dissociative disorders."

"Dissociative disorders?" My voice broke. My chest constricted at the thought of being sent to a psychologist.

"A psychologist?" Jake said at the same time. "How will that help? Obviously there's something physically wrong."

Dr. Peters seemed to be measuring his words carefully. "As I said, as of right now we haven't found a physical cause for your wife's symptoms. So, getting a structured clinical interview for dissociative symptoms seems like a good next step. There's also the possibility it could be psychogenic non-epileptic seizures or non-epileptic attack disorder. This happens when emotional stress turns into physical symptoms like seizures. And Alice's symptoms do seem to come on during times of stress. We need to at least rule these things out. Dr. Evelyn's diagnosis will let me know which direction we'll go after that."

Jake nodded. This seemed to satisfy him.

The rest of the brief exchange came from a distance, a cold chill running through my body.

—◆◆◆—

Dread. That was the feeling that had taken over since the appointment with Dr. Peters this morning. Dread and inevitability. Like I was just an object, hurtling toward my worst nightmare, and there was no way to stop myself. I was darkness traveling at the speed of light.

I sat frozen on the edge of the bed, staring at the business card in my hand: Dr. Willa Shae Evelyn, PhD

A rivulet of sweat rolled down my side, beneath my orange maxi-dress. I raised my eyes back to the expanse of sparkling blue water and bright sky beyond the sliding glass doors. It was startling, the contrast between the harsh, blinding daylight and the darkness within me.

Get a grip. Make the appointment.
With one deep, shuttering breath, I forced myself
to make the call.

EIGHT

"Alice, hello. I'm Dr. Evelyn." The well-dressed, soft-spoken woman smiled at me as she motored out of the hallway and into the waiting room with the aid of an electric wheelchair.

I pushed myself up from my chair and bent slightly to shake the woman's petite hand. "Nice to meet you."

"Shall we?" Dr. Evelyn turned the wheelchair around on a dime while making a follow-me motion with her hand.

Her office was a welcoming space with warm wood floors, bright light pouring in from four different square windows and lots of tropical plants. An underlying scent hung in the air, something that made me think of Easter. *Lilacs maybe?*

I settled into the overstuffed, velvety gray sofa and watched the doctor apprehensively. My throat felt constricted, my breathing shallow.

Even though Dr. Evelyn had a desk in the corner of the room, she maneuvered her wheelchair so only a few feet and a low, square table sat between us. A Zen rock fountain bubbled soothingly atop the table.

Dr. Evelyn was a slight woman with short-cropped silver hair and ocean-blue eyes. Those eyes crinkled in the corners as she smiled at me. She removed her reading glasses and let them hang from a gold chain to rest against her powdered-blue, silk shirt.

A silver pen was perched in her hand, a notebook in her lap. "How are you today, Alice?"

"Nervous," I answered, re-crossing my legs and forcing a smile.

"No need to be. I want you to know that everything you tell me is strictly confidential. You can talk to me about anything here and it goes no further." After I acknowledged my understanding with a nod, she continued. "You've been referred to me by Dr. Peters because of blackouts and headaches. Is that right?"

"Yes." I squeezed my fingers to keep them from shaking.

"Okay. Well, what we normally do with cases like yours is what they call a SCID-D-R interview. It's been proven capable of distinguishing between seizures and pseudo-seizures, and it's also what we use to diagnose dissociative disorders."

"What exactly are dissociative disorders?" I forced the question out through constricted vocal chords.

"In short, they're an involuntary defense mechanism, an adaption of the brain which results in a discontinuity in the experience of being oneself. The consensus is that they're caused by psychological trauma, but some studies have found that just growing up with a grieving or depressed parent in the early years of development can be enough for the mind to create dissociative adaptions."

"Dissociative adaptions?" I dug in my memory. I'd heard about this somewhere. Didn't I read a book about ... my gaze darted back to the doctor. "Wait. Are you talking about multiple personalities?"

Dr. Evelyn lifted her hand, her tone softening. "In the most severe form of dissociation, yes. Alternate self-states can form. But, dissociative experiences can be anything from common occurrences like daydreaming and deja-vu to fragmented memories. The label "multiple personality disorder" isn't used anymore because it's really not a dysfunction of personality but of memory, and this breakdown of memory affects identity, awareness and perception."

My insides trembled like a small earthquake. *Is this the darkness living inside me?* I tried not to show the terror gripping me as I asked, "So, I may possibly have this disorder?"

"That's what we're going to find out."

"From this test you mentioned?"

"Yes. There are five main symptoms—amnesia, depersonalization, derealization, identity confusion, and identity alteration. And there are different degrees of all of these. We know you're experiencing the amnesia. Time loss is extremely frightening, so I'm glad you were brave enough to reach out for help. We just need to see if you're experiencing any of the other symptoms."

She paused, glancing at my wringing hands. "But let's save that for our next session. Today, why don't we get to know each other? I'll go first because I know my clients are too polite to ask about the wheelchair. I was paralyzed from the waist down in a car accident when I was twenty-three. It took me awhile to finish grad school because of it, but I'm stubborn like that." She smiled at me. "I've been married to the most wonderful man on the planet for fifteen years, and we have two adopted children who are now nineteen and seventeen. Do you have children?"

I nodded. "Yes, I've been married to my husband, Jake, for eight years and we have a seven-year-old, Charlie, and a five-year-old, Addie."

"How did you and Jake meet?"

I glanced down at my wedding rings, twisting them around my finger. "I was working as a waitress in Orlando at this little pie diner and made the mistake of being nice to one of the customers, telling him I liked his vintage Mustang. So, for a week he kept waiting for me to get off work and asking me if I wanted to take a ride in it. He got more and more insistent as the week went on. Saying things like, 'Come on, I promise you'll love it.' 'What are you afraid of?' Then one day he blocked my VW Bug in with his car and wouldn't take no for an answer. That's when Jake pulled up and saw him trying to corral me into his car. He came over and asked if there was a problem. I said yes, so he grabbed my hand and took me back into the diner. He waited there with me, drinking coffee and talking, until the guy left and I stopped shaking. The rest is history."

"Your savior," she said with a thoughtful nod. "And so both of your children are in school now. Do you work outside the home?"

I shook my head. The thought of my children pushed back some of the terror, enough for the trembling to stop. "No. I really love being there for them full-time and am lucky enough to be able to do that. I do volunteer work for Project Freedom, though, which takes up a lot of my time. My friend,

Angeline, got me involved a few years ago and that's been really rewarding."

But also has seemed to escalate whatever is happening to me.

Dr. Evelyn glanced up, pen poised above her notebook. "Project Freedom? That's the organization that works with trafficking victims?"

"Yes."

Her pen scratched something on the paper. I wondered what she was writing. "Can you tell me a little about your childhood? Just a brief sketch. Where you were born, how many siblings, that sort of thing."

My throat was so dry it burned. "My childhood?" I glanced over at the pastel, wood-framed painting on the wall. In the center was a painted book with the words: Your story matters.

Be honest with her, Alice. You're here to get help.

"I ... I'm an orphan. I was abandoned as a newborn, left at the Shiva Vishnu Temple in Orlando. I spent time between the Garden of Hope Children's Home and foster homes." I watched Dr. Evelyn's expression carefully for any sign of shock. So far, her demeanor was calm, her mouth set in a soft, encouraging smile, so I decided to keep going. "I was told this anyway. I don't remember anything before my thirteenth birthday."

It was the first time I'd said these words out loud to anyone. They must've had weight to them because a bit of pressure released from my chest. Like a fat bird had taken flight from its perch on my heart.

And there it was. A flicker of worry. Just a slight puckering of skin between Dr. Evelyn's brows, but I caught it. The doctor blinked a few times, nodded and then wrote in her notebook. When she was done, she set her pen down slowly. She folded her petite fingers with the gold wedding band and met my gaze.

"Alice, I'm sorry you've been dealing with this alone for so long. I really am. But you're here now, and I promise you, I will help you figure out what's going on, and we will deal with these symptoms together."

My eyes filled with tears. I hadn't realized how alone I'd felt until that moment. Reaching for a Kleenex on the table, I fought to keep my composure. "Sorry, I've been really emotional lately."

"No need to apologize. Let's get you set up for that interview on Monday if that works for you."

"Okay. Sure."

"Good." She wheeled over to the door. "Come on. Let's see what I've got open."

<hr />

That night I took the sleeping pill Dr. Bertinelli had prescribed and dreamed I was a body of fire, destroying everything I touched. Buildings of steel and glass melted at my feet into pools of glittering lava; the skins of rabbits and deer I tried to touch became gray ashes, the animals became fire spirits themselves, hopping away to light their own path of flames. My tears were drops of molten lava sizzling as they fell to the earth, burning holes that opened up into caverns.

This unnamed threat moved with me from the dream world into my tousled bed sheets. My eyes stretched open. Darkness pressed against the wall of glass. My body felt heavy as I rolled over. Jake's side of the bed was empty, but I could hear the shower running. My heartbeat only started to slow as I became conscious enough to know this world was the real one ... the safe one. That is, until I made my way into the kitchen, brushing my tangled hair from my face and sleep from my eyes, and saw flames on the gas stove burning soft, mellow and orange.

Who'd turned that on?

With a flick of my wrist, I snuffed the flames and glanced around the kitchen. "Aurora?"

No, of course, she wouldn't be up this early on a Saturday morning.

—◆◆◆—

I slid back into the velvety soft sofa Monday morning. Though I'd enjoyed the weekend with the kids, I was still not sleeping well, so I was tired and restless as Dr. Evelyn organized a large grouping of papers on her lap. Today she wore a long-sleeved, peach silk shirt and black pencil skirt. I smiled as my gaze fell to her shoes. They were rose gold glitter stilettos with a peach silk bow that wrapped around her slight ankles.

"Your shoes are lovely. My friend, Vivi, would appreciate them. She's a personal styling consultant and runs Style Matters blog. A complete shoe fanatic."

Dr. Evelyn's blue eyes sparkled as she looked up. "Oh yes, I read that blog. Your friend does have fabulous fashion advice. Honestly, I've always had a shoe fetish, too, but I could never walk in heels. One of the silver linings of being paralyzed ... I can wear any shoes I want now, and no blisters or twisted ankles."

I tilted my head, intrigued by her positive attitude. "*One* of the silver linings?"

She nodded. "Mm. Yes. It's very important in a tragedy to find the good. I think it was Victor Hugo who said, 'Whatever causes night in our souls may leave stars.' It's true, but you also have to turn your attention to finding them or they might as well not be there.

"You know I would've married the wrong man if it weren't for the accident. I learned what a selfish, uncaring toad my boyfriend at the time was." Her smile widened as she made a twinkling motion with her fingers. "A definite star." Then she slipped her reading glasses on. "All right. Let's get started, shall we?"

My throat was dry. I cleared it and then said, "Sure."

"You've said that you have complete amnesia before your thirteenth birthday?" She glanced up for confirmation. When I nodded, she jotted something down. "What is your first memory?"

I glanced over at the morning light slanting through the window and let myself go back to an earlier time. "It was the very day of my thirteenth birthday, and I was in a foster home. The mother, Sherry, had four foster kids, including me, and not very much money." I snuck a glance at Dr. Evelyn before I took a breath and forced the truth out of the dusty, dark prison I'd kept it in. "I learned that later, actually, that her name was Sherry. At that moment, sitting at the table with the woman wrapping a gauze bandage around my throbbing hand, and the other three kids cowering against the wall, I had no idea who any of them were. I was scared, disorientated. I thought I must've hurt my head, too, and gotten some kind of amnesia." I glanced down at my right hand and rubbed at the slightly discolored, thicker skin on the edge of my palm. "I had no idea what had happened to my hand. I only knew it hurt like crazy. And my eyes felt swollen so I knew I'd been crying. Later Bo, the nine-year-old, told me Sherry had pressed my hand to the hot stove burner as punishment, because she thought I'd stolen one of her yogurts out of the fridge." I shrugged. "He felt bad because he was the one who'd taken it."

Dr. Evelyn adjusted her glasses and watched me with a new intensity. "And what happened next?"

I looked up at the ceiling, trying to remember the exact details. "She said something about the unpleasantness being out of the way, unwrapped a chocolate cupcake, dropped it on a paper plate and stuck a candle in. Then made the kids sing Happy Birthday to me, which they did, but I could tell they didn't want to." I moved my attention back to the doctor. "We all seemed miserable. It was so hot that day. Sherry used fans in the windows and there were flies in the house, big fat, loud buzzing ones. She made me say a wish when I blew out the candle. I said I wished for a bike, but, really I wished to have a family of my own someday. To be a mother. That seemed too private to say out loud. Too sacred." My stomach clenched at the memory. "Anyway, I split the cupcake between the kids when she went back to watching TV. I didn't stay there long, though." I suddenly felt vulnerable. *Why did I tell her that story? What if she thinks I am crazy?* My heartbeat sped up. I watched her with apprehension clawing its way up my throat.

"Thank you for sharing that memory with me." She looked up from her notebook and, seeming to sense the tension, gave me a reassuring smile. "You're doing fantastic, Alice. One quick question regarding that day and then we'll move on." She waited for me to nod. "What did Sherry and the kids call you? What name?"

I pushed aside the panic and thought back. "Well, everyone called me by the name on my birth certificate, which was Alyssa. I eventually got them to call me Alice, though, which is the name I felt fit me."

"When did you feel Alice fit you? The day of your thirteenth birthday or before that?"

I sat up straighter and thought hard. "I honestly don't remember. It could've been after that day, I guess. Is that important?"

Dr. Evelyn wrote that down and shook her head. "Not at the moment. Let's move on. Have you ever found things in your possession that seemed to belong to you, but you don't remember how you got them?"

My breath hitched. "Yes." I'd always thought it was just my forgetful nature. Looking at it from the doctor's point of view now, I realized it should've been a red flag. "I've found jewelry in my drawer that I don't remember buying. Things that … strange things that aren't even my taste. Like this gold spikes and dagger choker. And one time this heavy blue stone necklace. Sometimes it's clothes or books." Alarm was starting to creep in again and threatened to crumble my fragile confidence.

Dr. Evelyn nodded encouragingly. "You're doing great. How do you think these blackouts you've been experiencing have affected your social relationships?"

I wrapped my arms around my stomach and moved my attention back to the window. "I don't think my friends have noticed them. Well, this last time at the funeral, they noticed I left without saying goodbye. My best friend, Rhys, made me promise to go to the doctor after I came clean about not remembering leaving. As far as my marriage, it's funny. There have been important times that I've missed, like when I had both my kids. At a certain point in both labors, I blacked out and woke up holding a baby at home. Jake never noticed anything was wrong, so I must've still acted like me, right?"

Dr. Evelyn tapped the silver pen to her lip and then said, "Not necessarily. People see what they want to see. What they expect to see." She looked back down and flipped a page. "Can you describe what it feels like right before you black out?"

I picked at a piece of loose thread on the bottom of my yellow button-down shirt. "It starts with an overwhelming feeling of rage." I lifted my eyes. "I honestly feel like it's going to consume me, just burn me up. I don't know where it comes from. It doesn't feel like it originates with me. Like it's not my rage. That sounds ridiculous, I know." I lifted my hands, at a loss to describe the feeling.

"Can you say more about what happens after you feel this rage? Before you black out?"

"I feel ... like I'm shrinking, floating away, separating from reality. Sometimes I can stop myself from leaving by concentrating really hard on something physical. But that's rare."

Dr. Evelyn pointed her pen at me. "Good. That's good. You're naturally using grounding techniques and if we have time today, I'll teach you some more. Okay. Have you ever looked in a mirror and not recognized yourself?"

I froze. "Doesn't everybody?"

"No," Dr. Evelyn said softly. "Can you describe what that experience is like?"

Hot tears sprang up in my eyes. I blinked them back as I choked out in a panic, "Oh my God. Am I crazy?"

"No," Dr. Evelyn said firmly. "Absolutely not. These questions are designed to find out what sort of coping mechanisms your mind has developed in order to deal with trauma you may or may not remember. That's all. And it's not to tell you you're crazy. It's so we can safely deal with those traumas together, and so I can help you develop new coping skills." She shrugged with a smile tugging at one corner of her mouth. "I don't even have a diagnostic code for crazy."

I managed to return a shaky smile as I reached for a Kleenex. "Right. Sorry." I took a breath and pulled my hair off my damp neck, twisting it in my fingers. "Well, I was fifteen the first time I can remember it happening. It was terrifying. Feeling like I was looking at a stranger. Like a stranger was looking back at me. I avoided mirrors for a year, then I just got used to it, I guess. Now I think, 'Oh, you again' and move on."

Dr. Evelyn put down her pen and stared thoughtfully at me. "Have you been institutionalized before, Alice?"

The room shrunk, pressed in on me. The sound of children crying echoed in my head. My lungs hardened and I couldn't take a breath. "I..." The tears fell now, hot and accusatory down my face, then my throat. "Do we have to talk about this now?"

"We don't." Dr. Evelyn shook her head. "It's okay. We'll move on."

There were forty-five more minutes of questions and then Dr. Evelyn gave me a technique to try the next time I felt myself floating away.

By the time I slid back into the buttery leather seat of the Range Rover, clutching an appointment card for two days from now, I was drained. My world felt unstable, and I knew in my gut things would never be the same.

NINE

I received a 911 text from Angeline, asking the group to meet at Island Tiki Hut Bar, one of our regular haunts, at eight p.m.

Charlie'd had a hard time falling asleep, so I was late and still unsettled from my morning appointment with Dr. Evelyn when I arrived. Plus I hadn't found the right time to tell Jake about the appointment, or the courage for that matter, so I was upset and distracted already. Scanning the scattered crowd, I spotted my friends huddled around a high-top table.

"Sorry I'm late. Charlie's at the monster-in-the-closet stage, so I had to stay with him until he fell asleep." I slid onto the empty stool, immediately feeling the somber, worried energy in the group. I directed my attention at Angeline. "So, what's going on?"

"She was waiting for you to get here to tell us." Rhys was peeling the soggy label off his dark beer.

"All right." Vivi shifted impatiently. "She's here, so what's up?"

Angeline shook her head. "I'm not even sure I should be sharing this with you guys, but I can't ... I don't know how to wrap my brain around this, so collective hive mind it is." She squeezed her fingers tightly around her own beer bottle and took a deep breath. "Okay. So, I had a chat with Veora this afternoon. I figured as Director at Project Freedom, she may have some more insight into where Carmen would go. She was really gutted—she kept whispering under her breath in Spanish like she does when she gets upset—and I could tell there was something she wasn't telling me but wanted to. Eventually she broke down and I got the whole story."

She paused and took a swig of the beer. Then she shook her head like she still couldn't believe it. "Apparently, the police located Drac two days ago and were willing to consider charging him with second degree murder in Reyna's death. But, turns out, he has a solid alibi." She twisted a purple-tipped curl around her index finger, her eyes fixed on the table. "He was caught up in a poker game in a back room of C.J.'s Tavern. The room has surveillance cameras, and it checked out that he was there all night."

We collectively groaned.

She held up her hand. "It gets worse. Apparently, about three weeks ago, Drac sent Reyna, along with some other girls, to this party at a prominent businessman's house. Carmen went with her because she had a bad feeling—this guy apparently has a reputation and Reyna was scared. You guys know how hard Carmen was working to get Reyna out with her, yeah?"

"Can I get you something to drink?" a waitress asked at my elbow.

I startled. Then recovering, I pointed at Rhys's beer. "One of those would be fine, thanks."

"Anyway," Angeline continued, "Reyna wasn't all right. Apparently, the host of the party got rough with her. He handcuffed her to his bed, punched her repeatedly in the face and, when she begged to leave, he raped her and then let three more of his friends in the bedroom to take turns."

My hand moved to my stomach as the heat flared. Bile rose in my throat.

Vivi cupped her hands over her mouth, tears glistening in her eyes.

"Jesus," Rhys whispered. "Who? Who was it?"

"No idea." Angeline tore a napkin from the holder and dabbed her eyes. "She couldn't tell me his name— for liability reasons—and there are too many rich businessmen in Sarasota to guess. But, when Carmen brought Reyna to Veora the next morning for help, she talked her into going to the police."

"Let me guess," Rhys said, "they didn't believe her."

"No, they belicved her. Veora has a good relationship with the department so they trust her. Also, Reyna had enough injuries to back up her story, and Carmen was a witness. She'd heard Reyna screaming for help. She'd tried to get into the bedroom and got tossed out of the house and threatened at gunpoint to leave. But, the police said since Reyna was "working" it would be very hard to get a conviction. They were supposed to be looking into it but suggested Reyna leave town. For her own safety."

"Leave town?" Vivi crossed her arms. Her shock and grief were turning to anger. "Where the hell was she supposed to go?"

"Exactly." Angeline rubbed her forehead roughly. "Plus, she was hooked on coke and whatever else Drac had been feeding her to control her. She wouldn't go anywhere she couldn't get a fix."

"And then she ends up dead. Can't be a coincidence," I added.

Angeline stared at me, real fear pooling in her eyes. "No. Carmen didn't think so, either. Before the funeral, she'd told Veora she thought that businessman had killed her or had her killed. Reyna told Carmen someone was following her and she was scared. Carmen just thought the drugs and stress were making her paranoid ... until Reyna actually turned up dead."

"And now Carmen has disappeared."

"I swear to God, if they find that girl behind a dumpster, too," Vivi choked, unable to finish the thought.

I reached over and squeezed her hand, then turned to Angeline. "If the police knew about Reyna being assaulted by this businessman, did they question him about Carmen's disappearance?"

"Don't know," Angeline said. "I was too shocked to think to ask Veora that question. But I'll see what I can find out tomorrow."

"He can't get away with this," Vivi said.

We all stared at Vivi in silence, knowing that yes he could, and probably would, get away with it. The reality was, no one cared about a dead hooker.

The darkness churned in me. A white-hot spark ignited, and a shift in my perception warned of an impending episode. Slipping my phone from my purse, I stared at the date and silently repeated: *It's Monday August 22nd and I'm an adult. It's Monday August 22nd and I'm an adult.*

Rhys rested a hand on my arm. "You okay?"

I forced a nod. The sense of separation was lurking in the corner of my consciousness. But, at least I was aware of the present moment, so that was progress. "Just worried about Carmen."

Rhys squeezed my arm and then thought for a moment. "There had to be other witnesses, right? Reyna and Carmen weren't the only girls at this party. So, we find out who else was there."

"How? Ring up the pimp and ask?" Vivi's frustration lent a sharp edge to her words.

"Maybe we could ask the girls at Freedom to try and find out for us. The girls in the first phase—the one Reyna was in—are still active on the streets. They may know something. Or can find out," Rhys answered.

"If this guy has already killed to get rid of witnesses, I don't know how safe it would be to ask them to poke around about that night." Angeline blew out a deep breath. "I'll talk to the Veora about it though. See what she thinks."

Vivi held up her almost-empty wine glass. "A toast. To not letting the bastard get away with what he's done to Reyna."

"Cheers," Rhys said, knocking her glass lightly with his beer bottle.

"And to finding Carmen safe and alive," Angeline added with her own clink.

"To justice." I tapped my bottle to theirs, while clutching my phone like a lifeline in my other hand.

◆◆◆◆

My eyes fluttered open, and dozens of flickering candles greeted me. A silkiness moved around me as I lifted a hand. I froze. The room was bathed in darkness, except for the warm light of the candles flickering around the tub. The water I was immersed in had grown lukewarm. It sluiced off my bare torso as I pushed myself upright. I glanced around.

How did I get here?

The last thing I remembered was lying in bed, talking with Jake about Charlie's teacher sending home a note. He'd become distraught when another student messed up the pencils he'd arranged neatly on his desk. I'd been worried he was displaying OCD behavior. Jake had been comforting me. I'd teased him about his over-organized closet, then I'd taken a sleeping pill.

And ended up in the bath tub? What time is it?

Disorientated, I lifted the tub plug. The sucking sound of the water swirling down the drain was a bit startling in the silence. Rising, I padded across the bathroom to the towel closet, leaving puddles from my dripping body on the tile along the way. Wrapping a towel around my body, I flipped on a light and blew out the candles. Then I noticed the pile of clothes in front of the sink. Turning, I plucked my yoga pants off the floor and the red t-shirt Angeline had given me with the word "Sisterhood" embossed in gold glitter.

Why are my clothes on the bathroom floor? My stomach clenched. *Had I gotten dressed and left the condo again?*

With a sick feeling in my gut, I tossed the clothes in the hamper and tiptoed back through the bedroom. Leaving a towel wrapped around my wet hair, I slid back under the covers. Jake was snoring lightly. He stirred but didn't wake up. I checked my phone on the nightstand: 2:26 a.m.

I forced my eyes closed. At least it wasn't a nightmare that had woken me up this time. Though I wondered as I drifted off, *was my waking life becoming the nightmare?*

⸻⬤⬤⬤⸻

Tuesday evening we walked through the doors of Ale's Steak House and were greeted by a smiling hostess in a black suit, blonde hair pulled back in a severe bun. I wasn't looking forward to tonight. This dinner was all about schmoozing a new property investor from Miami. I'd much rather be home eating Aurora's homemade hot and sour soup with the kids, looking at the new photos of her girls she'd received in the mail this morning.

"Right this way," the hostess said.

Jake rested a hand on my back. "After you."

As we approached the table, my stomach dropped. Of course, Oliver Brooks was here with his father, Graham. I headed for Graham's wife, Joy, as a buffer.

"Hello, Joy." I bent down and kissed her powdery cheek. The woman was in her seventies but wore impeccably applied make-up, her hair a chin-length bob, dyed a soft natural-looking brown.

"Good to see you," Joy said, as she watched me drape my sequined, black purse over the end chair beside her. "How are the kids?"

"Great. Enjoying the new school year so far."

After Jake finished shaking hands and greeting the family, I forced myself to greet Graham, then their family lawyer, Seth, and lastly, Oliver. I let my eyes skim over Oliver, though, minimizing eye contact, least he get any idea I wanted anything to do with him.

Jake addressed the two men now standing. "And this is my wife, Alice—Alice, this is Alonso D'Cruz, President and CEO of Tropic Investments Group in Miami, and his associate Rex Ramirez."

I rounded the table and shook their hands. "Nice to meet you both. Welcome to Sarasota."

Alonso's eyes were a flat black in the dim restaurant lighting as they swept over me and then landed politely back on my face. His smile was almost fluorescent as he answered, "The pleasure is all mine. And it's a beautiful city."

Rex offered me a polite but dismissive nod, then took his seat and returned to the conversation he'd been having with Oliver.

Another couple showed up after we'd ordered drinks—Mr. and Mrs. Connelly, old friends of the Brooks.

I shifted in my chair and reached for my water goblet. I was still feeling out of sorts, still bothered by my middle of the night activities and feeling detached from myself.

"So, I hear you're trying to get into politics, Oliver." Mr. Connelly's loud, gravelly voice drowned out his wife's, who'd been engaged in a conversation with Joy across the table about a new restaurant they'd tried out. The women fell silent.

"Yes. District two commissioner's seat."

I allowed myself a glance at Oliver since his attention was occupied. He'd gained weight over the past few years, his grey-suited-bulk taking up a lot of space at the table. His face looked bloated and shiny, as if he'd gotten a facial peel. His grey eyes, set a bit too close together were locked on the ice in his empty drink like a petulant child's.

Suddenly his eyes lifted and met mine. I froze.

"When are you going to settle down?" Mrs. Connelly was asking Oliver. "You're what? Forty-two now? Not a spring chicken anymore, Ollie." Only the Connellys could get away with using Oliver's childhood nickname. They'd known him since he was in diapers.

Oliver's mouth pushed up in the corner as he held my gaze. "All the good ones are taken, Faye."

I dropped my gaze to my lap, my face growing warm.

"Faye's right," Graham grunted. "Every good man needs a good woman behind him." He wrapped a meaty arm around Joy's shoulder. She lost a few inches of height from the weight. "I wouldn't be where I am today without your mother. She took care of Ollie, the house, everything so I could concentrate on my career. She's a saint." He planted a loud kiss on her cheek and then released her.

Joy adjusted her top and then drained her wine glass.

The waiter arrived to take our orders. I wasn't sure I could eat. My stomach felt tight and unsettled, so I ordered a small Caesar salad.

"Watching your weight, dear?" Joy asked when the men went back to their conversation. She continued in a conspiratorial whisper, "Good for you. No one wants to be traded in for a younger, thinner model, but it happens. It's important you take care of yourself, keep up your figure."

"If my husband's that shallow, I'll help him pack." My voice trailed off. *I didn't think that. Why did I say that? I would be devastated if Jake left me for a younger woman.*

Joy patted my leg, threw me a look of pity. Her pale eyes scoured my face. "I've got an excellent plastic surgeon." She waved a manicured hand, her diamond tennis bracelet slipping half-way down a bony arm. "You've got a few years, though and a genetic hand-up. Beautiful skin. What are you dear? Middle Eastern?"

"Yes." Every time someone commented on my unusual eyes, skin color or thick hair and asked if my heritage was Indian or Arab or Israeli or any of the other guesses, my answer was always *yes*. It was easier that way. *What else could I say?* I had no history rooting me to the earth, no ancestors to build a story on. I was a woman unmoored. Some would call me lucky. No family skeletons rattling around in my psyche. Being unwanted was both freeing and a wound that got the scab picked off at times like these. A little pain, a little blood seeped through. I washed it down with a mouthful of warm pinot noir.

"The problem is," Jake was saying to Alonso D'Cruz. "Sarasota's housing and rental market has gotten too high for the working class. All the folks in the service industry who keep this city running can't afford to live here. They have long commutes in ever-increasing congested traffic from more affordable surrounding areas. So, we're ripe for an expert in low-income apartment communities like yourself to come in with a solution." He motioned to Graham. "We've got the property. We just need a builder with a vision the city commissioner's board can get behind."

Graham winked at Oliver. "And a board member who'll fight to eliminate the overly complicated regulations."

Well, that explained Oliver's sudden interest in politics.

I glanced at Alonso. He was nodding receptively. If this went well, Jake would be in a good mood tonight, and it would be a good time to talk to him about the test I'd taken and what the results may mean.

By the time we'd finished our meals, we'd also finished a few bottles of red wine and a handful of mixed drinks. The conversation had risen in volume and energy. Joy had moved to sit beside Faye, and they were blocking out the rest of us, heads bent, laughing over some private joke. Everyone seemed in a good mood. Except for the lawyer, Seth, who'd stayed his usual somber self, dark shark-eyes quietly taking in everything. He gave me the creeps.

I turned as a shadow fell across me. Oliver had dragged a chair to the end of the table beside me. He smiled as he plopped down and scooted the chair even closer. "I'm tired of talking business. This end of the table seems much more appealing."

I glanced at Jake. He was thoroughly engaged in some debate with the Miami businessmen.

Oliver followed my gaze. "Don't worry, Jake can entertain himself without you. He always does."

I clenched my jaw, feeling a surge of protectiveness. "What's that supposed to mean?"

Oliver leaned on the table, his eyes focusing on my mouth. "Oh, Alice. You're so innocent. So trusting. It's cute."

I suddenly felt a warm weight on my knee beneath the tablecloth. I froze.

Oliver's eyes were glittering, full of menace. My lungs hardened.

His damp palm slid up my leg, beneath my dress. I tried to jerk my leg away, but he was prepared and clamped down on my thigh with steel fingers. Tears blurred my vision.

He leaned closer, until I could feel his hot, rum breath on my face. "I told you I was tired of waiting."

My insides were trembling, turning to liquid, but I couldn't get my body to move. I could only watch as his eyes narrowed, his face darkening with a mixture of lust and promised violence. It sent waves of terror through me.

Danger. Danger. We are in danger!

A growl escaped his pursed lips as his fingers found the edge of my underwear, and he tried to pull them to the side, scraping my skin with a sharp nail. The pain propelled me upwards as I ripped free from his hand. I pushed the chair back with my foot, not daring to make eye contact with him and hurried to the safety of the women's restroom.

I leaned over the sink, trying to untangle the emotions rushing through me and gulping air. I let the tears fall. The rage battled with fear, humiliation, guilt and shame.

With a moan, I tore a paper towel off the dispenser and ran it under the icy water. Everything felt so out of control. I pressed the damp towel against the back of my neck and met my eyes in the mirror. Slick, shiny black pupils stared back at me. My mouth opened of its own accord. I was mesmerized by the flesh of tongue so red, it looked like a wound.

I felt myself lurch and separate. *No, no, no.* I grasped at the present moment, which was growing slicker. "It's August 23rd and you're an adult. It's August 23rd and you're an adult." Gritting my teeth, I repeated the mantra.

Then a voice spoke, though my mouth didn't form the words. *Do not despair, Alice. Your beauty has been a liability, bringing pain into your life. But now it will be the web we will use to lure and capture the damned.*

"Stop it. Stop it. Stop it," I whispered.

Two women entered the restroom and disappeared behind stall doors. As they came back out, washed and dried their hands, I could feel their silent, questioning stares. I kept my head lowered until they left, then tamped down all the emotions, stuffed them deep to deal with later. I couldn't let Oliver know he'd gotten to me.

Just get through the rest of the night. It's almost over.

When my pulse had slowed, and I was back in control, I released my death-grip on the edge of the sink and tossed the paper towel in the trash. Smoothing my dress down, I stepped outside.

"Hello, Alice."

My head jerked up. I stared at Oliver. He had one hand against the wall, the other shoved deep in his pocket. The threat was palpable as he leaned in, inches from my face. "I don't know why you're avoiding me. You know it's inevitable, you and me."

There was a rush of rage like a waterfall and then I fell back. Not physically but within, like an invisible arm had jerked me into the backseat of my own body. I watched from a distance as I straightened my shoulders and folded my arms below my chest.

My voice was calm and held a tone of amusement I didn't recognize. "Perhaps you forgot to ask because I'm not leaning into your car window in one of those ridiculous tube-top numbers, so I forgive you."

Oliver's blood shot eyes narrowed in confusion. "Ask what?"

"How much."

Silence and then his expression darkened. "You expect me to pay for it?"

I lifted one shoulder casually. "You expect me to give it to you for free?"

Oliver's hand dropped from the wall. He straightened up, staring at me in disbelief. Then with a twinge of hurt in his eyes, he adjusted his suit jacket. "Just for the record, I never called you a whore."

I stepped forward abruptly. When Oliver stumbled back a step, I pushed my face near his and hissed, "No, you just expect me to act like one. And speaking of whores ... I know what you and that sorry group of men you call friends are doing with those girls. The drugs, the assaults, the threats. You are not going to get away with it."

Assaults? Threats? What am I talking about?

"You bitch," Oliver spat. "You think you're so smart. We all have secrets, Alice, and I know yours. Maybe it's time Jake knew, too, huh? How crazy his wife really is."

I heard the low laughter then. The same laughter I'd been hearing when no one was there. It was coming from me. "You silly man. She's not the crazy one."

I felt myself walking away, toward the table. As I sat down, I was suddenly back in control. A wave of nausea swept over me. I reached for my glass. *What the hell just happened?* As I took a sip of water, I knew one thing for sure. Oliver had somehow found out about my stay at the Children's Psychiatric Hospital. That had to be the secret he was threatening me with, which meant I had to tell Jake first.

Ten minutes went by and Oliver still hadn't returned to the table. By then, I was shaking inside. I had no idea why I'd said those things to him, but I knew I'd made a big mistake. I didn't need Oliver as an enemy.

One glance at his clenched jaw when he finally returned told me all I needed to know. I'd triggered the violence in him I'd always tried to avoid by being polite, and he'd gone from wanting to own me to wanting to destroy me.

◆◆◆

I had to endure another forty-five minutes of silent glares from Oliver before the group decided to call it a night. As we all filed out into the warm, moon-lit evening, I glued myself to Jake's side.

"Are you cold, dear? You're trembling." Joy searched my face after hugging me good-bye.

"A bit. The air-conditioning was turned up pretty high in there," I lied.

A sleek black limo rounded the parking lot and pulled up to the doors.

"Our ride," Oliver said, motioning to Alonso D'Cruz and Rex Ramirez.

The men shook hands with us, saying their goodbyes. When the driver opened the limo door, I caught a glimpse of bleached hair. I stepped sideways to get a better view and my stomach clenched. Huddled on the leather seats were three girls clutching champagne glasses, long, bare legs glowing in the LED-lit coach. I recognized two of the girls from Oliver's house, one of them being Gillian. She had her head leaning on another girl's shoulder, her eyes fixed on some unknown spot. My view was blocked as Alonso and Rex climbed in. Oliver turned and smirked at me before he followed.

TEN

"How are you sleeping?" Dr. Evelyn asked, after letting her gaze sweep my face.

I tucked my hands between my crossed knees and shrugged. "My family doctor prescribed me Ambien. I'm falling asleep easier, but I'm not sure I'm staying asleep. I found myself in the bathtub the other night with no recollection of how I got there."

"Sleep walking can be a side effect of Ambien, though incidents do seem to diminish over time. But finding yourself in a situation like that could be more related to your blackouts than the medication. Are you keeping a journal?"

"No, should I?"

Dr. Evelyn nodded. "Journaling is a good idea for many reasons. I recommend it to everyone." She folded her hands in her lap. "So, tell me what's been going on these last few days since we've seen each other."

I wasn't sure what she wanted to hear. *Should I tell her about the kids? The incident with Oliver? Our search for Carmen and what I'd learned about Reyna?* I decided to stick to the reason I was here. "Well, I've been using the technique you taught me to stay grounded, and it seems to be working. Though, I feel like the incidents are getting more frequent. Is that normal?"

Dr. Evelyn smiled and I thought, in that moment, if I could choose a mother it would be someone with a smile like hers.

"I think you're going to have to let go of the word *normal*. There is no normal as far as the mind is concerned. Everyone is unique in how they deal with stress and trauma."

I let my gaze fall to the water burbling in the Zen fountain for a moment. "But, I'm not sure I'm even dealing with trauma. I honestly don't remember having a traumatic childhood except for the one—" I pressed my lips together and glanced up at Dr. Evelyn. I wasn't ready to talk about that.

Thankfully, she didn't press the issue. "The mind has an uncanny ability to divide our individual consciousness into parts. Like when you suddenly arrive at the grocery store, but don't remember driving there because your mind was somewhere else. You don't remember thirteen years of your childhood, Alice, but there are parts of your mind that do hold those memories. Those parts have been walled off to protect you from *something*."

"Something traumatic?"

"Most likely, yes. The threat is gone but your brain has developed sort of a hair trigger, still dissociating when it perceives a threat." She paused, gathered her thoughts. "You see, pieces of traumatic events can be stored as isolated emotion, like the rage you feel before a blackout, or as images or even just feelings. These bits can be accessed more readily and reacted to like a fire-alarm because they're not integrated with complex memory. To help you heal, we need to integrate these bits. Does that make sense?"

I nodded slowly, though I wasn't sure I understood at all.

"Good. So, our goal is going to be to access these pieces and build bridges between those walled-off parts, so you can be aware of experiencing your whole life, past and present."

"Sounds complicated. How do we do that?"

"By dealing with your lost memories. And I'm not going to sugarcoat this, it's going to be hard work. Because of the way our brains are wired, remembering and confronting past traumas will feel like they're happening again, with as much intensity. You're going to have to be brave, but you are not going to be alone this time. Do you trust me?"

Do I? I stared at Dr. Evelyn, at her confident, controlled posture, the compassion burning in her eyes. "Yes. I do. I'm just not sure I trust myself."

Dr. Evelyn nodded once. "You will. One day, you will."

A tiny thrill raised the hair on my arms. *Is it possible to get rid of this darkness inside me? To have a whole, uninterrupted life without blank spaces? And what would be the cost?* "Where would we start?"

"Well, I'd like to tackle this from two sides. On my side I'd like to try hypnosis. It's been used with a high success rate in recovering and integrating dissociated memories. And on your side, I'd like you to start from the beginning. Your life is like a puzzle, a mystery that we must piece together. We're going to need a timeline of events, a linear version of your story. Do you know what happened after you were found abandoned at the Temple?"

I shook my head. "Honestly, I've never really wanted to know. It's always been this monster in my rearview mirror that I never wanted to look back at. I've kept my attention on the road in front of me."

"I understand." Dr. Evelyn tapped her pen on the closed notebook in her lap. "But now you're not alone in the car." She smiled. "Do you think you can start piecing together your past?"

"I guess I'm willing to try."

"Good. May I assume then that you've never researched the day you were found abandoned?"

I shook my head slowly. I felt numb. *Do I really want to open up this gaping wound and dig around in it? No, but it's no longer a choice.*

"I would start there then. At some point, you may need to hire a private detective to help, but for now, surely finding a newborn abandoned at a temple was worthy of some kind of story in the local paper. The larger papers like the *Orlando Sentinel* have archives you can search online. There may be a small fee."

I was sitting forward, on the edge of the sofa now. My hands had grown damp. "I can do that." I licked dry lips. "But, to address the elephant in the room ... what were the results of that test I took? Do I have this dissociative disorder? I ... I was waiting to tell my husband until I knew something for sure." That was a lie. I'd been too exhausted and worried last night to start the conversation with Jake. There was so much I needed to tell him. I couldn't put it off much longer.

Dr. Evelyn's mouth contorted in one corner. "The usual score to indicate Dissociative Disorder is in the 17-20 range. You didn't quite reach that so let's just deal with the symptoms and not worry about the labels for now. Sound good?"

It was a tiny bit of relief. "Yes. Thank you."

"Higher, Mommy!" Addie squealed as I pushed her on the swing.

"Such a brave girl." Reluctantly, I gave her a stronger push and watched her red hair fly up as she was pinned against the sky. It was just a moment and then she was falling again. It would be one of the snapshots in my memory that I returned to when the darkness came. "All right, Mommy's arms are tired. You push yourself for a while. I'll be on that bench right over there."

I settled onto the sun-warmed, wooden bench and dug in my bag for a hairband. The afternoon was stifling hot without a breeze for relief. I'd decided to bring the kids here after school today anyway, because watching them play was one of my guilty pleasures. Medicine for a stressful day.

I couldn't get the image of those girls huddled in the limo out of my head, though. Gillian had appeared to be on something. *Is she dating Oliver?* I shuddered. *No young girl in her right mind would date Oliver. Unless it's for the money. Is he giving her money? Using those girls like prostitutes? Maybe I should ask Jake if he knows what Oliver's up to?* I bit the inside of my cheek, letting the scenario play out. *Nope. He'd confront Oliver and then Oliver would tell Jake my secret. I had to come clean first ... and soon. I couldn't figure out what was going on with those girls until I did. How would Jake react?* My chest tightened. I knew exactly how he would react.

Sighing, I piled my hair up in a messy bun and secured it as I watched Charlie. He was retrieving a soccer ball for the toddler who'd let it roll under the slide. Such a sweet kid. I hoped the world would be kind to him in return.

"Hello, Alice."

Startled, I turned toward the voice on my right and found myself looking into a pair of soft, velvety eyes as dark as midnight. I removed my sunglasses. "I'm sorry, do I know you?"

The beefy woman—wearing a bright yellow dress, her black and graying hair a thick mass of braids—chuckled and it loosened something in my chest. "We've seen each other around." She held out a large hand. "Gia Rossi."

I took her offered hand. "Sorry, I don't have the best memory." She did seem familiar in some way. *Could I have met this woman while suffering from one of my blackouts?* It was entirely possible. "Do you have kids here?" I asked, searching the playground for a clue.

"I don't, no." The woman stared out at the dozen or so kids climbing over the plastic playground equipment. "I meet my clients here sometimes. I find being outdoors comforts them."

"Clients? What do you do, if that's not being too nosey?" I asked, starting to feel disorientated.

"I guess you could say I'm a counselor of sorts. I help people ... remember themselves. Remember their divine nature."

It was my turn to chuckle. "You'd get along great with my friend, Angeline."

"Ah, Angeline DeLavoye from Open Heart Yoga Studio."

I nodded, unable to hide my surprise.

"Yes, she's doing great things, that one."

She knows Angeline? Maybe that's where I've seen her then.

I watched Charlie climb up into the swing his sister had vacated. He was more tentative, pushing himself slowly with one sneakered toe.

"Being a mother is a wonderful gift." Gia's lips were stretched in a wide smile, revealing perfectly white, square teeth. Her voice held no discernable accent but instead had a musical, lyrical quality, like she was reciting poetry. "We can know ourselves through our children. We can look at our children being neurotic, sensitive, stubborn and it's like holding up a mirror to our own nature. Humans are special this way, above the gods." She met my gaze and squinted like she was searching for something.

I laughed then. It felt like a needed soul-stretch. "Tempting fate a bit, isn't it? To say we're above the gods? Though, I do agree with you that being a mother is a gift." I sighed, turning my attention back to the kids. "If only they could stay little forever."

Addie marched over then, her auburn hair wind-blown, a streak of dirt across her cheek. She held out her hands. "I fell off the monkey bars."

I clucked sympathetically as I eyed her bloodied, scraped palms. "My little daredevil. Guess we'd better get you home and cleaned up." Standing, I called for Charlie. Then remembering my manners I turned back to the woman, "Nice to meet you, Gia."

She stared at me with a knowing smile. "Until we meet again."

─••••─

I lay in bed that evening, propped up with pillows, my laptop balanced on my thighs.

Jake was stretched out beside me, the folder of papers he'd been reading now abandoned on the nightstand. "So, you're really going to try to piece together your past? I always thought it was too painful for you to talk about."

I removed my reading glasses. "It's not that it's too painful. I just don't remember most of it. Dr. Evelyn thinks that if I can recover those lost memories, it'll help with the blackouts I'm having. She said if there's trauma in my past it could explain why I'm losing time now. It's my mind's way of dealing with that trauma." I didn't mention the possibility of dissociative disorder. I was holding out hope it wasn't that serious. *Though maybe tonight would be a good time to tell him about my hospital stay?*

"So, she doesn't think there's anything physically wrong either?" Jake's jaw was twitching. He was uncomfortable or worried, searching my face suspiciously.

My defenses went up. I lightened my tone, trying to reassure him. "Nope." I leaned over and pressed a soft kiss on his lips. He tasted like his after-dinner Scotch and he needed a shave. His stubble was a dusting of gold on his sharp jawline. "It'll be fun, anyway. Like putting together a puzzle. You know how much I love puzzles."

Jake seemed to relax. He slid his hand into my hair and tugged me close for a longer kiss. Then he rested his forehead against mine. "Are you sure? You sure you want to remember things that your mind thought it best to block out?"

I ran a thumb over the wedding band circling his long finger, a few nicks and scratches, well worn. "Dr. Evelyn feels it's the only way for me to heal. And I agree. It's time. I really need your support on this, Jake."

"Of course. Come here." The laptop slipped off my legs as he folded me into his lean chest, his arms encircling me protectively. "You do what you need to do. I'm with you one hundred percent." He pressed a kiss onto the top of my head. "Always."

Just say it, Alice. "*Jake, I was locked up in a mental institution when I was fourteen.*"

My heartbeat became audible in my head. "So, there's something I need to tell you."

Jake pulled away from me. Suspicion once again surfacing in his gaze. "What is it?"

I suddenly couldn't bear the thought of him seeing me differently … imperfect, broken. "Promise me you won't let this change the way you see me."

He slid his hand over mine. "I promise. Whatever it is, it won't change the way I feel about you."

His words were what I needed to hear, but I knew every micro-twitch in his face, his eyes, his mouth. He wanted to believe what he said, but whether he knew it or not, he wasn't sure he could keep that promise.

My resolve collapsed. I couldn't do it. Not tonight. *Just give him a small piece of the story. A little at a time so it's not such a shock.* "You should know, I can't remember anything before my thirteenth birthday."

His shoulders loosened, the relief lit up his face as he chuckled. "That's it? Alice, I'm sure it's not uncommon for people to forget their childhood." He pulled me to him. "Did you really think having a bad memory would change the way I feel about you?"

"I guess not." I closed my eyes and breathed in his familiar scent. Comfort was in the smallest details. I felt terrible for being such a coward, but I had something else to worry about right now. "Okay." I pushed away and resituated the computer on my lap. "First, I need to search the *Orlando Sentinel*. See if there were any articles about the day I was found."

I searched for their website and clicked on the 'archives' tab. My heart fluttered as I typed in the search bar: Shiva Vishnu Temple and 'baby found.' Then I put 7-04-86—7-04-87 in the date range, a full year to be safe. Exactly one article came up from 7-5-

86: _Abandoned Newborn Found Outside Popular Orlando Temple_

I lifted my hand to my mouth. My heart drummed in my chest. There it was in black and white. My history, the beginning of my story, which had always seemed like just that ... an abstract story.

You can do this.

Jake scooted closer and rubbed my shoulder. "You okay?"

I forced myself to take a deep breath and exhaled slowly. "I'm okay." With a shaking hand, I clicked on the full text icon and used my credit card to pay the $3.95 fee.

We watched the article appear together and read:

A baby girl, thought to be just a few hours old when she was found last night at Shiva Vishnu Temple on Cherry Street, is in stable condition at Orlando Regional.

The baby, who weighed seven pounds, was found by a group of teens shortly before midnight on the steps of the temple where they were alerted by her cries and called 911.

A search of the surrounding area was conducted by police, who are desperate to find the child's mother. They believe she may have given birth somewhere near the area where the baby was discovered.

The Department of Children and Families has taken custody of the baby girl but the police are appealing to the mother to call the hospital. And anyone who may have *information on the mother or child should contact them.*

They would also like to remind the public that Florida's safe haven law allows parents in distress to drop off a newborn up to seven days old at a hospital or firehouse without being charged.

"My God," Jake whispered. "That makes it real, doesn't it?"

"Yes." I swiped at a tear that had swelled and rolled down my cheek. I thought of the woman who'd abandoned me on a concrete step, abandoned a soft, pink, vulnerable new being ... left me there to whatever fate would fall upon me and never looked back. *How could she? Was she that horrified by what came out of her own body?*

"Hey." Jake folded my hand between his. "This wasn't about you. Your mother obviously didn't feel like she could take care of you."

I let my head fall onto Jake's shoulder. Sometimes I thought he could read my mind. "I know." But I didn't know. Not in my heart, where it counted. In every beat of my heart lived the sharp sting of rejection, of not being good enough to even be loved by my own mother, the one person who should've loved me unconditionally. *So, how could Jake ever love me unconditionally?* "I'll be fine. Just a shock to see it in print." I lifted my face and looked up into his bloodshot eyes. Then I moved closer, pressing my mouth desperately against his. Tonight, I needed to be loved.

ELEVEN

I weaved my way through the crowd at Finn's Bar with Jake's hand on my lower back. Jimmy Buffet was playing over the speakers so Tai's set hadn't started yet. Good, we weren't late.

"Beer?" Jake asked after we'd greeted our friends at the table.

"Sure." I slid into the chair next to Rhys and eyed his thin but broad-shouldered, impeccably dressed date, who'd been introduced to us as just Ben. "Hm, let me guess, another model?" I teased.

Rhys's dark eyes met mine, a conceding smirk appearing. "What can I say? Perk of the job."

I shook my head. "I give up." I moved my attention across the table to Vivi, who'd just handed Ben back his heavy-looking silver watch with a "nice piece" compliment. I noticed there was no empty chair beside Vivi. "Hey, where's Rolf tonight?"

"Had to go to the Country Club." Vivi waved a hand in dismissal, but I caught the flash of anger in her eyes. Prodding her would do no good though. As close as we'd all become, Vivi rarely shared any information about her marriage ... good or bad.

What I knew of their story was Vivi and Rolf Thorn III had dated in high school, but had broken up for four years while Rolf went off to Columbia University to study tax law so he could take his father's place in the family business. But he'd stolen her back from another guy and proposed to her a year after he returned home. When I'd asked Vivi if that's what she'd wanted, she said what mattered was Rolf wanted her, and not just as a trophy wife. He'd first asked her out when she'd had braces and break-outs, and he was the only guy to ever ask her opinion on anything. Jake and Rolf had been friends since the sixth grade.

Angeline leaned over the table. "Hey, guys, before Tai comes on, I wanted to tell you I had that chat with Veora this afternoon."

"Please tell us you have good news," Vivi said.

"Well, she is really gutted about this whole thing, so she's not willing to drop it. She shared some more details with me. Apparently there were deep ligature marks on Reyna's wrists and neck, indicating she'd been restrained when she overdosed. Someone killed her and the businessman, whoever he is, has a pretty good motive. The police said he's got an alibi, but Veora thinks he could've hired someone. Said she's willing to try and find out which other girls were at that party, see if they saw or heard anything. The bad news is if she can't find someone else willing to step forward, without Carmen as a witness there's no case."

"Unless he did hire someone to kill her and that guy gives him up," Vivi said.

"Long shot," Rhys answered.

"We still don't know who this guy is?" I asked.

Angeline shook her head. "Not yet. She plans to ask Freedom's lawyer about outing him, make sure they can't be sued. Oh, but some good news, the Sarasota PD has agreed to hold a press conference to ask for the public's help in finding Carmen."

"I'll get one of the photos I took of her last month to the department, then," Rhys offered. "So they don't use her mug shot."

"Good thinking. Thanks." Angeline shot him two thumbs up.

Jake returned and handed me a cold, dark beer. I pressed it against my temple. It was warm in here and crowded. As Jake took the seat across from me, Tai appeared on stage in black skinny-jeans, a baby blue t-shirt, leather and mala bead bracelets and his chin-length dark hair shining under the spotlight. His beloved acoustic Martin guitar hung over one shoulder as he adjusted the mike. He gave our table a salute and his wife a wink before settling on the stool and cradling his guitar.

A few whistles escaped the growing crowd as people began to notice he'd taken the stage. He was a local favorite, with his buttery voice and half-Japanese, half-Caucasian boyish-good looks.

"Good evening, everyone," he said into the mike, strumming a few bars to warm up his fingers. "How're we doing tonight?"

Hoots and more whistles answered him.

He grinned at the crowd. "Sounds like you're ready for some music."

He was in his element. Tai taught music at Sarasota Middle School to help pay the bills, but performing live was what he lived for.

"I'm going to start with one I wrote for a good friend I lost two years ago called Bullets in the Night Sky." The first few notes he pulled out of the guitar drowned in heavy applause. As the crowd settled down, he closed his eyes and began.

For an hour and a half Tai had the crowd in the palm of his hand, leading us through a roller-coaster of emotional highs and lows with what local music critics had called a "unique blend of R&B and indie-folk."

When he finally exited the stage and came to the table, his hair was damp with sweat and his eyes sparkled like onyx as he greeted us. His grin was the kind that comes from the high of doing what you're born to do.

"Nice job." Jake grabbed another chair and motioned for Tai to take the seat next to Angeline. "Beer?"

He nodded, scooting his guitar case safely under the table. "Yeah, sure. Thanks."

"I'll go with you. I need a refill," Vivi said to Jake after giving Tai a dramatic bow. "Anyone else need anything?"

"I think we're good," Rhys said, then turned to Tai. "Great set, boss." He made introductions between Tai and Ben, who gushed appropriately over Tai's performance.

Angeline handed her husband a couple napkins off the table after he greeted her with a kiss. "Fabulous as always, babe."

"Thanks." He snuck another kiss and then swiped at his sweaty forehead and neck with the wad of napkins. "Hey, Alice. How're the kids?"

I smiled but felt that familiar twitch of discomfort around Tai and the subject of kids. He and Ang had been trying for almost four years to get pregnant, with no luck yet. Angeline confided that it was starting to worry him. "Getting too big, too fast. They both seem to be enjoying school this year so far, though."

He nodded. "Good to hear." Then he wadded up the napkins. "This isn't working. I'm gonna go wash up in the restroom. Be right back." After stealing another kiss from his wife, he disappeared through the crowd.

"How goes the baby-making?" Rhys asked. He knew better than to ask in front of Tai, too.

Angeline shrugged. "It'll happen whenever it happens. I just wish Tai would stop beating himself up about it like it's his fault. We've both been tested for everything under the bloomin' sun and there's nothing wrong. Not the right time, I guess."

"It took my sister and her husband six years," Ben chimed in. "But then last year they had triplets."

Angeline smirked. "You do have to be careful what you wish for. The bloody universe has a sense of humor."

I was glad her sense of humor was still intact, and wished I could do something to help. Ang and Tai would make great parents. They'd be those cool parents, co-sleeping and breast-feeding in public, the parents who took diaper blowouts and screaming public tantrums in stride, their gratitude and awe at creating life unfazed.

"Hey," Rhys nudged my shoulder and interrupted my thoughts. He whispered, "How'd the appointment with the psychologist go?"

"Fine," I said reflexively. Then, when he kept staring at me, I sighed and leaned closer. Keeping my voice low I said, "She wants me to fill in some parts of my past I can't remember. Thinks there may be some trauma there that my mind is protecting me from, that may be causing the blackouts. So," I shrugged, "I'm working on that. I'm going to contact the Florida Department of Children and Families tomorrow. See if I can find out anything about my childhood. Where I went after Orlando General. Who took me in."

"You don't know?"

I sipped my now-warm beer and met his startled expression with openness. "I don't. Not all of it, anyway."

Rhys rubbed his dark shadow of stubble roughly with one hand. "Jesus. I never knew that. I just assumed you didn't want to talk about it." He leaned forward onto the heavily lacquered table and held my gaze. "If you need help, you let me know. Anything at all."

I reached over and squeezed his arm. "Thanks." Then, changing the subject I shook the dregs of my bottle. "What I need right now is a new beer."

He narrowed his eyes and smirked. "I'll let you get away with it for now, but this conversation isn't over." Standing, he added, "I'll see if I can catch Jake at the bar for you."

I made small talk with Ben, all the while feeling bad because he seemed like a sweet guy, but I knew Rhys wouldn't keep him around. I consoled myself with the idea that Ben probably knew what he was getting into. Rhys must've had a reputation by now.

A couple of guys from the table behind us wandered over to talk to Tai. They were standing around chatting about music when Jake, Vivi and Rhys returned. Their attention shifted to Vivi.

At forty-one she still possessed the kind of beauty that demanded attention, with her sharp cheekbones, surgery-perfected curves, long, glossy hair and fitted white dress to show it all off. But she also had a sharp mind and wielded her beauty like a weapon, especially when she was in a bad mood, like tonight.

I glanced behind us. The three guys at the table were elbowing each other and egging on their friend in the black polo shirt.

When I'd first met Vivi, I wasn't sure I liked her. She obviously used her beauty as currency to get what she wanted. But after learning about her past, I understood. She'd been conditioned early on to believe that physical beauty was the only power she had, the only thing that made her visible, that made her valuable.

Black polo-shirt guy peeled away from the conversation with Tai, one hand clutching a beer, the other shoved into the pocket of his khaki shorts. Still handsome in his mid-forties with dirty blond curls and a square jawline, his looks were offset by an ugly strut that only came from a life of privilege mixed with copious amounts of alcohol. Rejection wouldn't sit well with him.

I nudged Rhys as he sat down and gestured with my chin toward an unsuspecting Vivi, who was settling in with her fresh gin and tonic. Rhys's responding cringe echoed mine as he leaned back in his chair. He'd noticed her dark mood, too.

The guy parked a chair at the end of the table and straddled it backwards. Setting his beer on the table, he held out his hand to Vivi with a charming smile that probably opened a lot of doors for him. "Scott. And you are?"

Vivi's honey-brown eyes narrowed. Instead of taking his offered hand, she clicked her large, cushion-cut wedding ring on her glass. "Married."

Scott's gaze brushed off her ring, lingered on her cleavage. His smile stretched like a lazy cat in the sunlight. "Happily?"

She watched his glassy-eyed grin for a second. "I didn't invite you over here, so you can kindly leave now."

Scott didn't budge. In fact, he leaned in closer.

Did he just take that as a challenge? This guy wasn't getting the hint.

His speech was slurred as he said, "I find that sometimes a woman doesn't know what she wants until she's presented with options."

"Is that right?" Vivi's posture was stiff and cold as she folded her arms. "All right, *Scott*, I'll bite. You know I'm married, so what exactly are you offering? One blissful night to make my life magically better?"

Scott's tongue shot out and licked his bottom lip. "It doesn't have to be just one night and I can promise you it would be magical." He reached over and ran a finger over her forearm.

"Brave," Rhys whispered, resting an arm protectively on the back of Ben's chair.

We all knew Vivi could handle herself, but this exchange had everyone at our table on edge.

Vivi's eyes blazed. She slid her arm out of reach. "And I can promise *you* it would be neither magical nor consensual for me so, seriously, leave."

Scott jerked back like he'd been slapped. "Whoa, lady. What the hell? Not consensual?" His eyes hardened, became blue marbles in a red face. His hands curled into fists on the back of the chair.

His sudden rage was like a spark jumping to the fire within me. It caught. My scalp prickled. My own hands balled into fists. I wasn't floating away, but there were strange thoughts racing through my head. Violent ones. *Flashes of smashing the beer bottle over Scott's head. Blood running down his face. Lifting the bottle again. A cracking sound as his nose shattered.*

I shook my head and squeezed my eyes shut. My heart was racing. What was happening to me? *Please stop!*

When I could open my eyes again, the sole focus of Scott's rage was on Vivi. I struggled for control of my own rage—or *was* it mine?—as he laughed harshly. "What are you, one of those chicks who think all men are boogeymen out to rape you?"

Vivi met his glare with her own brand of fury. "Don't you dare get all high and mighty with me about what men's intentions are, Scott. You made your intentions crystal clear and believe me, you're in no way original."

I thought about where her rage was coming from and knew part of it came from the rape she'd experienced at fifteen ...

She'd been so excited to finally be invited to a party. She'd played beer pong for the first time, got so drunk her friends put her in the parents' bedroom to sleep it off. She came to with a senior football player grunting on top of her. The room was spinning. It was dark. When she realized what was happening, her body was too weak, too sick to fight. She could only whisper, "Stop, please." But he didn't. He finished and actually kissed her forehead and said, "Thanks" as he got off and left her half-naked and sticky on a stranger's bed. She never told anyone what had happened back then. She was humiliated. Better to keep her mouth shut. But also, that kiss. The fact that he thanked her, like she'd given him something willingly ... that had confused her, caused her to doubt herself. Maybe she had given him permission somewhere along the way.

"That's some Nazi-feminist bullshit," he scoffed. "But don't worry, I won't take it personally. You obviously just hate men."

Vivi smiled with feigned patience. "I don't hate men, Scott. I love men." She stirred her drink calmly but her hand was shaking. "Remember that mess awhile back where the unconscious woman was raped behind a bar in Gainesville? I don't think most men are him. I think most men are the ones who yanked him off the woman and held the bastard for the police. But, there are enough men out there like him for one in five of us *chicks* to be sexually assaulted." She leaned forward and gave him a smile that held no warmth. "Of course, we're supposed to sit back and say, 'Well, that's just the way guys are, right?'"

He held up his hands. "Hey, I'm not that kind of guy."

"Well, let's hope that's true for the sake of the next drunk girl you try to pick up."

"Whatever, think what you want. I'm out." He stood up and pushed the chair forcefully into the table, grabbing his beer. "You don't know what you're missin'. Crazy bitch," he threw out behind him.

"And there it is," Vivi growled under her breath.

"You okay?" I asked.

Vivi nodded but she was definitely shaken.

Angeline sighed as Scott's friends all cleared out with him. "I'll get 'em."

"What a jerk." Ben leaned forward and motioned to Angeline's departing back. "What's that about?"

"Oh that," Rhys said. "Whenever a guy hits on one of the girls and ends up calling them some version of crazy bitch, they get the "crazy bitch" drink. Ricky, the bartender, actually created it for them, some ungodly concoction of Tequila and rum."

As everyone went back to their conversations, my gaze caught on a black dress, the curve of a cheekbone, an angled bang. The girl turned. Her mouth opened and a sheet of blood spilled out, ran down her neck. I gasped. Then she was gone, sliding around the corner, disappearing down the hall where the restrooms were. *Carmen!* I was catapulted up and pushing my way through the crowd. "Excuse me. Excuse me." A small line of bored women were leaning against the wall.

"Did you see a girl come through here, dark hair, pixie cut, wearing a black dress? She may have been injured?"

Lots of shrugging, head shaking, gum chewing. No one saw her. I waited my turn and checked the bathroom just in case. She wasn't there. Of course she wasn't. She wouldn't still be in the black dress from the funeral. Just a wishful ghost.

But what did it mean? Is she hurt? Dead? Or am I losing my mind?

TWELVE

Friday, after dropping the kids off at school, I sat at the dining table with my hands poised above the laptop keys. The morning sun shone through the wall of glass to my left, and Aurora's humming drifted from the open kitchen behind me. A slight headache was gnawing at my temples from the late night and the anxiety of dealing with my past.

Come on, Alice. Let's do this. I was trying to act braver than I felt.

The Florida Department of Children and Families website was pretty straightforward. It turned out I just had to make an account and submit a request for information on where I'd been placed after they took custody of my newborn self. I had no idea how long it would take to get an email back.

What now?

"You want more coffee?" Aurora called from the kitchen.

I glanced into my empty cup. "Be great. Thanks," I called back.

Maybe it'd be better to work backwards? That would mean contacting the last place I'd been—Garden of Hope Children's Home. I'd left there on my seventeenth birthday. Well, "left" may be too mild a word. I'd suffered through, and graduated from, high school the month before, and I'd had enough of my life being in everyone else's hands. With my meager personal belongings shoved in a pillow case, I'd waited until everyone was asleep and then snuck out the window. I can remember the night sky glittering with stars, a full moon lighting my way across the yard to the road. The adrenaline rush from the fear of getting caught, the excitement of the unknown, and the feeling of freedom on that first bus ride after my escape. It all came rushing back. Funny, I no longer felt that sense of freedom and adventure in my current life. *Where has it gone?*

Aurora's small figure appeared at my elbow as she poured more coffee, the faint scent of furniture polish on her hands. "Is Mr. Jake home for dinner tonight? I'll make his favorite."

"Oh." I stared at the computer screen, distracted. "He didn't say. I'll text him in a bit and ask."

She was still hovering. When our eyes met, she put a small, warm hand on my shoulder. "Something is wrong?"

I motioned to the computer. "No, not wrong really. I'm just trying to get some information on my childhood." She knew I'd grown up in foster homes, but of course, didn't know about my lack of memory before thirteen. "Fill in some blanks. I'm just anxious I guess."

"Ah, good. That's good. The past is important to know. Otherwise, how do we avoid the mistakes we've already made?" Her warm chuckle put a genuine smile on my face. "I'll bring you some fresh orange juice, too." She gave my shoulder a last squeeze and silently padded away. Aurora's answer to everything was food.

Okay. It had been thirteen years, but it was possible some of the same staff was there. I typed 'Garden of Hope Children's Home Orlando' in the search bar. As the page loaded, my chest constricted. It became hard for me to breathe. I pushed back from the table and went to stand in front of the floor-to-ceiling windows, drawing comfort from the familiar view.

You're safe. You're an adult. You're safe. You're an...

Suddenly, it happened again, the sensation of being jerked into the backseat of my own body. I was no longer in control.

"One fresh orange juice." Aurora sat the glass down beside my computer.

I walked back to the table and slipped into the seat. "Thank you kindly. May I ask you something?"

Aurora nodded, taking the seat at the end of the table. "Anything, Alice, you know this."

I watched as my hand lifted the orange juice glass, and I examined it in the sunlight. "Is it not hard for you to be without your children?"

We've already discussed this, had long conversations about it. Why am I asking Aurora this now?

Aurora's head tilted like a bird, and she swept her gaze quickly over me. Her mouth puckered with concern.

Can she tell something's wrong?

"Of course. It is very difficult. But it is better than my girls going hungry. Or not getting an education.

We do what we must for our children as mothers. Not being there is a small price to pay."

I sat the juice back down. "But don't you feel guilty about not being there?"

"Yes. Guilt is also part of motherhood, no? In the beginning my heart breaks when I do anything for your children. I say, I should be doing this with my own children. But guilt does no good. I made a choice and I believe it is the right one, so I make the best of it. Besides, I speak to my girls every day. I'm still in their lives."

"Guilt and sacrifice. This is what you believe motherhood to be?"

"Those are parts of it. Not the best parts though." Aurora reached across the table and squeezed my hand. "Are you sure you are all right?"

The voice echoed, reaching me where I sat waiting: *You may have to sacrifice being without your children too, Alice. You must stay strong like Aurora.*

Then I was pushed up front again. Back in control. I tried not to show how startled I was. I cleared my throat, testing the control I had. "Yes but … if something happened to me, if I couldn't be with the kids, would you stay with them?"

Aurora's eyes widened. "You are sick?"

"No," I said carefully, not wanting to lie to the woman who'd been so good to us. "Not that I know of. I've been having some problems with headaches and memory, so the doctors are trying to find out what's going on. I need to know you'll be there for the kids … just in case."

Aurora stood and gave me a hug. "You don't need to worry. I am here." She rested her hand on my cheek for a moment. "Adelyn and Charlie are also like my children. It fills me up to love them, too."

I wiped at a tear that broke loose and smiled at her. "We're all lucky to have you."

When she left me alone again, I sipped the orange juice, letting my nerves calm down. I needed to talk to Dr. Evelyn about this feeling of not being in control of my own body. I glanced back down at the screen. Garden of Hope Children's Home was the first result.

Clenching my jaw, I clicked on it. A photo of the two-story, brick colonial home stood center page with clickable sections beneath: About GHCH, How to Help, Success Stories.

It was a small home, as far as orphanages go, only housing twenty children at a time, staffed with a director (Miss Franny), office personnel, a counselor and two sets of "parents."

I clicked on the "Contact Us" tab and found the phone number. Before I could change my mind, I picked up my cell and called.

"Garden of Hope, Laura speaking."

I clutched at my necklace, forcing my dry tongue to move. "Hi, Laura. My name is Alice Leininger. I lived at Garden of Hope on and off until I was seventeen. I'm calling because ... I was wondering how I go about getting my records from you?"

"Sure, Alice, I'd be glad to help you with that. What's your birthdate?"

"July fourth nineteen eighty-six. My last name was Brown at the time."

"Eighty-six? You'll be a few months past your thirtieth birthday then, right?"

"Yes."

"All right. We usually only keep the physical files in storage up until a child's thirtieth birthday. Some parts of the case files have been digitized, so we'll definitely have those. What I'm going to need from you is a written request, along with a copy of some form of photo I.D. like your driver's license. You can scan that and email it to me if you'd like. Meanwhile, I'll have someone check storage and see if they've purged your physical records yet. There'll be a mailing fee, depending on what we're sending you. I'll let you know what that will be once I find out the status of your files."

My voice was thick with emotion as I gave Laura my phone number and thanked her. Feeling numb, I drafted the email request and then went to Jake's office to scan my driver's license, which I'm glad said Alice *Brown*-Leininger so there'd be no questioning who I was. I wasn't sure why I'd hung onto the name Brown, used it as my middle name. Maybe this was why. Maybe deep down I'd known all along I'd have to face my past.

I texted Jake to ask what time he'd be home tonight. Then, I tried to decide if I'd have enough time to squeeze Angeline's 9:30 a.m. yoga class in before my 11:30 appointment with Dr. Evelyn. Closing the laptop, I decided the stress relief would be worth the rush.

—◆◆◆—

I sat in Dr. Evelyn's office in my yoga outfit, a bit sticky with dried sweat but much more relaxed.

"How are you today, Alice?" Dr. Evelyn's smile was warm, her eyes a transparent blue.

I really thought about the question, since she really wanted to know. "It was a rough morning. I'm a bit nervous about getting my records from Garden of Hope, that's the Children's Home I stayed in on and off," I explained. "I called them this morning and they said they had some records digitally archived and would check storage to see about the physical stuff."

Dr. Evelyn nodded slowly. "Very good."

"Oh, and I found the article in the *Orlando Sentinel*, about my discovery at the Temple." I opened my bag, slid out a folded sheet of paper and handed it to her. "I printed out a copy for you."

My stomach clenched as Dr. Evelyn slipped on her glasses and began to read. It was silly. Of course she wasn't going to judge me, see me differently now that she was holding proof I'd been unwanted, even as a helpless newborn. I wrestled with that insecurity and finally, with great effort, flung it off a cliff in my mind. Dr. Evelyn was here to help me, not judge me.

When Dr. Evelyn was done, she removed her glasses and folded the article back up. "May I keep this?"

I nodded, noting the new, glassy sheen in her eyes. *Has the article upset her?*

"How did it make you feel reading this, Alice?" Her voice was strained.

Yes, definitely affected. I was surprised at the doctor's vulnerability, but grateful because it made it easier for me to accept mine. "It made me feel ... sad, hurt. It made the abandonment more real, sharper, I guess. I feel exposed but also, I think I feel a bit more anchored to this life now." My attention locked on the fountain, my voice growing more distant. "And maybe less invisible ... less like a ghost haunting this world. There'd been a record of me, even though no one wanted me. I existed. Life wanted me to exist. It's there in black and white." I shook myself and came back to the room, a bit embarrassed by my openness. "Anyway, I also emailed the Department of Children and Families to see where I was placed after I left the hospital. Not sure how long it will take to hear back from them, though."

Dr. Evelyn scratched her pen on the notebook and then sat it down, folding her hands on her knee. "I want you to give yourself credit for this first step. It's a big one. To open the door you've kept firmly shut all these years. You're being very brave."

My cheeks warmed at the act of being praised like a child. But, I also let the praise soak in and absorbed the idea of being brave. "I've never felt brave. And right now I feel like I don't have a choice."

"But you do. You have a choice between just surviving in a life that's full of black holes, frustration and in your own words 'monsters in the rear-view mirror' and a life where you can close up those holes and dissolve those monsters by facing them. By taking this first step, you've made a choice to face those monsters. See? Bravery."

I couldn't help but return Dr. Evelyn's smile. "Or maybe I just don't know what I'm getting into."

Dr. Evelyn chuckled. "Somewhere you know, believe me. Or your mind wouldn't have dedicated so many resources to protecting you from it."

Anxiety lifted the hairs on my arms. "Right." I wiggled my foot, trying to find the words to describe what had been happening. "There's something else. Something has happened twice now, but it's really hard for me to describe. It was really frightening."

"Just try your best."

I rubbed my temples. "Okay. Both times it felt like I was watching myself like a movie. Like I wasn't really in control. And I said confusing things. Things I had no idea why I was saying them." I shook my head. "I'm not explaining it right."

"It's okay. I understand what you mean." Dr. Evelyn tapped her pen on her lip for a second and then checked the clock. "Let me tell you what I'd like to do. We have about thirty minutes left, so I'd like to introduce you to hypnosis. It will eventually help us untangle what you described to me. But for now, we won't try to get to the bottom of anything or dig anything up. We'll just let you feel the sensation of being deeply relaxed, so you'll know what to expect for our next session. On Monday, we'll go deeper and begin to explore. Do you have any questions or concerns before we start?"

"Deep relaxation sounds good." My voice was calm, but my hands had grown clammy. "Will I stay conscious?"

"You will be in complete control the whole time, but in a different state of consciousness. I'm just going to take you into a light trance today. Your breathing and heartbeat will slow, your brain will be producing alpha waves, which is the same state you're in when you're daydreaming or watching television."

"Doesn't sound too scary."

"It's really not. You just lie back on that pillow there and get comfortable."

I moved into a comfortable prone position. There was a swooshing as the curtains were partially closed. The room dimmed. A warm, yellow light flicked on in the corner. I unclenched my fingers and turned my head at the sound of scraping across the hardwood floor. Dr. Evelyn was moving the small table out of the way.

"There we go," she said, the hum of her wheelchair filling the silence as she maneuvered herself beside me. "All right. Please close your eyes and take a deep breath in through your nose. Good. Breath out slowly while you listen to the sound of my voice."

I fell quickly into the soft space Dr. Evelyn opened.

—◆◆◆—

"You're getting more butter on your face than in the bowl." I smiled and wiped Addie's face with a dishtowel. Dinner was over so she was standing on a chair, helping Aurora make brownies.

"Okay. Here, since you like to play in the butter, you grease the pan." Aurora removed the bowl from in front of Addie, replacing it with a pan. Then she handed her a tub of Crisco. "Make sure you get the corners."

"Can I take some brownies for Miss Elsa?" Addie asked, digging her fingers into the white lard.

"Of course you can." I kissed the top of her head, inhaled the fruity scent of her hair. I was glad Addie liked her teacher. Of course, Charlie'd had Miss Elsa for kindergarten, too, so I already knew the woman had the patience of a saint. "What else do you need?"

"Two eggs." Aurora took over the mixing bowl contents.

"Two eggs it is." I went to the fridge, keenly aware of a strange sense of well-being. *Is it the after-effects of the hypnosis session from this morning?* I should probably just enjoy and not question it.

I placed the egg carton on the marble countertop beside Aurora. My phone vibrated in my back jean's pocket. Sliding it out, I read the group text message from Angeline: *Press conference Channel 10 five min!*

I texted back: *Thx watching*

"Mom has to watch something on the news. Be back in a bit." Clutching my phone, I crossed the kitchen into the living room and found Jake and Charlie curled up on the leather sofa, both enthralled in a fishing show. They looked so cozy I hated to break it up. "Hey, Charlie, can you go help Aurora in the kitchen for a few minutes. She's making brownies. Mommy needs to watch something on the news."

Jake looked at me curiously then ruffled Charlie's hair. "Go on buddy, we can finish this later."

"Okay." Charlie's tone was one of disappointment, but he hopped off the sofa and disappeared anyway.

"What's up?" Jake asked as I lowered myself onto the sofa and picked up the remote.

"Sarasota PD is holding a press conference about Carmen." I switched to the news channel.

Chief Price was decked out in his black uniform and black tie, standing behind a podium and staring at a leather notebook in his hand. His complexion was gray and puffy pouches of skin hung beneath his eyes. A large poster of the Sarasota PD badge and an American flag stood behind him.

He looked up and nodded, apparently at some cue off camera, then leaned closer to the microphones attached to the podium and cleared his throat. "Thank you all for coming. We really appreciate our partnership with the media, and I want to thank you for getting here on such short notice. The reason we've called this conference today is to ask for help from the citizens in our community to locate a missing person. We're in the twelfth day of the search for this young lady, Carmen Castiel." Chief Price picked up a photo and held it out to the cameras. It was one Rhys had taken of Carmen. Thank the stars it wasn't her mug shot; I couldn't imagine that garnering much sympathy. "Miss Castiel is missing and considered endangered. There are a number of investigators working on different aspects of her disappearance at this time, but we've been unable to locate her. Miss Castiel is a former sex worker, who was in the process of getting out of the life with the help of Project Freedom. She's also a witness in an ongoing homicide investigation."

I was glad to hear him say "ongoing." Reyna hadn't been forgotten.

The chief paused to consult the leather notebook. "She has no family that we're aware of and has not been in contact with anyone at Project Freedom, nor been back to the room at the safe-house she is currently staying in. She was last seen walking along US 41 around the mall area on Sunday, August 14th around 3 p.m. wearing a black dress and black flip-flops. Miss Castiel is twenty-two years old, five-foot-five, light brown skin, short dark hair, brown eyes, weighing approximately a hundred and twenty pounds. She was not carrying a cell phone at the time of her disappearance. If you see, or have any contact with, Miss Castiel, please call 911 or you can reach us through Crimestoppers. Any tips or information will be greatly appreciated. Thank you. I'll be taking questions at this time." He pointed up front. "You with the gray shirt. Go ahead."

"You mentioned her being a witness in an ongoing homicide investigation. Can you tell us which case you're referring to?"

The Chief hesitated and then said, "Yes. The death of seventeen-year-old Reyna Flores. She was an acquaintance of Ms. Castiel's and Project Freedom was also trying to help extricate her from a life on the streets." He pointed to a different reporter. Bursts of flash like a strobe made him squint as the reporter asked her question.

"I thought Reyna overdosed?" Jake asked, his thumb rubbing my shoulder absentmindedly.

I'd filled Jake in on what'd happened to Reyna at a local businessman's party but not the recent update. "That's what we thought at first, too. But apparently there were signs she'd been restrained when she'd overdosed, ligature marks on her wrists and throat.

Cause of death was officially overdose, but the police think it was forced.

"She'd been scared, too. Told Carmen someone was following her. Carmen told Veora she thought the businessman who had the party was involved with Reyna's death. That's why we're so worried about Carmen's safety. What if she'd decided to confront him herself?"

After all, she may have set her pimp's car on fire. Who knew what else she was capable of in her state of grief and anger?

Jake's gaze was locked on the press conference. "She could've got scared, decided she didn't want to testify and skipped town."

I leaned back into the solidness of his body. "I wouldn't blame her for being scared but ... without going back for her clothes? Her cell phone? That wouldn't make sense."

"I'm not sure it's possible to be scared and rational," Jake said, tucking me protectively under his arm. "But yeah, doesn't seem to be the likely scenario."

I didn't want to think about the likely scenario, but the thought came anyway. *Will we be attending another funeral?*

THIRTEEN

Monday morning, I lay on the grey sofa in Dr. Evelyn's office while she readied the room for our hypnosis session. Curtains drawn part-way. Soft, yellow light clicked on. Table moved. But this time, Dr. Evelyn had also set up a video camera.

"I like to record the sessions," she explained, "so if there's anything I feel you need to see, we have that option." She maneuvered her wheelchair in front of me, a notebook in her lap. "Okay, the goal here is twofold. First we want to construct a comprehensive narrative for you, give you a sense of continuity of self. A life-story without holes and stops. Does that make sense?"

"Yes," I whispered, already relaxing under Dr. Evelyn's soothing, calm voice.

"Good. The second goal is to reframe any traumatic experiences that may resurface. Over time and repeated access, these fragmented and dissociated bits of memory will be transformed, defused and stored differently ... as narrative memories, allowing your adult-self to view them with greater understanding and compassion. Go ahead and close your eyes and take a deep breath in."

I breathed in lilac-scented air, drew it deep into my lungs. My lungs expanded and my hands relaxed on my stomach. It felt good to let go.

"Good. Now during this session I want you to allow the memories to come without forcing them or trying to stop them. Let them flow like water. Another deep inhale ... and exhale. Very good." Her words stretched, softened as she took me deeper into the trance.

"Now I want you to imagine you're standing on a beach. It's a beautiful, clear day. The sun is warming your skin. The water is lapping gently at your bare feet. This is the only sound, the lapping of the water. You look down and notice beneath the crystal-clear water, the sand is covered with stones. The stones are all different shapes, sizes and colors. You realize that each stone is a memory from your childhood. Some were hurtful at the time, but you can see they happened long ago and can't hurt you now. As an adult you can re-examine those memories with a different perspective and put them where they belong, in the past. You pick up one of the stones now and bring it with you to the shore. The sand is soft and warm as you sit down to examine the memory. Tell me what you see."

My words came slowly, drawn from somewhere far away. "Booths. Booths with games. Pick-a-duck. Ring toss. A wall of balloons. Oh, you throw darts. Win prizes. Stuffed animals. The air smells sweet and greasy, like fried dough. My feet are getting dirty. I shouldn't have worn flip-flops. But it's so hot today."

"You're at a carnival?" Dr. Evelyn asked quietly.

"Yes."

"How old are you?"

"Fourteen. I'm fourteen since Monday. Martin and Clara brought me, my foster parents. They're like really old, but they've been nice to me so far. I have my own room." A small frisson of tension rippled through my body.

"Is there something wrong, Alice?"

"No. Yes. That man with the mustache and green t-shirt has been staring at me. He keeps smiling at me but not a nice smile. His eyes are all wrong. This is the third time I've seen him. He's making me uncomfortable." I fell silent. My head jerked.

"This is just a memory. It's not happening right now. The man can't hurt you." A pause. "What are you doing now?" Dr. Evelyn asked.

"I'm staying close to Martin. The man is coming towards us now. I'm ducking behind Martin. The man ... he's talking to Martin. Why is Martin being so nice to him? He must not see what's in the man's eyes."

"What is the man saying?"

"He's saying, 'I won this bear and don't have a daughter to give it to. I'd like to give it to that pretty young lady with you.'" I shook my head slightly. "I don't want it. I just want him to go away. Stop staring at me. My face is burning. But Clara has a grip on my arm, and she's yanking me out from behind Martin. 'Well, isn't that kind of you. Don't be shy, Alice. Thank the nice man for his gift.' I'm staring back at him. His eyes are eating me alive. My throat is dried up, and I barely hear him over the pounding in my ears. 'Alice, what a pretty name for a pretty girl.' I'm looking up at Martin for help, but he looks confused by my behavior. Then he looks mad. Why is he mad at me? He says, 'Go on, say thank you.'"

I was shaking my head. A weak "thank you" falls from my lips. Tears dropped onto the pillow.

Dr. Evelyn moved her tone back to conversational. "Okay, Alice. Put the rock down now. In a moment I'm going to count to five, and when I get to five you'll be fully alert and feeling refreshed and relaxed. Ready? One. Two. Three. Four. Five."

I moved back toward awareness of the office. I was relaxed, so finding my face damp with tears was surprising.

Dr. Evelyn fiddled with the recorder. The tiny red light died. "How are you feeling?" She held out a box of tissues.

I plucked a Kleenex from the box and sat up. "Fine actually. Wow, I haven't thought about Clara and Martin for ages. And I forgot all about that stalker guy at the carnival." I twisted my hair around my fingers, reviewing the memory. "I remember now. I stuffed that bear in the trash can in the garage as soon as we got home."

"You seemed pretty upset."

"Yeah, I guess I was. I wanted Martin to protect me, tell the guy I was only fourteen and stop being a creep or something. But they thought it was a nice gesture." There's a stirring of dark emotion. I poked at it. "Also, I felt guilty. Like I'd done something wrong. Like I made that man notice me. I felt like Martin thought I did something to draw his attention, too."

"But now that you can look back with adult wisdom, you know you did nothing wrong," Dr. Evelyn said. "In fact, your instincts were spot on. The guy was being a creep."

I looked into her eyes and smiled. Even this many years later it felt good to have my reaction validated. "And I guess Clara was taught to be polite, so she was teaching me to be polite." There's something darker there, though. Maybe she understood being polite to avoid the anger, too. Maybe that was the real lesson.

I dropped my hands and let my hair fall over my shoulder. "They were nice people, but I didn't stay with them very long either. I screwed up pretty bad."

"Do you want to talk about what happened?"

My chest contracted. The plates in my mind shifted, became unstable.

Tiny paper cups of pills. Scratchy white sheets. Nurses in pink uniforms. The click of the door locking.

"Not yet."

❖❖❖❖

As I waited in the car line to pick up the kids, I checked my email on my phone. There were two in my inbox that sped up my heart rate. I clicked on the one from the Department of Children and Families:

Mrs. Leininger,

Thank you for your inquiry. You will find a copy of the court documents below, dissolving parental rights for Alyssa Grace Doe, birthdate July 4, 1986, social security number: 086-55-3787 on September 9, 1986. Child was placed in the care of Garden of

Hope Children's Home in Orlando, Florida on July 6, 1986.

I stared at the official document beneath that, vaguely picking out the words "reason" and "abandonment." Then I dropped the phone into my lap and gazed out the window. The palm tree fronds caught the sunlight, sparkled. The brick school building wavered like a mirage. The sky was a white screen. Everything had a sharp, bright edge to it.

Doe? I'd always assumed that whoever had named me Alyssa Grace, had also given me the last name Brown. Brown is the name on my social security card. When did my last name change from Doe to Brown?

I rubbed the space between my brows, where a headache threatened to take root. *What am I doing?* Tearing into my perfectly constructed life. *What if I can't handle what I found out?* Charlie and Addie didn't deserve this. They needed me to be stable … sane.

A chuckle echoed. Is that what you are right now?

A loud bell rang. Children began to trickle out of the buildings. I shoved my phone back into my bag. The other email, the one from Garden of Hope, would have to wait. I'd take the kids to the park and read it there, outdoors, where it'd be easier to breathe.

—◆◆◆◆—

"Race you!" Addie flung open the car door and hit the ground before Charlie got his seatbelt off.

Charlie moaned. "Mom, tell her it's not a fair race if you don't start at the same time."

I bit my lip to keep from smiling at his innocent belief that the world was fair. Oh, how I wish it was in my power to make it so. "We'll discuss it with her later. Go play."

I walked to the wooden bench as Addie claimed her favorite swing and yelled for Charlie to push her. Sitting down, I shoved my sunglasses on top my head and watched them for a blissful moment. Charlie, his face scrunched up and red with determination. Addie, her coltish legs pumping, her sparkly pink shoes glittering in the sun. The rhythm untangled my nerves and softened my chest.

When I was ready, I took out my phone. The email from Garden of Hope had a little paperclip by the date. My digital records must be attached. With a hesitant touch, I opened the email and read:

Mrs. Brown-Leininger,

I've attached the files here for you that were digitized. I also have good news. We've recovered your physical records from storage and will be mailing those out to you in the next day or two. The charge on that is $23.00. You can mail a check or call me with your credit card number.

I hope this helps.

Best,

Laura Beringer

Great. Probably best to wait until I'm on my computer to open the digital files, where they'd be easier to read. I stuffed my phone back into my bag. When I looked up, that woman I'd met before with the gray braids, Gia Rossi, was walking out of the trail, coming toward me. I waved.

"Beautiful day, isn't it?" Gia smiled as she took a seat next to me. The scent of rich earth and pine drifted from her. "A good day with fresh air and sunshine for the children."

"Sure is." I watched Addie jump off the swing mid-air. I cringed and held my breath until she stood up and raced after Charlie, red hair glistening in the sun. I sighed.

Gia chuckled beside me. "May she never lose that free spirit."

"Yes." I smiled, despite the worry. "She is fearless."

"And your son?"

"Charlie?" I found my son, who had stopped, his blond head bent, studying something in the sand. Probably ants. He could watch ants for hours. "Charlie is more cautious. But he's got a great imagination."

"Imagination is important. Who's to say what's true when this world is but a packet of energy for your brain to interpret into color and shape. Why not imagine dragon wings on horses?"

A memory floated toward me. *Colored pencils scattered on a school desk. My fingers holding a blue one, shading in ... wings ... on a horse.*

Startled, I glanced over at Gia. The woman was sitting serenely, her attention out in front of her. No, of course, it was just a coincidence. She couldn't know that about me. Lots of preteens probably drew horses with wings. She was a strange woman though.

I glanced back at the trailhead. "I haven't walked that trail in a while. Charlie thought he saw an alligator in the creek beside the trail when he was five. He wouldn't go back after that."

"That imagination." Gia turned and met my gaze. It was a shocking moment, one of recognition that came and went in a flash. "I'm sure he gets that from you, but Alice ... there are things that may seem impossible. Things you will refuse to believe because they are too foreign to your senses. Believe them. Believe in yourself."

...I help people remember who they are...

I wanted to brush off her words as the ramblings of an eccentric old lady. But some quality in her voice rang of truth and urgency, which made it impossible to dismiss them. I could only nod.

She echoed my nod then her mouth melted into a warm smile, the seriousness disappearing. "You know Rumi?"

"Thirteenth century Persian mystic, yes. I'm very fond of his poetry."

"Rumi came here because he'd fallen in love with humans and their vulnerability. He wanted to help them, point them in the direction of true love with his gift of words."

"Came here? What do you mean?" I wanted to laugh, but a prickling of heat in my chest stopped me. Besides, it would be rude.

She pursed her lips. "Some would call it reincarnating, I suppose. It is a recycling of energy. He was not originally created as part of the human race." She turned to me, her eyes willing me to understand something.

That something was wriggling within me, like a caterpillar struggling against its chrysalis walls, wet wings eager to be free, to stretch and fulfill their destiny.

Charlie walked over, his hair darkened around his forehead with sweat, his eyes bright green in the sunlight. "I'm hungry."

My voice sounded distant as I said, "Go tell your sister it's time to go then." I stood, feeling a bit lightheaded and out of sorts. "Enjoy the rest of your day."

Gia chuckled softly. "We surely will."

--◆◆◆--

The kids were tucked in bed and Jake had retired to his office before I allowed myself to think about the information waiting for me from Garden of Hope. It was time to face it.

The moon was a pale streak on the dark waters outside the bedroom window as I slid back onto the bed, rested against the headboard and opened my laptop.

Breathe, Alice. Here we go. Be brave.

I clicked on the email. Closed my eyes. Took a deep breath. Blew it out. Opened my eyes. Clicked on the attachment. A yellow folder appeared. Clicked on that, ignoring my shaking hand. Within the folder were a dozen or so individual documents: *case plan, predisposition report, judicial review report, comprehensive assessment, medical health histories, mental health report,* and the one that almost stopped my heart, *adoption form.*

Adoption? Had someone wanted to adopt me? If so, why did they change their mind? Only one way to find out. I opened the document.

More photocopied pages. I scrolled down to the first one: *Agency – Foster Parents Placement Agreement. Name of child: Alyssa Grace Doe ... case number ... birth date ... etc. Foster Parent's Name: Michael and Trudy Brown.*

Brown!

Glow in the dark stars on the ceiling. Soft pink nightgown. Giggling...

I struggled with the memory as it dissolved out of reach.

With growing frustration, I scrolled through more scanned pages: *background check, home study, etc.* until I came to *State of Florida Certificate of Adoption.*

My hand flew to my chest. *Oh my God!* I gathered my shirt in a fist and held on tight as I read over the official document dated September 7, 1986.

I raised my head and stared at nothing, my mind reeling. I'd been adopted when I was only two months old. Adopted! A family had wanted me. Tears spilled down my face. *What had happened?*

Jake entered the bedroom and stopped when he saw me. "Alice?" He moved quietly to my side. "What's wrong?"

I stared at him, my hand still clutching my shirt. "Michael and Trudy Brown." My voice was barely a whisper. "They adopted me."

"What? When?" Jake moved his gaze from me to the laptop. Then he lowered himself onto the bed next to me and read. "So, you were two months old? What happened to them?"

"I ... I don't know." I blinked to get the screen back in focus, then opened the remaining folders, feeling braver now that Jake was next to me. There were three other foster agreements. One was in 1995 with a Chad and Bianca Worthington.

I would've been what? Nine? Why wasn't I with my adoptive parents?

Another was in 1999 with Sherry Green. That one I remembered. The woman who burned my hand on the stove. I'd been thirteen and only stayed with her a few months. And then the one with Clara and Martin when I was fourteen. No other mention of Michael and Trudy Brown.

I sighed. Exhaustion was setting in. "Garden of Hope is mailing me the rest of my records. I should have them in a few days. I'm sure there'll be something in there to explain what happened to ... the people who adopted me." *My family*, I almost said.

It occurred to me I could do a Google search for them. But, I was too tired and too emotionally drained to even think straight tonight. Also, a prickle of warning rose in the back of my mind. A flashing red light. I closed the laptop. *Tomorrow.*

Jake squeezed my hand, leaned over and pressed his lips to my forehead. "You're trembling. Do you need a sleeping pill?"

I rolled my head toward him, my eyes already closing. "I don't think I'll have any trouble sleeping tonight."

But I was wrong.

My mind tortured me with terrifying images—rivers of blood, shattered glass, raging fires—screams. Gut-wrenching, heartbreaking screams.

I awoke in the dark, my scalp and back drenched in sweat, my heart pounding in my ears.

Just a dream. Just a dream.

FOURTEEN

A dull thumping behind my eyes distracted me as I dropped the kids off at school Tuesday morning. The temperature had already reached eighty degrees and there wasn't a cloud in the sky, which made dark sunglasses and air conditioning a necessity. My phone beeped.

"Have a great day." I savored hugs from the kids before they hopped out. Sliding down the passenger window, I called, "Addie, don't forget to give Miss Elsa your field-trip permission slip."

Addie waved in acknowledgement before skipping over to a group of tiny, pony-tailed girls gathered by the glass doors. I sighed. That was going to be trouble in ten years. I pulled into a parking space and checked my phone.

A text from Angeline: *Can u meet me at studio after u drop off kids?*

I texted back: *on my way*

Angeline was waiting out front, sipping from a ceramic mug, her elephant bag slung around one shoulder. When I drove up, she jumped into the car, grinning. The scent of chai tea drifted from her mug as she placed it in the cup holder.

"What's up?"

Her excitement felt like a hundred bumble bees stirring the air. "Danna gave me the name of one of the other girls at the party that night." She yanked on her seatbelt. "You don't mind going with me, yeah? I don't want to mess this up."

I put the car in reverse. "Of course. Where are we going?"

She dug out her phone and pointed down the street. "Go left on Washington." Then she turned in the seat as I drove. "Okay, so this girl's name is Josette Owens. She's got a meeting with her case manager this morning at nine, so hopefully we can catch her coming out."

"Not to put a damper on your enthusiasm, but how do we know she'll show?"

"She got busted for prostitution two weeks ago. Instead of jail, she agreed to participate in the Turn Your Life Around Program, so if she completes the program, the charges will be dropped. This is the lesser of two evils."

"So Danna told *you* this Josette Owens girl was at the party? Why not tell Veora instead?"

"Oh, she did. Yesterday, Veora tried to talk Josette into telling the police what she saw. Veora said she really seemed like she wanted to, but she's scared. She's only just turned eighteen. God, just a baby." She made a noise of disgust deep in her throat. "Anyway, Veora thought maybe I could befriend her, let her know she's not alone. Show her she's got a ready-made support system in place, so she can be brave and help put Reyna's killer away. Turn right at the light."

And maybe Carmen's killer, too. I made the turn, crept along in the heavy morning traffic until I finally made it into the parking garage. I checked the time. 9:15 a.m.

We waited outside the case manager's office for half an hour. The hallway smelled like stale water and the fluorescent light was flickering enough to aggravate my headache. Just when I was about to ask if we should go in and check to see if she was in there, the door opened and a slight girl exited. Her dark hair was in a tight ponytail, large silver hoops hung from small, round ears and her gaze was cast to the floor.

Angeline sprang out of the chair. "Josette? Josette Owens?"

The girl stopped and looked up at us. "Yeah?"

God, she looked about fifteen. My heart ached as I recognized the shaking hands, the clutch of anxiety and drug addiction.

"Hi, I'm Angeline and this is my friend, Alice. Veora Leon, the director at Project Freedom, told us we could find you here."

Her shiny raven eyes darted back and forth between us. She was wearing jeans and a purple vest over a black tank top; she tugged the vest closed, folding her arms around herself. "What do you want?"

Angeline held up her palms. "We thought maybe we could buy you some breakfast."

The girl's eyes registered suspicion as she looked us over, her voice barely a whisper as she asked, "Why?"

I stepped in. "Veora thought you might like a hot meal and some friends to talk to. That's all."

She glanced back at the door behind her and finally shrugged. "Yeah sure. Why not."

I drove them to Sunny's around the corner, a small organic diner with private booths and the best coffee on the planet. Josette spent the drive talking about Angeline's purple-tipped hair and how she wanted to cut hers and get pink streaks, but Drac said no. I said she should be able to do what she wants, it was her hair, and she said Drac is sort of her boyfriend—he took her in when she ran away from home last year—so she doesn't want him to think she's ugly. I fought the urge to go find Drac and run him over.

After Josette ordered a stack of lemon pancakes, bacon and coffee, her gaze drifted just south of eye contact. Her leg was jiggling under the table. "I just met Veora yesterday. She seems nice. She wants me to start the program there. Said they have a," her fingers curl into air quotes, "'rest phase.' No commitment. Just a place to stay and think, ya know—about getting out."

Despite her thinness, baby-fat still padded Josette's jawline. Her movements were full of both aggression and defensiveness. Thinking about what she'd already been through in her short life, I had to suppress a wave of thick, hot anger.

Angeline dipped her tea bag into the cup of hot water repeatedly. I could feel her holding herself back, trying to ease into the conversation about Reyna. "It's a good program. You thinking about it?"

Josette shrugged and scratched at a sore on her bare arm. Blood seeped from the opened scab. She plucked a napkin from the holder and pressed it on the spot. "It's not that easy. I mean what would I do for money, ya know? If Drac hadn't taken me in, I'd be sleeping in a park, probably get assaulted every night anyway."

The casual way she said 'anyway' cracked my heart open wider. I heard the strain in Angeline's voice when she said, "Nothing worth doing is easy. And Project Freedom would help you with learning a skill for a job." When no reply came she asked, "You have any other family around?"

A heavy emotion darkened her expression, narrow shoulders fell. "I had an older sister. She's dead."

"I'm so sorry," Angeline said carefully. She was trying not to spook her. "Do you want to talk about it?"

Josette stiffened her spine and shook her head. "Nothing to talk about. The drugs got her. She's a cliché'."

The waitress brought a coffee pot and thick white cups.

We watched Josette dump half a dozen packets of sugar into her coffee. A streak of blood was drying on her arm. We shared a concerned glance.

"Project Freedom is a good program, Josette. We've worked with them for years and have seen the results. You can have a real life. One where you decide where to go every day instead of having Drac dictate your life. It is possible."

She sucked on her bottom lip and then sighed. "For some maybe, sure. But you gotta understand ... Drac's the devil I know." She lifted her cup and gulped the coffee. Her hands were shaking. Putting the cup down, she scratched at her collar bone, leaving angry red marks. She was getting antsy. "Look, I appreciate what y'all are trying to do. Trying to help and all ... you just don't understand how hard it'd be to get out."

"Hard but not impossible."

"Here we go." The young waitress appeared and slid plates of steaming food in front of us with a practiced smile. Her glance at Josette's bleeding arm was sharp; her smile faltered. I wanted to assure her that wasn't the wound to worry about. "Let me know if you need anything else."

"Thanks." I cut a corner off my spinach omelet and watched Josette. She was dumping packets of syrup on her pancakes. A tiny silver ring circled her thumb, cutting into her skin and her nails were bitten to the quick, raw. She closed her eyes on her first bite. This made me smile.

"So, you knew Reyna Flores?" Angeline asked as she cut up her avocado toast. Her tone was casual, but I could feel the tension in her body humming beside me.

Josette froze mid-bite. With effort, she reanimated and swallowed hard. "Yeah. I knew her." She reached for her coffee cup, eyes cast down.

Angeline put her knife and fork down deliberately, keeping her voice soft. "Then you know she was murdered."

Josette's eyes flicked up. They were wide with fear. She shoved a forkful of soft pancake in her mouth and chewed hard, staring at Angeline.

"Look, we know you were at the party with Reyna the night she was raped and beaten by that businessman and his friends. We think he may've had something to do with her death, and the police are willing to look at him for it but ... Carmen was the only witness they had and now she's disappeared."

Josette pushed herself back into the padded backing of the booth. "Did you hear what you just said? Disappeared! Probably dead. And exactly why I don't want nothin' to do with this. I already told Veora that."

"I know. I understand what we're asking is a lot. But, you're in a unique position to get justice for Reyna. There's no one else, Josette. He's going to get away with disposing of her like she was a piece of rubbish." Angeline was leaning on the table, her eyes trying to pull Josette back in.

Josette's gaze darted around the diner. She chewed on her thumb.

"What is it?" Angeline probed.

She dropped her hand then leaned forward. "Look, there were other girls there, too. Not just us paid sex workers. That group, they like to have fresh girls at their parties. Girls not in the life. You know what I mean?"

I shook my head. "But why would girls who aren't in the life agree to be at these parties? What are they getting out of it? Drugs?"

Josette stared at me like I was the most clueless person on the planet. "Well, yeah, getting a fix is part of it, but how do ya think they got hooked in the first place?" Her stare moved between me and Angeline.

"They are conned. Brought there to serve food or give massages, promised a lot of money. Girls puttin' themselves through college fall for that shit. Then bam. Their drinks are spiked with Roxi or roofies. Then they're raped, sex tapes are made, they're blackmailed. It's pretty fuckin' sad to tell you the truth."

I was trying to digest this. "Do you know any of these girls' names? If we can find one girl who'll talk, we can go to the police. We can stop this."

But Josette's resolve had hardened like a shell around her. "Sorry. I can't. Men like him with their fancy yachts get away with using and throwing us girls away every day. That's just life. Nothing I do or say is going to change that. I'm not risking my neck for nothin'."

Something bristled in my mind, slid sideways and connected. My spine straightened. *Oh God. Could it be?* I already knew the answer in my gut, but I asked anyway. "Josette, this businessman who had the party … is his name Oliver Brooks?"

Angeline's head whipped around to me. I heard a catch in her throat. Then we both stared at Josette, waiting. The burble of voices and background music around us faded as blood pounded in my ears.

She was staring back at us with rising anxiety, but she finally nodded. "Yeah … that's him. But you didn't hear it from me."

"Bloody hell," Angeline whispered as we stared at each other, trying to make sense of this.

I was holding on by a thread, desperately trying to stay present as the rushing waters of rage roared through me. I clutched Angeline's hand, focused on the shared shock widening her amber eyes. Suddenly Oliver's face was there. His leering stare. He laughed. The impact knocked me into the darkness.

——◆◆◆◆——

My eyes blinked open. The dark wood ceiling fan in my bedroom came into focus. Early evening light shone outside the windows. *What time is it?* Disorientated, I pushed my hair out of my face and rolled over. I reached for my phone on the nightstand. *5:18?* That couldn't be right. My heart fluttered. I jumped up. *The kids! Did I leave them at school?* I checked the phone again. No missed calls. The school would've called.

Then I noticed an unfamiliar red notebook lying on the duvet next to me. I pushed myself up to a sitting position and picked it up. *Did one of the kids leave this here for me? Must've been Addie, she was really getting into drawing.* Feeling better now that I knew they were home, I flipped open the notebook. The first page had loopy handwriting that I didn't recognize. It said:

Dear Alice. These girls told their stories to you. I'm leaving this in your hands. Do what you feel is right.

I frowned. *Did I leave myself this note? Knowing I wouldn't remember? No, that's not my handwriting.* Confused, I flipped quickly through the notebook and caught glimpses of different ink colors, different styles of handwriting on each page. I flipped back to the front and read the second page:

My name is Jillian Harris and this is my account of how I got involved with Oliver Brooks and his friends. Back in January of last year, Oliver asked me if I wanted to make some extra money serving drinks at one of his parties. He offered me an obscene amount of money for a few hours work so, of course, I said yes. When I got to his house, there were a dozen other girls there already. The guests were all men. Powerful men I recognized from the club. I wondered why their wives weren't there, but I soon found out. The first hour was fine. I served drinks like I came there to do. But then, Oliver called me into the kitchen and said it was my break time. He handed me a drink. I didn't think anything of it, until after about twenty minutes, I started to get really sleepy and my body began to feel heavy. Oliver approached me and led me into his bedroom. I should have tried to leave, but I just needed to lay down. I started to panic when I heard Oliver shut the door and then sit on the bed, but I couldn't get my body to move. That's the last thing I remembered about that night. I woke up in the morning feeling really out of it. I was also undressed and in pain. Oliver was sleeping next to me. It was like waking up into a nightmare. I struggled to sit up and look for my clothes. Oliver woke up and I asked him what he had done to me. He smiled and asked if I wanted to see the video. When I started crying, he got up and threw my clothes at me and said if I told anyone what happened that video would be all over the internet. All I could think about was how devastated my parents would be. He let me leave but I've had to do whatever he asked from then on, which included having sex with his friends for the past eighteen months. He started me on Roxycodone to make it easier for me to comply. I can't get off of it now, and it's been a downhill spiral from there. I'm telling you this story because I can't take it anymore. But I will only come forward and tell the police if I'm not alone. These are powerful men who won't hesitate to kill me. They won't believe one girl. You have to keep your promise that I won't be the only one who comes forward.

I had my hand over my mouth. I dropped it, my heart and mind racing. I flipped to the next page where another girl's story waited. I counted the pages of stories. There were fourteen all together, and each story named the men who'd assaulted them. I recognized all of them. One in particular made my stomach roil.

Those nights I was suspicious about leaving the condo ... this must've been where I went, to talk to these girls, get them to open up and tell their stories.

I flipped back to the note in front and studied it. Definitely not my handwriting. *Had someone else been with me? Angeline maybe? No, it isn't her handwriting, either. Besides, if any of my friends were with me on these nightly excursions, we would've talked about it by now.* I shoved the notebook under a pile of books on my nightstand. I needed to think about the best way to handle this. Oliver had powerful friends, judges, lawyers, people in the police department. These girls were trusting me. I had to make sure their stories wouldn't get buried. *I'll talk to Jake when he comes home Friday. He'll know who to give the notebook to.*

With a sudden crushing need to know my kids were safe, I half-stumbled, half-ran down the hall and into the kitchen. Aurora was there, humming over the running water as she scrubbed a pot. Charlie was taking silverware out of the dishwasher and carefully placing it in the drawer.

"Hi, Mom," Charlie said, going back to his careful arranging.

"Feeling better?" Aurora asked, turning off the water and wiping her hands on a dishtowel.

"Yes," I said, forcing a smile. "And Addie? She's...?"

"Working on her art project at the table." Aurora's wizened eyes met mine. There were questions there, but she was too polite to ask. "There is a plate for you in the fridge."

"Thanks." I wasn't hungry. My mind was still on that notebook. *Should I call Dr. Evelyn tonight and tell her about my middle of the night outings? No, I'll see her in the morning.*

"Daddy!" Charlie bolted past me. I whirled around to see Jake standing there in his suit, holding a manila envelope, which confused me because he was supposed to be driving to Miami tonight for business. *Why is he here?*

He hugged Charlie with one arm, but he was staring at me over our son's head. He wasn't smiling. *Something's happened. Did I do something during the blackout this time?*

I approached him cautiously. "Hey."

"We need to talk."

I followed him into his office. The tile was cold on my bare feet and the chill traveled straight up my spine. He dropped into one of the leather armchairs in front of the window, rubbed his forehead roughly.

"What's going on?" I lowered myself slowly into the chair opposite him.

Wordlessly, he handed me the manila envelope. Pain flashed in his eyes, and his face was drained of color.

With a racing pulse, I slid out the sheet of paper. My heart dropped like a stone, sinking into the darkness, settling at the bottom of my stomach.

In my now trembling hand, I held a photocopy of my admittance form to Children's Psychiatric Hospital. I was fourteen. My mind was reeling. My mouth had dried up. I let my eyes find Jake's and the pain and betrayal there hit me like a fist to the gut. "Where did you get this?"

I knew exactly where he'd gotten it, but I was stalling, trying to come up with a good reason I hadn't told him yet.

His jaw twitched. Nostrils flared. "So, you do ... remember this? Being committed in this place?"

I knew he needed me to say no. I could make this easier on both of us by denying it, but I nodded and waited for the fallout of his anger.

He stared at me like I was a stranger, the blue of his eyes bright around pinpoint pupils. The lines around his mouth had deepened. "And you didn't think this was something you should've mentioned? Christ, Alice, mental illness is something that can be passed down to the kids!"

Blood rushed to my face. "The kids aren't in danger of being crazy, Jake."

"But you are." It was a vicious whisper, and I saw that he regretted it immediately. But the damage was done.

A small cry of despair escaped my lungs.

This was why I'd never told him. Because I knew he had to have things perfect, untainted, unbroken. I hadn't wanted him to look at me differently, the way he was looking at me now. It hurt like an open, sucking wound in my chest.

His head dropped and he shoved his hands into his newly cropped hair. "I'm sorry." He looked up at me. The whites of his eyes were shot through with broken capillaries. "I'm sorry. That wasn't fair. I'm just..." he stood abruptly and began to pace. "I'm just caught off guard."

He's caught off guard? I almost laughed. "I told you my records are on their way. I was planning on sharing everything with you."

"You've had almost a decade to share this with me, Alice."

I bulked at the utter rage simmering beneath his words. "Oliver did this." I spit his name from my mouth like poison.

Jake stopped pacing, hands on his narrow hips. "If so, he did me a favor. I deserve to know the truth about the woman I'm married to."

"Oh really? And do you deserve to know the truth about your friend Oliver?"

"What are you talking about?"

I crumbled up the paper in my hand. "He did this because he stuck his hand up my dress at Ale's the other night and got angry when I wasn't receptive. This was his way of getting even."

Jake's face looked sunken, like it was collapsing under the weight of his disappointment. He slowly lowered himself back into the chair, crossed one leg over his knee. "Oliver was three sheets to the wind that night. He wouldn't even have remembered making a pass at you the next day, let alone get even for being rebuffed."

"You think you know him so well." I challenged him. "You're not a woman, so you don't realize how dangerous he is. He—"

He held up a hand. "Stop, Alice. You're seeing the world, and Oliver's flaws, through a dark, twisted filter because of all the stories you've heard at Project Freedom. It's not healthy, being around all those women who've suffered such abuse. It skews your perception of people."

Now I was the one feeling betrayed. *He's defending Oliver? Saying I'm overreacting?* I felt myself lurch. *No no no.* I dug my nails into my palms and stared at Jake until I was anchored to him by force of will alone. "I have proof that Oliver is dangerous, Jake."

"Proof?"

"Yes. Did you know Oliver throws sex parties? That he doesn't just use prostitutes but tricks young girls into having sex with him and his father and friends—your friends—by drugging, raping and then blackmailing them?" My whole body trembled. Saying it out loud solidified it, made it real.

"That's ridiculous."

"I have a notebook full of fourteen girls' stories. Fourteen girls willing to come forward to testify against Oliver, Graham and the others."

It wasn't surprise on Jake's face, it was anger. *Did that mean he already knew about these parties?*

"And how do you know these girls are telling the truth? How do you know they don't just want a big pay out? Sure Oliver gets drunk and makes inappropriate passes at women. But he wouldn't drug them and rape them, and neither would Graham. I can't believe that. And besides this isn't even about Oliver. It's about you ... and the fact that you kept something important hidden from me."

I opened my mouth, but nothing came out, I was choking on my anger. I could only stare at him.

He broke eye contact and rubbed his face. A seagull glided by the window. The air-conditioning kicked on, its hum underlining our silence.

Finally, he nodded and blew out a long breath. "Look, I have to go to Miami tonight so we'll talk about this when I get back. And as far as your allegations ... say I believe it's possible, you do realize our financial success is tied to Graham's, don't you? I've built my whole business around him and his real estate connections. If they go down, so do we."

I stared at him in disbelief. *This is his first thought? Not about what these girls have suffered but about money?* I folded my arms tighter around my stomach. "So, we'll have to move into a smaller place. Get rid of a car. That's nothing compared to what these girls have been through."

His posture stiffened. "What they *say* they've been through."

I crossed my arms. "Why would they make up these horrible stories?"

Jake straightened his tie roughly, his face reddening. "I told you why. Money. And even if some of it's true and they're exaggerating the rest, I'm not losing everything I worked for and letting you destroy everyone around us, because some girls got themselves into a bad situation."

Every muscle in my body clenched. I was stunned. In that moment, as I stared at Jake, I didn't recognize him. He was a stranger to me. "Are you asking me not to give the notebook to the police?"

He threw up his hands. "I'm telling you that if you do ... we're not talking about a smaller place, Alice. We're talking about bankruptcy."

FIFTEEN

"**H**as something happened?" Dr. Evelyn was studying me. She looked angelic in a white silk shirt and sparkly white sandals, her eyes glowing with concern. "You seem more stressed today."

"Yes." *Where to even begin?* Not with Jake finding out about my stay at a mental institution. Or with Oliver's sex parties and the notebook. Those issues were too big. I wasn't ready to touch them.

I opened a smaller can of worms. "I received some of my records from Garden of Hope. Apparently a couple—Michael and Trudy Brown—adopted me when I was two months old."

"Really?" Dr. Evelyn tilted her head. "Do you know what happened to them?"

I shook my head. "Every time I thought about Googling their names, I felt this deep panic. I think something bad happened."

"Well," she said. "If you'd like, we can try to go back further in hypnosis today, to a time when you were with them."

The red light flashed in my mind. *Danger.* I gritted my teeth. Time to be brave. "Ok. Let's try."

"Good girl." Dr. Evelyn rewarded my bravery with a sincere smile.

We went through the now familiar routine, and I found myself falling quickly into a relaxed state. My body was heavy. My mind was creating the beach and the pile of memory stones.

"The sand is warm, the sound of the ocean is soothing. You are deeply relaxed. Do you see the stones?"

"Yes." My voice was far away.

"Good. I want you to choose one that holds an early childhood memory. One from when you were with Michael and Trudy Brown. Pick up the stone and tell me what you see."

I was drawn to a mossy green stone. It's warmth radiated in my palm. A memory began to shimmer like a mirage and then suddenly I was in a boxy living room, seated on a worn, plaid sofa. My small feet dangled in the air.

"There are pink and white balloons tied to the chair and streamers hanging from the light. I'm waiting. Oh ... it's my birthday. I'm so excited. Mom went to pick up Dad at work and get my cake. It's going to be pink and have a blue horse with wings. That's what I wanted, and Dad said I could have any kind of cake I wanted. Ms. Tilley at his work makes the best cakes. Someone is knocking on the door. Why would Mom and Dad knock?"

The red light flashed. A horrible scream ripped through my mind. I was sucked into a whirlpool of darkness.

Blinking, I slowly came back to present awareness. "Did I fall asleep?" I asked, clearing my throat. My body was drained, and I felt like I was crawling out of a deep slumber beneath the earth. I unfolded my legs, which were pulled up onto the sofa. My feet were tingling from the position. My eyes were stinging like I'd been crying, but I didn't feel upset at all.

Dr. Evelyn was calm but something had changed in her eyes. They were alert, too shiny. "In a way, you did. What do you remember?"

I turned my attention inward. And there, bright like a patch of sunlight glinting off a wave, sat a new memory. "Oh. There was a car accident. The police came and told the babysitter my parents wouldn't be coming home. They'd been killed." I glanced up at her. "Shouldn't I be more upset about this? I ... I feel nothing."

Dr. Evelyn struggled with something and then she nodded to herself. "There's a reason for that. I'm going to show you the video of the session, Alice. But I want you to prepare yourself. You're going to see yourself acting in an unusual manner, but it's not unusual for dissociative disorder. It's perfectly normal and it's actually a good thing, a breakthrough that will help us with your treatment. You've reclaimed some information from your past that was previously blocked out. It's progress."

Dissociative Disorder. She'd said it so she must believe I have it now. Progress? Then shouldn't she be happier than she looks?

"All right," I agreed warily.

She retrieved her laptop from her desk, rolled back over and plugged the video recorder into a port. Maneuvering beside me, she situated the screen so we could both see it. "Any time this gets too intense for you and you want me to stop the video, just say so."

I didn't say anything. Uneasiness was running through my body, like a live current beneath my skin.

She pushed play. I braced myself.

Me, stretched out on the sofa, the doctor's voice in the background leading me through the process of relaxing. Me, explaining the balloons and the cake and then how someone knocks.

Then, on-screen me was suddenly pushing herself up.

Something zinged up my spine. That wasn't right. That wasn't supposed to happen. I glanced at Dr. Evelyn. She reached over and gave my hand a supportive squeeze. My attention fell back to the screen.

On-screen me had configured herself into a ball, her arms wrapped around her knees. Her eyes were darting around the room in confusion.

Dr. Evelyn's voice held a note of surprise as she said, "Well, hello there. And who might you be?"

I thought that was a silly question until I heard a child-like voice answer, "Lyssie Grace."

The room tilted. My pulse quickened and my mouth dried up.

"Well, it's nice to meet you, Lyssie Grace. Do you know who I am?"

On-screen me was hiding behind her hair. She pulled a piece into her mouth and shook her head.

"I'm Dr. Evelyn. You're in my office right now because Alice is having some trouble with her memories. Do you know Alice?"

She shook her head no again.

In real time, I covered my mouth with my hands. Shame had set my face on fire.

Dr. Evelyn was calm as she asked, "How old are you, Lyssie Grace?"

On screen, I held up six fingers.

"You're six years old. That's good."

I watched with horror and fascination as the child-like me nodded. She lifted her head and there were tears streaming down her face. She wiped her nose on her knees.

"Lyssie Grace, why are you so upset?"

"The policeman came and said Mom and Dad can't come home. They're in heaven now. Misty and her mom gotta take me to their house." Her head dropped and she began to sob. Deep, ghostly sobs that echoed around the office.

I watched Dr. Evelyn move her chair closer so she could comfort the little girl.

God, I'm actually thinking about this person as separate from me. And feeling sorry for her.

The sobs sank into my bones like concrete. Just when I thought my heart would break, Dr. Evelyn's calm voice overlaid the sobs. "Alice, I'm going to count to five. When I do, you will awake calm and relaxed. One ... two ... three ... four ... five."

Dr. Evelyn clicked off the video and closed the laptop.

I stared at her, feeling very far away from myself. "What was that?"

"That," she said in a quiet voice, "I suspect was the personality who holds the trauma of losing your parents at such a young age. It's a protection protocol your mind used to detach that horrible experience from your whole, to keep it separate and unknowable. Lyssie Grace not only holds these memories, but also the devastating emotions that go with them. You've now accessed her memories, but she's apparently still protecting you from the emotional impact."

"But she ... didn't know me?" I couldn't believe I was actually asking this question. "How is that possible if she's ... inside my mind?"

"It's complicated. Sometimes those within a dissociative system can know each other, some can know of the existence of only a few others, some don't interact with any of the others. It's possible to connect each of them, though. Also possible to reintegrate them, which would be ideal but won't necessarily be our goal. I think we should schedule three sessions a week for now. I'll make room in my schedule."

"So, it's true? I actually do have this thing ... this disorder." My heart sank, dragging all my dreams of being normal with it. "My husband, he'll never accept this. He'll be disgusted by me. I'm disgusted by me."

She made a sympathetic clucking noise. "Why do you think that? Is he not being supportive?"

"He's a perfectionist. He can't handle things that are ... damaged or sick."

"Well, you are neither. In fact, it takes a creative mind to protect itself like this. I would say you are exceptional."

A burst of laughter escaped me. We shared a smile and then a deep, inky sadness washed over me. "What am I supposed to do now?"

"Well, it would probably be a good idea to confirm what we've found out today. I think you'll find less resistance to Googling the Browns now. Besides that, we'll just continue doing what we're doing. This really is a good thing, Alice. It means you can heal."

―――

I maneuvered through the traffic in a daze.

The rest of the day, I tried to keep as normal as possible. I pushed a cart around Publix, though the colors, smells and choices overwhelmed me, and I had to keep wiping the sweat from my upper lip. I smiled and made small talk with the cashier as I paid for things I didn't really need. I picked up the mail from the concierge desk. More smiling. More small talk. Did a load of laundry. Went back down to the garage, got in the car, picked up the kids from school. Ate dinner with Aurora and the kids, tried to pay attention to the details of their day. Helped with homework. Stayed as far away from my thoughts as possible.

By the time the kids were tucked in, exhaustion had rendered my mind and bones a heavy burden. I stood in front of the glass doors in our bedroom. There were rows of low, lumpy clouds like someone had flung orange and yellow buckets of them across the sky. Dark shapes of anchored sailboats littered the water below.

I retrieved my laptop and sat on the bed. Before the numbness wore off, I Googled "Trudy and Michael Brown Orlando car accident." And there it was, like it'd been waiting for me to find it all this time.

Couple Dead After Fatal Crash,
in the *Orlando Sentinel.*

July 5, 1992. An Orlando couple died Friday evening on I-4. Florida State Troopers responded to the scene around 5:15 pm. The couple has been identified as Michael and Trudy Brown from Brentwood. Michael was a manager of Publix and Trudy was a fourth-grade teacher at Brentwood Elementary. They leave behind a surviving six-year-old daughter.

Witnesses say nineteen-year-old John Davis was passing a tractor trailer in the right-hand lane and swerved back into the middle lane at the same time Michael Brown was moving into the middle lane from the left. Both vehicles spun out and the Brown's Honda Accord rolled down an embankment. John Davis was taken to Orlando Regional Medical Center with non-life-threatening injuries.

I closed the laptop, poking at my feelings. Nothing. A hollow black hole where my reaction should be.

SIXTEEN

"Good morning, Alice." Dr. Evelyn's voice held a gentleness that brought to mind thick down comforters and cold winter nights. A softness that was in preparation for something.

"Good morning," I croaked. My voice sounded heavy, defeated, void of sharp edges. I was dressed in yoga pants and one of Jake's well-worn, fishing t-shirts. I'd barely had the energy to run a brush through my hair this morning. I barely had the energy to hold myself up right now. My whole life was collapsing around me. I stared at Dr. Evelyn from somewhere behind the new invisible wall that was separating me from everything.

She put her pen down in her lap and laced her fingers, hooking them on one knee. "You seem sad this morning. Did you talk to Jake about what happened here yesterday?"

"No, he's on a business trip for a few days." My voice was as flat and one-dimensional as I felt. "I don't know if I'm sad. I can't feel anything right now. I Googled the Browns last night. They did die in a car accident. Some kid passing on the right switched lanes at the same time they did, but he wasn't killed. Jake found out about me being institutionalized when I was fourteen." I was mildly surprised that I'd said this out loud. I watched her reaction from behind my invisible wall.

The softness was there in her eyes, too. "Are you ready to tell me what happened?"

Am I? I didn't feel any panic about it. I guess this numbness was good for something. I shrugged and began the story that I'd never willingly told anyone.

"It happened when I was living with Martin and Clara. Eighth grade. I didn't have any friends. The girls picked on me, so I tried to become one of the boys. This one group of popular boys sort of ran things, so I started hanging out with them ... the jocks, Bill, Martin, Reece, Steven. We'd play touch football at Bill's house after school. He had this big house in a gated community. The first one I'd ever seen, with a huge landscaped yard, perfectly mowed grass. I can still smell the grass.

"Anyway, at first I felt special because they let me hang out with them. But, that eventually turned to shame because, even though it was touch football, I'd always get tackled and grabbed in private places. I ignored it. The price of having friends at all, right? But I made it a point to never be alone with any of them. Especially Bill Rice. The way he looked at me reminded me of that man at the carnival.

"That day, I'd gone to Bill's house. We were all supposed to meet there as usual, only the others didn't show up. And his mother wasn't home like she normally was to bring us out lemonade and jam sandwiches.

"While we waited, he wanted me to hear this cool new song so, against my better judgement I followed him to his room. At first, it was great. He was being really nice to me for once. No teasing, not talking to me like I was just a stupid girl. He even asked me what it was like not having parents, like he cared.

"But then he pushed me down on the bed and started tickling me. He was digging his fingers into my sides, which really hurt, and I tried to push him off, but was twice my size so he wasn't budging. My face felt like it was going to explode, it was so hot and God, the pressure. I was sweating. He was laughing but there was this meanness underneath. I started to panic. He slid his hand between us and started unbuttoning my shorts. That's when I let my eyes meet his and saw the determination there and something else, something that looked like hatred. I realized he wasn't joking around, and he wasn't going to stop. I screamed. And honestly at that moment ..."

I wasn't sure how to say this. I'd never said it out loud. I tried to describe it the best I could. "In that moment fire leapt directly from my mind to the curtains beside his bed. There was this whooshing sound. And heat. They were just ... engulfed in flames. Gray smoke curled out into the room. Bill started screaming *Jesus Christ*. He kept screaming. *What the hell did you do? What the hell did you do?* I was suddenly watching him from his doorway. I'm not sure when I got off the bed. He was running back and forth from the bathroom attached to his room with a trash can full of water, throwing it at the flames. The smoke alarm was screaming along with him. I ... I remember feeling detached, like I was sitting in the back of a dark theatre, watching a movie, and then I started to laugh and then that's it. I had one of my blackouts and woke up in the institution two days later."

Dr. Evelyn was calm but concerned as she asked, "What did the adults think happened?"

"Bill told his parents that I set the fire on purpose, because I told him I liked him, and he didn't like me back that way. But, of course that was ridiculous. I never told them what he'd tried to do. It was just my word against his. Anyway, I didn't get to go back to Martin and Clara when I got out three months later. They said they couldn't handle me. So, I was sent back to Garden of Hope."

Dr. Evelyn had picked up her pencil and was making notes. Her brows were drawn together thoughtfully as she said, "Thank you for sharing that with me, Alice. You know, memories are a strange thing. In the human mind, memories and imagination sort of entangle. That's not to say we can't have accurate memories, but a lot of times creations of fantasy get all mixed up with actual events. You remember this fire as a sort of a supernatural event. Would you like to go back to that day in hypnosis and see if we can find out how the fire actually started?"

An image materialized in my mind of Drac's car burning. I shoved it away. "Would I like to? No, not particularly. But, I suppose we should try."

It took me no time at all now, under the guidance of Dr. Evelyn's voice, to fall into the space where my body felt like concrete and the beach opened up in my mind.

"I want you to look for the stone that holds the memory of when you were fourteen. When you were up in Bill Rice's bedroom the day the fire started."

I scanned the stones and spotted a smooth, brown one swirled with honey-yellow. I reached for it, but my hand brushed a larger stone the color of licorice. The heat of it drew my attention. Yes, that's the one. I picked it up and sat with it, cradled it in my lap.

"What do you see, Alice?" Dr. Evelyn's voice was a whisper on the ocean breeze.

"Bill has posters on his wall. Pearl Jam and girls in bikinis. His room is so big, I can't believe he has it all to himself, and he has his own bathroom. It smells like gym socks and strawberry air freshener."

"What is Bill doing right now?"

"He's ... he's walking toward me, saying, 'Do you like it?' I nod but I don't really. Not my kind of music and it's too loud. I can feel the bass pounding in my chest." I gasped. "Get off! Ow! Bill, get off!"

"This isn't happening right now, Alice. You're safe. This is only a memory."

I was panting. His breath was hot and smelled like peanut butter. He was crushing my lungs with his weight. "Stop it!"

Then I was blinking and back in Dr. Evelyn's office, sitting up. I felt drugged, disorientated. The clock said twenty-six minutes had passed. "What happened? Did I ... oh, God ... did Lyssie Grace come back?"

Dr. Evelyn's face had gone pale. She opened her mouth but quickly closed it and shook her head instead. She was very still as she looked at me.

"Dr. Evelyn?" Fear was starting to crawl beneath my skin like fire ants. She seemed so shaken. *What had I done?*

Her lip trembled as she tried to smile. "Forgive me. I'm being unprofessional and I don't mean to add to your anxiety. It's just ... I've never had a conversation quite like this one before." She went to retrieve the laptop, then she was sneaking little glances at me as she plugged in the video recorder. "How are you feeling right now?"

I scanned myself. "Exhausted, I guess, and nervous about what happened just now, but I don't feel upset if that's what you're asking."

She turned her chair so the laptop was facing us both. "Do you remember anything about our conversation?"

I bit my lip and shook my head.

She gave my hand a squeeze. "It's okay. Again, let me know if you want me to stop the video at any time. Ready?" I nodded. She pressed play.

Again, I was stretched out on the sofa, listening to her voice take me deeper into relaxation. She was telling me to pick up the memory stone. My voice began to sound distressed as I told her what I was seeing but my body was still.

Until onscreen I suddenly sat up and opened my eyes.

I gasped.

Onscreen-me was staring right into the camera. The gold specs in her eyes were more pronounced, glowing wild and feral. Her eyes moved slowly to the doctor behind the camera and there was a catch in

Dr. Evelyn's voice as she said, "Hello there. I'm Dr. Evelyn. And who might you be?"

Onscreen-me stretched languidly and ran a hand through her dark mass of hair. Her movements were confident, seductive.

I was riveted by both fascination and fear.

"I'm aware of who you are, Doctor." Her voice was startling. Rich, deep and with a tone void of any telling accent, like it came from a dusty textbook. I didn't recognize it as my own. On-screen me inhaled deeply through her nose, raised her arms, stretching her ribcage and then pushed herself up slowly. Her eyes drank in the room.

There was a jiggling of the camera as Dr. Evelyn apparently removed it from the stand. The camera angle shifted and then focused back on onscreen-me. She was now standing at the window, tugging the curtain back a little more. "Do you mind?" Onscreen-me glanced back at the camera. "If I let some light in?"

The tilt of her head, the angle of her hip jutting out as she stood there was so foreign; it sent a tremor through my core.

"No, not at all." Dr. Evelyn's tone was one of caution and curiosity.

Onscreen-me slid back the curtain and a rectangle of sunlight appeared on the wood floor. Her smile was radiant as she turned slowly and scanned the room. She sauntered over to the doctor's desk and picked up a glass paperweight with a blue jellyfish suspended inside. Holding it up to the light, she rotated it slowly. "Do you think we take color and form for granted, Dr. Evelyn? It's a miracle in itself, isn't it?"

"I suppose it is," Dr. Evelyn answered patiently. "I'm afraid you have me at a disadvantage here. You know my name, but I don't know yours."

She replaced the paperweight and let her eyes roam the room. "Kali."

"Kali?" Dr. Evelyn said. "That's your name?"

She glided over to the bookshelf and ran her hand over the spines, fingers stroking them like keys on a piano. "Yes."

"It's nice to meet you, Kali. May I ask how old you are?"

"I am eternal."

"The Goddess of War Kali then?"

Kali gave a slow nod. "That is one of my designations. I have been called Goddess of war, time, change, creation and destruction. Shakti, Ma Kali, Mother of the Universe. I have many, many names."

"Maybe I should ask this a different way. How long have you been with Alice?"

Kali turned her eyes on Dr. Evelyn. The camera blurred and refocused.

A chill ran up my spine. I really didn't recognize anything about myself and God, my eyes were gold, feral and paralyzing. Like a tiger watching its prey.

Kali stalked toward the camera.

My heartrate sped up. I fought the urge to back away.

But she glided by and the camera swung around, following her as she took a seat back on the sofa. Legs crossed, arms resting on the back, expression a mixture of danger and control, muscles tensed and twitching like a panther undecided on whether to pounce. She was a stunning creature. "Alice trusts you so I will try to explain our situation."

"Thank you."

"You see, this is my second incarnation. My form before this, of course, was part of the collective consciousness, where the energy patterns of human belief created me. This time is different. I chose to be incarnated as a human to experience being a mother not just as the energy force behind the birth, but as an actual vessel for life to come through. Of course, I didn't remember this until I'd been here almost thirteen years. Until this physical brain and nervous system were developed enough to interpret my goddess pattern."

"So, you're saying you were there in the beginning? But Alice wasn't aware of you until she was thirteen?"

"I was there in the beginning, yes." She'd turned thoughtful, picking her words carefully, like she was finding the ripest berries on a vine. "And yes, Alice is one of the filters, the patterns of consciousness through which I experience being human. You see, I had to let these veils of human ego, emotion and thought rise up between me and this physical reality. Sort of blind myself by letting them develop, so I could experience motherhood as you humans do, as a vessel. This allowed me to experience both human and divine love for my children."

"There's a difference?" Dr. Evelyn sounded genuinely intrigued but still a bit nervous.

"Of course. Human love is consuming. Divine universal love is creating. Humans are capable of both, depending on the starting point. If the starting point is the spiritual heart, it's divine love. If the starting point is the emotions, it is human love. You see the spiritual heart is a human's nucleus, containing the infinite light of universal love. Emotions are just different flavors of energy that human's feel and interpret through their physical bodies. Both are necessary for a full experience of this life."

"You've obviously put a lot of thought into this. So … let me make sure I understand what you're saying. You're a goddess having a human experience. Is that correct?"

This seemed to please Kali. She visibly relaxed. "Yes. Very good, Doctor. I'm beginning to see why Alice trusts you."

"I'm glad. Let's go back for a moment. Was it you who set the fire that day in Bill Rice's bedroom?"

"Yes."

"To protect Alice?"

"Of course. I've protected Alice many times. She recently remembered one of those times. After she'd run away from Garden of Heart for example. We stayed in a rundown motel for a few days and a man there tried to grab her and force her into his room. He didn't succeed." She smiled and a cold chill ran down my spine. "Anyway, back to the day in that boy's bedroom. That was the day Alice realized the end game. She'd been so confused before then. Sometimes being pleased or flattered by the growing attention from the males, sometimes being afraid but not knowing what she was afraid of. In that moment, pinned beneath that sweaty boy, she finally understood. The men and boys weren't stalking, harassing and pursuing her to have a conversation, to get to know or love her. It was all about possessing her flesh. This," Kali motioned to her body with a sweep of her hands, "this vehicle carrying her around. It was the only thing they wanted from her." A deep, guttural laugh clawed its way from her throat. "Such a waste. This heart is so much more valuable."

The hair stood up on my arms as I watched her hands curl into fists, the knuckles whiten. Her rage rumbled like an idling engine within me as she continued, "How cruel is this human ritual? This drive to procreate and the damage and violence that comes with it."

"Maybe, but humans also have free will. They can choose how they think and behave, and Alice did end up in a good relationship, with a man who appreciates her heart ... her love, also. Can we go back to the fire? How exactly did it start? Alice would like to remember."

Kali stared quietly at the doctor. Her face was hardening into a mask. "There is a womb of fire all women possess. A fire she can use to burn her enemies to ash. Yes, she is a creator, but she is also a destroyer. And sometimes love means burning the house to the ground so you can rise stronger and in a better place. *That* is what Alice needs to remember." Her eyes glittered dangerously.

There was a wariness in Dr. Evelyn's voice as she said, "Alice, when I count to five you will awaken. One ... two ... three ... four ... five."

Dr. Evelyn turned off the camera and we stared at each other.

My mind was like sludge. I couldn't make sense out of any of it. I reached up and touched my lips. They were numb. I ran my hand over my face. It was the weirdest sensation, checking to see if you recognize yourself. I was burning with shame and also the remaining embers of Kali's anger. "How am I supposed to know what's real now?"

"It's all real, Alice." The pockets beneath Dr. Evelyn's eyes were blue shadows, her skin was almost translucent.

"But I know nothing about Kali and all that stuff she ... I was saying. Where did that come from?"

Dr. Evelyn twisted the silver pen in her hand thoughtfully. "Well, knowing where you were left as a newborn, you may have researched Hindu beliefs during those thirteen missing years. And even if you didn't, it doesn't matter. This personality, Kali, probably has. There have been cases where an alter— that's short for alternate personality—speaks fluent Russian or Spanish, despite the host personality not studying it."

She paused, watching me. I wondered if she was waiting for me to run screaming from the room. I certainly felt like doing just that.

"There have also been cases," she continued, "where each alter has a different vision prescription or only one is left-handed, diabetic or deathly allergic to something. So, you see, it's not necessary for you, Alice, to hold the information or beliefs of your alter, Kali."

She let me digest that for a moment and then added, "The main takeaway here is that you were conditioned from birth to see the world as a dangerous place, and you didn't have a consistent protector so you created one."

My hand moved defensively to my throat. "But ... a goddess of war? That can't be normal. Even for people with this disorder."

"Actually it is. Our fancy term for it is possession form identity."

I rubbed my temples and tried to work out the implications. "Is she dangerous? Am I a danger to my kids?"

Dr. Evelyn's gaze drifted to the window for a moment and then she shook her head. "While she is an intimidating woman, she seems fiercely protective of both you and the children, so no ... I don't believe she's dangerous to any of you. I know this is difficult, but I promise you every single identity we discover in your system will have value and will help move you forward toward healing."

Horror gripped me. "There may be more than just Lyssie Grace and Kali?"

"There could be, yes. But, this is important ... the best way to approach any alter we discover is with gratitude not fear. They really are there to protect you. You don't have a history of self-harm or suicide attempts, so I don't think we're going to come across any self-destructive alters." She caught my eye. "But, I want you to be prepared for the possibility that you'll start to become aware of others. What we're doing here is building neural bridges between the different aspects of self. We're tearing down the dissociative walls you've built. You may start to see Lyssie Grace or Kali physically in your mind, or hear their thoughts, or even stay present and aware when one of them comes forward, instead of blacking out. You may even find yourself in conversations with them as if they're real, separate persons. Don't panic, all these things are normal for dissociative identity disorder, or D.I.D. for short."

I suddenly remembered the feeling of being jerked back inside my own body, of watching myself talk to Oliver that night at Ale's Steak House like it wasn't me speaking, and then again with Aurora. "Actually, I think that's already happening. Remember when I told you about feeling like I wasn't in control of my body? I think Kali came forward then."

Dr. Evelyn nodded. "I'm sure it was very frightening but it doesn't have to be. It's important we encourage the others in your system to see each other, become friends even. Then it won't feel so foreign or dangerous to you."

"Become friends with the voices in my head? How am I going to explain this to Jake? It sounds insane." *And he's already questioning my sanity... and my loyalty to our family.* Frustration burned in my chest. A tear broke free and dropped onto my hand. My life was unraveling, and I had no power to stop it.

"They aren't just voices, Alice. They have their own memories and their own ideas of how things are.

Would you like to have Jake come in with you? We can explain it to him together, and I can answer any questions he may have."

I squeezed my fingers. My hands were shaking violently again. "He comes back Friday night."

"Do you want to see if he'll come to your Monday session with you then? Or would you rather wait to tell him?"

I suddenly just wanted to get it over with. "I'll see if he'll come." *Why not? Things are already bad between us. What's the worst that can happen now?*

SEVENTEEN

I drove home under a blanket of thick, black clouds. A fast-moving summer storm had rolled in. The wind had picked up and fat drops of rain were bouncing off my windshield. I was bone tired, aware of every ache in my body, stiff and suspicious of every thought zinging through my mind.

It was startling how quickly life as you knew it could end. Destruction of the familiar. "Little deaths" they called these things. Empty nest. Divorce. Finding out you have a goddess of war living in your head.

"Mrs. Leininger!" Guthrie, the concierge, called and waved from the desk.

I forced my legs to carry me across the lobby to the desk, but I had no energy for a polite smile. I could only stare expectantly at him as the rain pelted the glass doors behind me. He was a small man, brown thinning hair, wearing a white starched dress shirt and a blue tie the color of a robin's egg. I thought it was pretty, and then I wondered if that was even my own thought. Maybe Lyssie Grace's favorite color was robin's egg blue. *Who knew?*

I felt fragile. The plates inside me were in pieces, like a shattered mirror, and I had no idea which image was the real me. I concentrated on holding Alice in place.

"I have a package for you." He lifted a rather large box from his feet and placed it on the counter. "Would you like help carrying it up?"

I stared at the label. Inside were my records from Garden of Hope. "I can manage. Thanks, Guthrie." I wrangled the box from the counter with a desperate, growing need to hide it from view. It felt like I was standing there naked and people would notice any second.

My arms ached under the weight and my heart beat against the box as I held it to my chest and waited for the elevator. I was a fraud, surrounded by luxury—golden elevator doors, gold wallpaper, gold striped satin couches and ornate gold mirrors—holding my ragged, unworthy past in my arms. I suddenly hated myself for digging all this up. *What have I unleashed?*

Thank God Aurora was out. I rushed the box into my bedroom like a dirty secret and closed the door. As I dumped it on the bed, my phone vibrated.

I fell beside the box and dug my phone from my purse.

It was a group message from Angeline: *Lunch @ Brady's noon. Important!*

A second one came in from her, addressed to just me: *Going to tell them about Oliver*

Great. Perfect. *How am I going to be normal today?* Rhys would know something was wrong for sure. *How long do I keep this disorder from my best friends?* I sighed. Well, I should at least wait until we tell Jake on Monday. Though, Rhys would be more supportive and less freaked out. *Maybe I should talk it through with him first?*

In the end, I decided to play it by ear. I also thought about bringing the notebook to show them, but then I thought about what Jake had said, that taking down Oliver, Graham and their circle would mean the destruction of our life, also. *Was that fair to the kids? Damn you, Jake, for wrapping our life around such vile people.* I needed more time to think this through. I needed Jake to sit down and explain our financial situation. Maybe we could come up with a way to save ourselves and the girls.

—◦●●◦—

Brady's was a small café with repurposed furniture painted bright colors and local artists' work displayed on the walls. The owner, Charlotte, was in her sixties and also from Bristol, so she and Angeline always chatted like schoolgirls catching up. Today was no different, and I appreciated it more today as Charlotte set us up with complimentary wheatgrass shots. My silence went unnoticed, even by Rhys who was listening to the women's enthusiastic conversation about trying to grow tomatoes under the onslaught of Florida's heat and bugs.

"I don't mean to be rude, Ang," Vivi said after Charlotte left, "but I have a client meeting in forty-five minutes across town."

"Okay, I'll get right to it then." She scooted her chair in closer to us and glanced at me. I gave her an encouraging nod. "So, on Tuesday Alice and I took a girl named Josette to breakfast. She was one of the girls working the party for Drac the night Reyna was beaten and raped."

"So, she'll testify?" Rhys asked skeptically.

"No, she's too scared." Angeline rested her elbows on the orange and white striped tablecloth. "But, she told us who the businessman is."

"Well, who? Who is it?" Vivi asked.

"Oliver."

Rhys fell back in his chair with a low whistle.

Vivi stared at Angeline. Then she gave her head a little shake. "Oliver? Oliver Brooks?" She moved her wide-eyed gaze to me. I nodded in confirmation. Angry splotches, the color and shape of strawberries, crept up her neck. "That entitled bastard."

"I had a chat with Veora yesterday, asked if there was anything we could do. She said Oliver's got a solid alibi for the night Reyna died and the night Carmen disappeared."

I squirmed in the chair, feeling guilty about not sharing the notebook, not telling them it's more than just Oliver who's involved. I glanced over at Vivi, feeling so torn.

"That doesn't mean he didn't pay someone to take care of his problems," Rhys said.

"Who does his dirty work? Seth?" Vivi asked.

"Probably," I answered. He was most likely the one who dug up my records for Oliver.

"He's definitely a creep, but is he a killer?" Rhys asked.

"Who knows and I mean let's face it," Angeline's face was uncharacteristically drawn, "Even if Oliver told Seth to take care of it, Seth could've hired someone. There's no way to know who physically did it."

"It gets worse," I said. "Josette also told us that at these parties, Oliver doesn't just use prostitutes. He tricks girls into thinking they're just coming to serve drinks and then drugs them, rapes them and blackmails them with videos to keep them under his thumb."

Rhys slammed down his water, his face dark with rage.

"Unbelievable." Vivi's face blanched. "We need to get the bastard to confess on tape. He's probably dying to brag about what he's doing."

"That's not a bad idea." Angeline nodded. She waited to continue until the waiter finished filling our water glasses. "We buy him a bottle of his favorite Scotch, get him feeling all cozy and safe and then ask him about the parties. Not all of us, just one so he thinks it's an intimate chat."

"It should be Alice," Vivi chimed in, checking the time on her phone. "He's got a thing for her."

"Whoa." Rhys held up his hand. "I don't think it's safe to put Alice in that situation."

"We'd all be there," Vivi said. "Just in the next room or something."

"Besides, would that even hold up in court? Recording someone without their knowledge?" Rhys asked.

"I think as long as the person recording it is a party to the conversation, it's legal," Vivi said.

"I'm sure it's not that simple," Rhys added.

"I guess that's something to look into. I know it's crazy, guys, but we have to do something. We can't let him get away with this." Angeline was twisting her straw wrapper into a sharp point. Her hands were shaking.

I'd never seen her so distressed. Not even two years ago, when her older brother had gotten into a serious motorcycle accident and spent three months in the hospital in Bristol. She'd always handled everything with an unwavering faith that things worked themselves out. Maybe it was the injustice of all this shaking her to her core. It was definitely shaking me up.

I had a sudden need to make things better for her. "I'm willing to do it. If we find out it would actually be usable against him." I didn't believe this would actually work. I wasn't sure any of us did, but it made us feel better. Besides, it wasn't going to be necessary. I would find a way to turn in the notebook without taking away my kids' future. I had to.

Angeline dropped the wrapper and grabbed my hand. "You won't be alone. We won't leave you alone with him."

"I'll call our lawyer today and see what he says about the legality of this." Vivi slipped her bag over her shoulder. "But right now, I gotta go." The guilt solidified when she hugged me goodbye. I would have to tell her soon.

The three of us caught up on the rest of each other's day-to-day lives. On the way out, Rhys grabbed my hand. "Walk with me a bit?"

"Sure." My stomach clenched. "Everything all right?"

We veered around a cluster of glossy young moms and their strollers coming out of the Mangos Smoothie shop next door.

"You tell me," he said when we got past them. "You seem really off today. And sad. What's going on?"

So, he had noticed after all. I wrapped my arms around my stomach and collapsed onto a bench beneath a gumbo limbo tree. The charade of control I'd tried to keep up had drained me. I was too tired to take another step.

Rhys sat down, a long arm slid protectively behind me. "Did you find out something bad about your childhood?"

I hesitated. *What if this was too much for him? What if my darkness scared him away?* I couldn't lose my best friend along with my sanity. I suddenly needed him to share his deep, dark secret, to be vulnerable first. We'd been inseparable since Jake had hired him to shoot our wedding almost a decade ago, but this was the one thing he'd never shared with any of us ... the story of what had happened to make him pack up his heart and declare it off limits for good.

I rested my head on his shoulder. "You first. What happened to make you give up on finding love?"

Rhys's shoulder tensed beneath my cheek. I watched the traffic creep by, listened to a car horn blow in the distance, the burble of conversations passing behind us on the sidewalk, giving him time to decide.

Finally, he sighed. "Fair enough." He slipped my hand in his and for once I knew it was because *he* needed the comfort. "His name was Lenny." He stumbled on the name, choked like his mouth had forgotten how to put the sounds together, like they were covered in dust. Then cleared his throat and tried again. "Lenny. God he was beautiful. You two would've adored each other. He had this quick wit, just could make anyone laugh. Everyone loved him." He pressed his cheek against my hair. "Well, everyone but the two people he needed to love him the most."

"How did you two meet?"

"At a club in Miami. We were eighteen. When you're eighteen, love is so intense you know ... it burns you up inside from the insanity of it. He was a painter and sculptor, first year at the Fine Arts College. We were going to set the art world on fire together. Except Lenny hadn't come out to his family yet so we had to keep our relationship a secret. Sneak out of town for dates, that sort of thing. His father was extremely homophobic and his mother went along with whatever his father said. We snuck around for five years. I pressured him the whole time to tell his family about us. I was getting fed up. He'd graduated, my photography business was taking off, it was time to have a real life together, get a house, a cat, settle down." He lifted his head and took a constricted breath.

I shifted my body to face him and squeezed his arm. "It's okay. You don't have to finish."

He moved his gaze across the street, but I knew he wasn't seeing anything in front of him. "He finally did it. He was twenty-three when he brought me home and told his parents about us. They were devastated. His mother became hysterical. His father hit him. Actually hit him ... in the face." Rhys winced like he was watching it happen all over again. "Then told him to get out of his sight. He never wanted to see him again. He no longer had a son, that sort of horrible thing that a child can never truly recover from." A single muscle jumped in his jaw. "He left me two weeks later."

Rhys turned to me, the exquisite pain had brightened his eyes. "He overdosed."

"Oh God, Rhys." I dropped my head onto his shoulder. "I'm so sorry." The sun was soaking into our bones, but it wasn't enough to chase away the chill. We were both trembling. After giving him a moment to recover, I lifted my head. "You feel guilty then? Is that why you won't let yourself be happy?"

He swiped a large hand over his face. "I don't know. Maybe. Guess I should probably talk to a shrink about that." A forced smile and then he straightened, pushed both the memory and the pain back into the dark hole he'd dug it up from. "All right, I've spilled my guts. Your turn."

"Thanks for sharing Lenny with me. I really am sorry." I watched a biker glide by, giving Lenny's memory some deserved space, and then sighed. "Where to even begin? I found out something really shocking. Apparently, I'd been adopted when I was two months old, but my parents were killed in a car crash when I was six. So, back to the children's home I went."

Rhys pushed my hair behind my ear so he could see my face. "You had a family? You didn't know this?"

I looked up into his eyes. "No. I've got my records now though so, I'm about to find out all the gritty details of my life, but that's not the worst part." I took a deep breath and then just spit it out, my words tumbling over each other, "Have you ever heard of dissociative identity disorder?"

"Yeah, I've seen a documentary," his eyes widened, "is that—is that what you have?"

I nodded and watched for any sign of horror in his reaction. I only saw genuine concern.

"Jesus, Alice. How? How have you lived so normally, without us noticing anything is wrong? That's pretty serious. Oh, the blackouts?"

"Yeah."

He was nodding slowly and thinking. I watched the pieces clicking into place in his mind. "At least it's not a brain tumor, right?"

"I don't know. A brain tumor may've been easier. They can't cut this out of me."

We sat there on the bench talking until my bottom was numb. I told him about Lyssie Grace and Kali, about my stay in the mental institution, about Jake's reaction to that. Rhys was more fascinated than anything, which gave me a new perspective. "*I'd love to capture the goddess on camera.*" "*Angeline is going to want to meet her.*" We laughed and cried and by the time I left to pick up the kids, I didn't feel so hopeless. Or alone.

—••••—

After the kids were tucked in, I dragged the box from Garden of Hope out onto the balcony. It was a beautiful night with stars glittering in a cloudless sky. The traffic crossing Ringling Bridge droned in the background as I lifted my face to the balmy summer breeze and listened within me for any objection to opening this box. Hearing none, I ran the box cutter over the tape and let the flaps fall open.

I lifted the items out one at a time. Manilla envelopes each with a white label: school records & report cards, medical health histories, case plan, judicial review report, guardian ad litem report. It was overwhelming, my life, hidden from me for so long, now spilling out of this box. Beneath the envelopes lay a thick spiral book with a hard cover that said *Lifebook*.

This I took over to the cushioned patio chair, sat with it on my lap and carefully opened the first page. There was a baby photo glued there in the middle of statistics: height, weight, etc. Thick, dark hair made glossy by the flash, dark-lashed, greenish-brown eyes staring calmly from a chubby face. A fierce urge to protect her from what was coming gripped me.

The pages were stuffed with photos, stick figure drawings—which I assumed were mine—reports from social workers detailing my flourishing in the Brown household. I found a Polaroid photo of me, age two, with red barrettes pinned in my dark hair, my mouth open in a wide smile. A short, balding Michael is holding me. Trudy's head is tilted and she's showing crooked teeth, smiling at me, long brown hair hanging over one shoulder. I studied them for a long time and then held the photo to my chest, close to my heart. They obviously adored me. This was the life I'd lost, the life that'd been stolen from me in one moment of careless driving.

I felt detached emotionally. I wished I could feel something for them, some spark of affection or recognition. Hell, I'd even take grief. Sighing, I returned the photo to the book. *So, then what happened to me?*

I found 1992, the year I'd been sent back to Garden of Hope after the accident. A social worker's disposition report said it all: withdrawn, refuses to speak, cries constantly, six months of daily counseling.

In second grade I'd apparently been placed in another foster home and started a new school. There's a photo of me in front of a low, tan building with double hung windows. I was wearing pink shorts and a pink backpack. I was so tiny. I stared at my face, the joy was already absent. This felt like a thorn prick in my heart.

I flipped the page. Another photo: me with a group of children huddled together on Garden of Hope's sandy playground. "Alyssa 7 yrs old" scrawled beneath it.

I stared at it, confused. *Was I back at the children's home so soon?*

Putting down the book, I went back to the envelopes and found Foster Agreements.

The digital files had held three foster agreements, but there were five hard copies here. Five foster homes, including the Brown's. I found the one from

1992, my first foster home after losing my adopted parents had been with a lady named Bee Washington. Nothing said why I hadn't stayed with her. I dug through more paperwork in the box until I found the report. I'd been removed after being attacked by another foster child in the home, a troubled fourteen-year-old girl. I'd received ten stitches above my eye.

I reached up, ran a finger over the small scar above my right eyebrow.

Every person who touched us left a mark.

I shuffled through the caseworker notes, some were folded, some rippled by moisture. One caught my eye and as I read it, the tiny hope glowing in the back of my mind that I didn't actually have dissociative identity disorder—that I was somehow making it all up under hypnosis—was snuffed out for good.

"Ms. Sherry Green is refusing to continue fostering Alice after an incident where Alice insisted she was Kali, the Hindu goddess of war, and threw a glass ashtray at her head."

My arms dropped. So, that's why I'd had to leave Sherry's home after only being there a few months? No one would tell me what had happened. Maybe they thought I was just pretending not to remember?

So, it was true. Kali's been with me since I was thirteen at least. And apparently she could be violent. Those angry, ferocious thoughts and images of violence breaking through and scaring me once in a while—did those belong to her?

Fatigue washed over me. Then a sudden urge to hold my kids gripped me.

I packed the papers and my Lifebook back into the box and slid it behind my yoga mat in the closet. In the back of my mind floated the question: What would Jake do with this new version of me? I heard the words *unfit*, *crazy* and *dangerous*.

I felt Kali stir, heard her laughter like an echo in a dark cavern.

Charlie's breath was an easy, slow rhythm. He was lying on his side with his arms flung out in front of him. The moonlight soaked through his curtains and outlined his soft fingers but left his face in shadow. Quietly, I lay down beside him, pressed my nose against his hair, smelled soap and little boy sweat.

I heard myself asking Dr. Evelyn how I would know what's real, and I knew this was the realest thing I would ever feel. This white-hot terror. Everything else was a waking dream compared to the thought of being separated from my children.

Charlie's pale fingers twitched. He took a deep breath. I would do anything to protect him from the monster, not the imagined one in his closet, but the one trying not to wake him right now, dripping hot tears on his pillow. If only I could be the mother he needs ... the mother he thought I was. If only I could rip the others from me. Just be me ... Alice.

I felt sorry for Jake suddenly. Jake, who'd taken a chance on a girl selling pies to pay for a moldy, roach-infested trailer. A girl he'd called his princess and whisked away to a golden tower, never suspecting that he'd also invited in the monster who would gobble up our happily ever after.

EIGHTEEN

Beep. Beep. Beep. The steady chirp of my phone alarm dragged me from sleep. With a groan I rolled over and pushed myself up. Something didn't seem right. An uneasy feeling stirred in my gut. Digging through my foggy mind, I remembered taking a sleeping pill after climbing into bed. Probably just nightmares again.

The condo was unnaturally quiet, like it was holding its breath. That vague anxiety deepened as I made my way into the bathroom and turned on the shower. Today was Friday. Jake would be home and there'd be no getting around it now. That must be what's bothering me. I had to tell him about the dissociative disorder, and I wondered if he'd ask for a divorce. I couldn't imagine him accepting a mentally ill wife, but as mad as we were at each other right now, I didn't want to lose him. My heart cramped at the thought. Suddenly my future held a possible divorce and bankruptcy. *How did we get here?*

Sighing, I lifted my t-shirt over my head. The scent of campfire smoke tickled my nose. I balled the shirt up and pressed my nose deeper into it. I couldn't tell if that was where the smell was coming from. Then I remembered Dr. Peters asking me if I'd ever noticed phantom smells like smoke or sweet smells. *Was this part of the disorder?* I tossed my clothes into the laundry basket. I'd have to ask Dr. Evelyn about that on Monday.

—●●●●—

The call came when I was driving away from the school after dropping off the kids. I pushed the answer button on the console display screen. "Hey, Ang. What's up?"

Her voice boomed through the car speakers. "Holy shit! Alice, have you seen the news this morning?"

A sensation of heat bloomed across my scalp. "No?"

"Holy shit. Holy shit."

I pulled over into Walgreen's parking lot. I was gripping the steering wheel so tight, my knuckles had turned white. "Ang ... what is it? What's happened? You're scaring me."

Her voice was shaking and I couldn't tell if it was from excitement or terror. "It's Oliver. His house burned down last night. They found a body. He's most likely dead!"

The heat traveled down to my arms and chest. My mind went brilliantly white. "I don't understand," I managed to whisper.

Another call was coming in. It was Rhys.

"They're not saying much except authorities suspect arson. It's gutted. By the time the fire department was called, the house was half way gone and the fire was too bloody hot, already coming through the roof. They couldn't save it. They found the body a few hours ago, but they'll have to confirm it's Oliver. But ... he was apparently handcuffed to his bed. Can you believe it? I'm in shock. We should have lunch at Brady's today. I'll be done by twelve-thirty." A pause. "Alice? You okay, sweets?"

"Yeah. Just ..." my breathing was shallow so it was hard to push out the word, "shocked."

"I know. It's so crazy. Okay, I have to go but I'll see you at lunch, yeah? We'll talk more then."

"Yeah. See you then."

Rhys was calling again. I stared at the console, numb. Then I declined the call and put the car in reverse.

I drove slowly down Midnight Pass Road and made the left on Hidden Harbor Way. The smell of smoke was drifting in through the car vents. A new rush of fear gripped me. *The smell of smoke on my shirt this morning ... is it possible there's a connection?*

And then I stopped in the middle of the narrow, paved street. Two firetrucks were stretched along the circle drive along with a black sedan and police car. Yellow police tape spanned the ash-covered landscaping. The once majestic house was a twisted black heap of ash and lumps of smoldering objects. Roberts Bay glittered blue through one standing, charred window frame.

A knock on my window startled me. I rolled it down.

"Do you live in this neighborhood, ma'am?" The police officer's eyes were squinting at me, blue diamond chips in a leathery face. His collar and arm pits were dark with sweat.

"No."

"I'm going to have to ask you to move along then."

I nodded. "Of course. Sorry."

I did a three-point turn, taking one last look at the gutted house.

No. No. No. Sleepwalking, taking baths, even going out to collect those girls' stories ... I could see that. But, leaving in the middle of the night to burn down Oliver's house with him in it? Surely, that's not possible. No. I wouldn't do that. I just wouldn't.

But would *she*?

The curtains catching fire in Billy's room. Drac's burning car, she probably did that, too. And now Oliver's house. Fire seemed to be her weapon of choice.

A cry escaped my lips. I pulled the car over. Shoved my hands in my hair. Squeezed my scalp. *Oh, please, God. Please, please, please. Don't let her have done this.* I was rocking, trying to keep from hyperventilating. Forcing deep breaths. In and out. The sobs came then. Deep, deep wailing sobs unearthed by pure terror. I welcomed the release.

Back home, I rushed into the bathroom and dug my shirt out of the laundry basket, shoved my nose in it. *Is it smoke?* I couldn't tell, now that the smell of smoke had invaded my nasal passages from being in the vicinity of Oliver's still-smoldering house. I threw it back in and began to pace. *What now?*

I caught my reflection in the mirror. Leaning on the counter, I squinted into it, meeting my own eyes, looking for any sign of Kali. "Did you do this?" I screamed. "You better not have done this!" I watched my eyes dilate. No sign of Kali. With a growl of frustration, I ran my hands through my hair and began pacing again.

I should call Dr. Evelyn. She'd know what to do. Rushing into the bedroom, I dumped the contents of my purse onto the bed and found my phone. My hands were shaking violently. I sat on the edge of the bed and used my elbows to steady my arms on my thighs.

Looking at my phone I saw five missed calls. Two from Rhys and one from Vivi this morning. One from Jake thirty minutes ago and ... my heart threw itself against my chest. I gasped. One from Oliver's cell phone at 3:34 a.m.

I dropped the phone like it had bitten me.

NINETEEN

I was perched on the park bench under the blazing afternoon sun, feeling claustrophobic in my own skin. Nowhere felt safe. Nowhere felt open enough, not even under the flat, empty blue sky. I'd lied to my friends, told them I had to pick up Addie sick from school so I couldn't make it to lunch. *How can I face them?* I couldn't even face myself.

"You don't look so good."

I glanced over, startled to find Gia seated next to me. *Why does she always show up when I'm here?* I narrowed my eyes, remembered her describing the horse with wings. "Are you real? Or just in my head?"

Gia chuckled and I felt it as a vibration in my own chest. No barrier existed between us. "Nothing is outside of consciousness, Alice. Consciousness is the supreme power, all there is. We all exist within it, just as individual, separate points of view."

I jumped up and grabbed my head. "Stop it! I can't do this!"

A startled young mother glanced sharply at me from the toddler she was pushing on the swings.

At that moment I really did feel crazy. Without looking back, I stumbled to the car and drove straight to Dr. Evelyn's office.

"Please, it's an emergency. I have to talk to her," I begged Fran, the receptionist, ignoring the woman gaping at me from a chair in the waiting room.

Fran's eyes were wide behind her thick glasses; pink blotches had appeared on her cheeks. "Alice, please, you have to calm down. She has fifteen minutes left with her current client and then I can let her know. Would you like some water while you wait?"

"Sorry," I said, unable to stop the tears and the trembling. "Yes, please."

I sipped the water. Something sharp was lodged in my chest so I couldn't take a deep breath. I was clutching a saturated tissue. I couldn't stop rocking. There were magazines fanned out on the table. I stared at a beaming Oprah in a red jacket, matching lips. *Allure* had an airbrushed model in a blue bikini. *Architectural Digest*, a square, three-story glass home glowing yellow against a night sky. This was what every moment felt like right now. A flat, glossy cover, one dimensional, not real. I was suspicious of each thought that zinged through my head. I practiced not grabbing them by the tail in case they weren't mine.

A door opened in the back, then came the hum of Dr. Evelyn's electric wheelchair and a hushed conversation. Fran's concerned face peered at me from the square opening. "Alice, Dr. Evelyn wants to know if you can wait forty-five minutes and then she can see you?"

I nodded. *Where else am I going to go?*

"Great. Let me know if you need anything while you wait." She turned her attention to the elderly lady who'd been in the chair since I'd arrived. "Dr. Evelyn will see you now, Kay. Go on back."

I listened as Fran rescheduled Dr. Evelyn's next appointment. To kill time, I Googled "Gia Rossi Sarasota." No results. Another ghost. My whole life was haunted by people who didn't exist or were missing. I finished the cup of water, made myself stand to throw it away. Stared at my hands, the blue veins, the wrinkly knuckles, the long, oval nail beds. They didn't look like my hands. I wondered what they were capable of.

Minutes melted into one another as the low tick-tock of the wall clock droned on.

And then Dr. Evelyn was there, looking very concerned. My legs were stiff as I pushed myself up. I followed her back to the office and sank gratefully into the familiar sofa.

Her mouth was set in a tight line of pink lipstick and wrinkles, but her eyes were watery with compassion. "All right, deep breath and then tell me what's going on."

It all tumbled out like an avalanche once I opened my mouth: Reyna's murder and Carmen's disappearance; Oliver being the one who beat and raped Reyna and possibly murdered them both; his harassment and his revenge by sending Jake my psychiatric records; the notebook full of stories I was sure Kali was responsible for, and then Oliver's house burning to the ground last night with him in it—and the smell of smoke on my clothes this morning.

When I paused to catch my breath, I searched her face for any reaction—horror, fear, anger—but she only looked more thoughtful.

She laced her fingers then unlaced them. "That's quite a lot to take in. All right, let's address the fire, since that's where your anxiety is coming from at the moment. How do you know it wasn't accidental?"

I shook my head vigorously. "The police are saying arson. And Oliver was handcuffed to the bed when he died. Someone was there with him."

Her thin brows, the same silver-gray as her hair, pressed together. "There's no evidence that person was you, though. Believing you smelled smoke on your clothes isn't really evidence."

I took out my phone and showed her the screen. My hand was shaking. "At 3:34 a.m. I had a missed call from Oliver's cell phone. At 3:35 I returned that call. It lasted over a minute so I obviously talked to him. God knows about what. I wish I could remember." I tossed the phone back into my bag. "Then I must've driven over there." I covered my mouth with my hands and closed my eyes. In the darkness, Kali smiled at me with shining black eyes and a blood red mouth. It was my first glimpse of her. With a shudder, I forced my eyes open and pushed myself back into the sofa. "What do I do? Tell me what to do. Should I turn myself in? Oh God, the kids." A wave of nausea hit me.

Dr. Evelyn held up a hand. "I think that's a mighty big leap you're making between a short conversation with Oliver on the phone last night and driving over to burn his house down. For all you know, he could've told you who was there with him. Jake comes back tonight, yes?"

I nodded.

"Okay, once you explain everything to him, you can decide together if maybe you should consult with a lawyer, just to be prepared for the worst-case scenario. But do not do anything before you talk to a lawyer. Otherwise, I'd suggest just letting the police do their investigation and see what they come up with. You may be worrying yourself for no reason." She maneuvered her chair closer, reached out and folded my hands in hers. "You can't work yourself into a frenzy about every possibility, Alice. Let's wait and see what the facts say, okay?"

"Facts." I nodded. "Okay."

She squeezed my hand one last time. "You have my cell phone number and my permission to call me if Jake needs help understanding your disorder, or if you need support. Seriously, don't hesitate."

❧

I'd asked Aurora to take the kids to a movie so Jake and I could talk. I was waiting at the kitchen table, on my third cup of lukewarm coffee, picking at a piece of toast, when the elevator doors opened. A large bouquet of red roses appeared first. My heart squeezed. *Has he forgiven me? Or is this a bid to make me change my mind about turning in the notebook?*

Behind the bouquet, Jake's face was drawn, pale. I stood and let him slide his arms around me. His body was warm and solid. The sweet scent of the roses felt like a lie.

"I tried to call you. Christ, did you hear about Oliver?" He squeezed me tighter and then released me, handing me the roses. I took them, pressing my thumb pad against a thorn. The pain gave me courage to keep breathing. "Graham called me this morning. Joy is beside herself with grief." He slid out of his jacket, loosening his tie. "I'll have to call Alonso. Tropic Investments Group was in, but I'm not sure what this will do to the deal now. We needed Oliver on that commissioner's seat to insure getting the low-income apartment building approved. Jesus ... burned alive." A shudder ran through him. He finally looked at me. "Where are the kids?"

I fell into the chair, too exhausted to hold myself up, lay the roses carefully on the table. "I've asked Aurora to take them to the movies. We need to talk, Jake."

His shoulders stiffened. "All right." Slowly, he draped his suit jacket on the chair across from me, watching me guardedly, then he sat down. "What's up?"

I turned in the chair toward him and squeezed my hands together. I was underwater, moving in slow motion. "I'm so sorry but I need to tell you a few things. Please let me get it all out. You can ask me questions after I'm done, but know that I didn't mean to mislead you. This time I just didn't ... I didn't know." I pressed my lips together and waited for him to acknowledge this much.

He swallowed hard and braced himself for what was coming, so I continued. "Dr. Evelyn has diagnosed me with dissociative identity disorder. It's why I have the blackouts. Apparently, there are parts of my mind that hold memories and emotions that I don't have access to. It was my mind's way of dealing with childhood trauma." My voice sounded far away, the words flat, floating from me like bubbles. "It's kind of complicated and I don't really even understand it all myself. Dr. Evelyn would like you to come to my appointment with me on Monday, so she can answer any questions you may have. But basically when I black out, it's because another identity has taken over." I paused because Jake's face had blanched; his mouth was hanging open like his jaw hinges had failed.

His voice was a hoarse whisper as he asked, "What are we talking about? Like multiple personalities?"

I nodded. My throat tightened. I wished I had something reassuring to tell him but instead I dropped more words, each seeming to hit him like a hammer blow. "So far we know about Lyssie Grace, she's six and was created to hold the memories and emotions of me losing my adoptive parents. And then there's Kali who claims she's always been with me and started the fire when I was fourteen that got me sent to the psychiatric hospital."

Jake's hands curled into fists and moved to press against his mouth. To his credit, he kept silent, giving me the space that I'd asked for.

I decided to skip telling him about Gia Rossi, since I hadn't decided if she was real or not. Instead I said,

"There may be more." I felt so heavy. My eyeballs ached in their sockets from the weight. I dug my nails into my palms just to feel something besides this weight. "And there's a bigger problem." I held Jake's gaze. "Oliver was the businessman who raped and beat Reyna, and most likely had her killed."

Jake dropped his hands heavily to the table. His eyes blazed like hot gas. "What the hell are you talking about? First you accuse Oliver of having sex parties and drugging girls? And now you're accusing him of murder? Jesus, Alice."

I knew he'd be defensive about Oliver again. Grief would play a part in that as would loyalty to his friend. But, I'd been counting on his loyalty to me to keep an open mind. "It's true, Jake. Ang and I talked to a girl who was at the party that night. She confirmed it was Oliver."

"You're going to take the word of a prostitute over a friend we've known for years?" Disgust and rage twisted his mouth into an ugly shape. "I'm really tired of this. She's lying and you know it."

Normally, his rage would seep into me and spark my own, but I was eerily calm. "What reason would she have to lie? There's nothing in it for her. She's even too scared to testify. Anyway, that's not the biggest problem. Around three-thirty this morning I had a missed call from Oliver. I called him back, though I don't remember doing that. Then, this morning I smelled smoke on my clothes and I'm scared. I'm scared I was there last night, that I may have started the fire. Well ... not me but Kali. Like she did when I was fourteen and felt threatened." I didn't mention being there when Drac's car burned. *What would be the point?*

There was a moment of complete silence as we stared at each other, neither of us breathing. It was as if the oxygen had been sucked from the room. Then the room exhaled and Jake exploded out of the chair. I collapsed against the back of mine.

He paced. Ran his hands through his hair. Rubbed his face roughly. Kicked the roller suitcase he'd abandoned in the middle of the room. Then finally sat back down. "I think we need a second opinion. This is ridiculous, I would've noticed if you were suddenly acting like another person." He shook his head vehemently. "This doctor, she's wrong." His hands shot out and grabbed mine across the table. The violence of it startled me. "Listen, there's no way you drove to Oliver's house in the middle of the night and set it on fire. This doctor has got your head messed up."

"No, Jake. She has video ... you can watch for yourself. Under hypnosis, these personalities came out. You can see them yourself on Monday. Dr. Evelyn can show you the videos." Thank God she had evidence, because I could see Jake would never believe me without it.

His eyes lit up manically. "Well, there you go. Right there. Hypnosis? That's quackery! Doctors can implant false memories and God knows what else with hypnosis. Make you think you're these other people even. We'll fix this. We'll find a qualified doctor to find out what's really going on. Don't worry." His gaze had fallen to the discarded roses. "We'll fix this."

I was in shock. I expected anger. Fear. Accusations. *But denial?* I didn't see that one coming.

TWENTY

Jake stood on the balcony, his blond hair gleaming in the morning sun, one hand braced against the stone balustrade, the other holding a cell phone pressed to his ear. He was talking to Graham, trying to find out if they'd learned anything new about Oliver's death. Neither one of us had gotten any sleep last night, and his posture was uncharacteristically slouched.

I sat at the table full of plates of half-eaten pancakes, scrambled eggs and bacon, trying to hold a decent conversation with the kids, when all I wanted to do was scoop them up in my arms and hold on for dear life. Charlie was explaining to us how sharks can be born live or hatch from eggs depending on the species, something he'd watched last night on YouTube. Luckily this only required a "that's fascinating" and "really?" once in a while from me. My gaze kept drifting back to Jake. Since I'd woken up, I'd been moving from numb detachment to unbearable anxiety. Right now the anxiety was beginning to creep back up.

Aroura poured Addie more orange juice. "You didn't eat your eggs." She pushed her plate closer.

Addie folded her arms. "Jessica says eggs are baby chickens. I'm not eating baby chickens."

"Well, Jessica is wrong," Aurora said. "Eggs are baby chicken *food* only."

Addie looked to her brother for confirmation. He nodded in agreement so she picked up her fork and stabbed at a yellow, buttery egg. At least they would always have each other.

I drank in every detail of my daughter—the way she held her fork in a fist, the stubborn set to her chin, her wild, unbrushed hair, her chapped bottom lip. I did this out of the desperate belief that she would disappear, that they'd both disappear, from my life. Or I from theirs.

"Addie, do you remember that woman at the park, the one in the yellow dress with dark skin and long braids?"

Her mouth twisted as she chewed and shook her head no.

I turned to Charlie, who was constructing a shark on his plate out of bacon pieces. "Do you remember seeing Mom talk to her, Charlie? She's kind of a big lady, always smiling? She's sat by me on the bench a few times."

"Nope," he said without looking up. "What's her name?"

"Never mind," I said. "It doesn't matter." *Kids don't pay attention to the strangers around them anyway, right?* I swallowed the last of my cold coffee and started gathering up the plates, stacking as many as I could carry to the sink. One foot in front of the other. Turned on the water, scraped the food into the disposal, arranged the dishes in the dishwasher. I couldn't think past this simple task.

"You are going to work me out of a job," Aurora said, appearing at my shoulder. She carefully sat two juice glasses in the sink. "This death of your friend is really bothering you and Mr. Jake?"

I bit the inside of my cheek and nodded without looking at her. Picked up the sponge, scrubbed non-existent food off a fork, placed it in the dishwasher. Just keep moving.

Her warm hand was patting my arm. "I am sorry. You let me know if I should take the kids to the park or anything, okay?"

"Thanks." I managed to meet her eyes for a moment, she deserved at least that. Her concern almost snapped my resolve. "I really don't know what we'd do without you." I forced a smile that I hoped seemed sincere and then turned back to the sponge, the glass in my hand, the simple task.

—◆◆◆—

I hadn't been able to bring myself to answer calls or leave the house, so the gang had come to me. We were out on the balcony, watching the setting sun. Discarded containers of the Thai food they'd brought were scattered on the wicker glass table.

Rhys thought it was time I told Angeline and Vivi about my dissociate identity diagnosis, and I'd agreed. So, they'd sat silently while I explained, and then I'd kept going, filling them in on my worries about being involved in the fire at Oliver's house. I was drained.

They were processing it all quietly, stealing glances at each other.

Jake and Rolf had migrated inside under the pretense of digging up a bottle of old Scotch. But, they'd been gone long enough now for me to know they were talking about something they didn't want to share with the rest of us. I wondered what Jake was thinking. He'd been avoiding me most of the day.

I suddenly remembered the time just before I met Jake, when I'd been sitting beside a lake in Orlando and saw the jagged shadow of a large bird glide across the water. Only when I looked up there was no bird to be found. This moment had the same quality and texture.

"Well," Vivi said, breaking the silence, "I think we all experience this in different degrees, Alice. We all act differently, have different personas, put on different masks depending on who we're dealing with. I mean, every person in our life has an idea of who we should be, how we should act. It's hard to not try and live up to that."

I shrugged. "Yeah, but I don't have a choice."

Angeline turned to me, her eyes brimming with bright emotion. "Sounds like Kali protects you, though. Do you know her story?"

I let myself fall into her gentleness, tumbled like I'd fallen off a cliff. "Not that I remember, no."

She tucked her bare feet up beneath her and settled in with her sparkling water. "Well, in Indian mythology, Kali was a fierce demon-slayer. There's this battle, right, where the goddess Durga is fighting two demon kings and losing. Because these two demon kings, they weren't daft. They had petitioned the Creator, Brahma, for the power to be invincible in battle, and he'd granted them their wish, guaranteeing that no man or god would be able to defeat them.

"You can imagine how bloody smug they were, and how much they got away with, yeah? But when Durga finally got fed up and brought in Kali, she found the loophole. See, up until that moment, the goddesses had fought wars by lending male gods their power and staying behind the scenes. But unlike the other goddesses, Durga didn't lend out her power. In fact, she took power from the male gods and fought the battle herself." Her dimple appeared as she smiled. "She changed the game and won. Because the Creator never promised the demons they wouldn't be defeated by a *goddess*." She nudged my arm. "So, with Kali on your side, I can't imagine you losing any battles."

"Hey," Rhys said from the chair. "She's got us, too. What are we, chopped liver?"

"Well, you're no goddess," Vivi teased him.

Rhys clutched his heart. "That hurts." Then, with a fading smile, he glanced toward the sliding doors. "How's Jake handling all this?"

I shrugged. "He thinks Dr. Evelyn is wrong. That I don't actually have D.I.D. and wants me to see a different doctor."

"Denial ... classic," Vivi said.

"Give him time," Angeline said. "He'll get to acceptance eventually."

"And then what? When he accepts his wife is a shattered, broken person, do you think he'll want to keep me around? You guys know Jake. He won't even tolerate a scuff on his shoes." I fought the lump in my throat.

Angeline leaned forward and squeezed my hand. "Hey, that's different and you know it. He loves you, Alice. He's not going to abandon you for something that's out of your control. You've done nothing wrong here."

"What about burning Oliver's house down with him in it?" I asked defiantly.

"You wouldn't do that."

"But Kali ... she would."

They glanced at each other. Then Rhys shrugged. "We'll just have to wait and see what the investigation comes up with. But, whatever happens, you have to know you're not alone in this. We're all going to be right beside you, no matter what. Okay?"

A firetruck siren broke the silence, screaming across the bridge as I forced a nod. I loved them, but I wasn't sure even a friendship as strong as ours could survive what I knew in my gut was coming.

It hadn't taken long for the investigation to swing our way. Sunday had stretched out painfully, time pulled like taffy—us watching the kids play on the beach, pushing away the relentless, brutal new wounds in our life; us choking down lunch and then dinner; us playing board games with the kids as the light faded, hands shaky and minds tortured. We discussed the notebook finally. Besides Jake losing all his clients, there was a new problem. If I turned it in, that would give the police motive, a plausible reason why I'd burned down Oliver's house. I agreed to keep it hidden for now, which made me hate myself even more. Then the phone call from the concierge desk. "There are two detectives here who'd like to speak to you."

We sent the kids to their rooms. Jake left me trembling on the sofa as he went to meet the detectives at the elevator with the warning, "Not one word about the phone call with Oliver that night." He squeezed my shoulder. It was the first time he'd touched me since Friday.

He returned with two people at his heels: a tall man and a petite, dark-haired woman. They both wore black slacks, dress shirts and grave expressions.

I stood, my heart pounding, and shook their hands as they introduced themselves.

The woman's grip and gaze were like steel as she nodded. "Detective Mendoza."

The tall man was softer with his cloud of gray hair, gray eyes and prominent Adam's apple bobbing as he said, "Detective Burrows. Nice to meet you."

"Please, have a seat." Jake motioned to the sofa. "Can I get you anything. Coffee? Water?"

"No, thank you."

Jake took a seat beside me, draped an arm casually behind me on the back of the sofa. "What can we do for you, detectives?"

Detective Mendoza took out a notebook as Detective Burrows laced his fingers together and leaned toward us, elbows on his knees. *Just a casual conversation.* "We were told you two were good friends with Oliver Brooks?"

We both nodded. Jake didn't have to fake the sadness in his voice as he said, "We're all devastated."

The detective sat back and adjusted his red tie. "I'm sorry for your loss. We're going to do all we can to find out what happened, you have my word. We're investigating his death as a homicide so we'd like to ask you ... did he have enemies you were aware of? Any business dealings gone bad? Any illegal activities he was involved in?"

"Any disgruntled ex-girlfriends?" Detective Mendoza added.

I kept my face blank, stared at the floor like I was thinking. But all I could see was Reyna's coffin. A flare of white-hot rage blinded me for a moment, then the separation, like I was floating away from the moment.

I felt *her* rise up. *He deserved it.*

I dug my nails into my palms, bit my cheek until I could taste the salty tinge of blood. The sharpness of the pain pinned me to the forefront of my consciousness. When my vision cleared, the two detectives were staring back at me, both of them alert.

My gaze slid off theirs. "I think I'm still in shock," I managed.

Jake rested a steadying hand on my thigh. "I wish we could help you, but I don't know of any enemies Oliver may've had. He was running for a city commissioner's seat, but I don't think that's a very cutthroat position. And as far as ex-girlfriends, he's never really had a serious relationship so ... no, no disgruntled ex-wives or girlfriends."

"Have you ever attended a party at his home where there were prostitutes?" Detective Mendoza asked. She addressed Jake, but her eyes flicked immediately to me.

I stopped breathing.

Jake's tone was the right mix of surprise and indignation. "Prostitutes? No, of course not. We've been to gatherings there, sure. But, I can say for a fact I've never seen a prostitute at his home."

Detective Mendoza was holding eye contact with me. I tried to shake my head no, but I think it was more like a wobble.

Detective Burrow's said, "Did you know he's been implicated in the death of a seventeen-year-old prostitute named Reyna Flores?"

Jake startled beside me, and I knew the possibility of Oliver being involved finally became real to him in that moment, now that it was coming from someone other than his paranoid wife. I glanced over. His face had paled, his expression crumbled, his eyes now full of uncertainty and new pain.

"We didn't know that, no," he finally managed.

Out of reflex, I glanced at him again. I really wish he wouldn't have said *we*. Now if I say I knew, he'll look like a liar or that he was covering for me. I opened my mouth and then closed it again.

"Mrs. Leininger?" Detective Burrows said gently. "You look like you have something to tell us."

Jake stiffened beside me. With panic rising, I said, "Well, it's just that we did know Reyna, the girl who was killed. I volunteer for Project Freedom and met her there. She was a nice kid, trying to get out of that life. We ... we went to her funeral."

Detective Mendoza's attention sharpened. "Did she ever say anything to you about working a party at Mr. Brooks's place?"

This question I could answer honestly. "No," I said emphatically.

Detective Mendoza scratched something in her notebook and then shared a glance with her partner. She stood and handed me a card. "If you can think of anything else that may be relevant, give me a call."

"We appreciate your time," Detective Burrows said, standing and shaking our hands.

I stared at the card in my hand as Jake walked them out: Detective Jean Mendoza, Sarasota Police Department, Criminal Investigation Division and her phone number in raised black lettering. Holding it felt like an omen. I slipped it into my pocket and went to find the kids.

TWENTY-ONE

Somehow I'd managed to get Jake into Dr. Evelyn's office on Monday. Only as we sat side by side on the gray sofa, it no longer felt like a safe space. The tension and anger emanating from Jake had filled up the room, wiping away the peacefulness.

"I'm sure you can understand my outrage," Jake was saying. "You've basically convinced my wife she's this other person capable of burning one of our good friends alive."

"Jake—" I began, horrified that he was being so aggressive with the only person who'd ever tried to help me.

"It's all right." Dr. Evelyn held up a hand and gave me a reassuring smile. Then she nodded at Jake. "Go on, please. I'd like to know what your feelings are about this."

"My *feelings*? My feelings don't matter one bit. What matters is that my wife believes she's capable of murder. It's a complete fantasy. I've known her for ten years, and I've never seen her act like this violent person you've convinced her she is. *Kali* was it? Or a six-year-old child? Completely ridiculous. I've only agreed to come today to let you know she will not be coming back here."

I could only stare at Dr. Evelyn. I'd never felt so frustrated and drained in my life. I didn't even have the energy to blink.

She glanced from me to Jake. "Before you make that decision, I have one request. I ask that you watch the video where one of Alice's alters reveals herself. Would that be okay with you, Alice?"

"Yes," I said gratefully. I turned to Jake. "Please."

His jaw twitched. He pinched the bridge of his nose. Then finally sighed. "Fine. Then we're leaving."

I didn't watch the screen as Dr. Evelyn played the video, I watched Jake. His posture was stiff, defensive. He held himself still, including his expression, though a brief flash of surprise did grip him right before Dr. Evelyn said, "Hello there. I'm Dr. Evelyn. And who might you be?" He saw something in the on-screen me he didn't recognize, like I had.

Jake didn't reach out to comfort me as he watched. That stung. I glanced up at Dr. Evelyn. She was watching him, also, and the disappointment was evident in the downturn of her mouth. She understood his mind was closed.

When she shut the laptop, she left the space silent, giving Jake the floor. Instinctively she seemed to realize that trying to convince him what he'd watched was real would be a mistake. He would only grip his disbelief more firmly.

Dr. Evelyn let her gaze meet mine. Her eyes were thick with apology; she'd lost this battle. She turned to Jake. "I can show you the one where Lyssie Grace appears if you'd like."

"That won't be necessary." Jake stood abruptly. "We'll be leaving now."

I pushed myself off the sofa with effort. "I'm sorry," I whispered as Jake disappeared through the door.

She reached out and squeezed my hand. "Give him time. It's a lot for him to accept. Call me when you're ready. I'll still be here for you."

We drove home in silence. Jake hadn't even looked my way. I wanted to ask him why it was so hard for him to accept my disorder, but I already knew why. Accepting such a big flaw in me would be admitting he'd made a mistake when he'd married me. Resting my forehead against the cool window glass, I tried to take a deep breath. I could've slept for a year.

———

At 8:30 that evening the detectives returned with a search warrant. Four other officers emerged from the elevator with them. It was surreal. Like one of those TV detective shows had invaded our home.

This time they separated us, but not before Jake grabbed my arm and whispered in my ear, "Do not say anything. Tell them you won't talk to them without your lawyer present."

I was being ushered into the living room by Detective Mendoza. She was speaking but I couldn't concentrate on what she was saying. All I could hear were the thoughts running through my head: *Jake brought up a lawyer. Does that mean he thinks I'm capable of murder? Does he think I may be guilty?*

Oh God, he does. He thinks there's a possibility I did this. Well, that makes two of us.

"Mrs. Leininger?"

I looked up. Detective Mendoza was seated beside me on the sofa. I didn't remember sitting down. "Yes?"

"I asked if you know why we're here."

Something hard in her voice made it all hit me at once, how serious this was. I began to tremble inside. I glanced at my hands. They seemed steady. I took comfort in them, like they were something separate from me. "No, I don't."

"Can you tell me where you were the night Oliver Brooks died?"

I grew cold. Up until that moment I could convince myself this had nothing to do with me. But they'd found something. Some evidence that implicated me. It was true then. I was a suspect. *Jake said not to talk to them without a lawyer. But won't that make me look guilty? Surely it would be better to cooperate at this point?* A wave of nausea ripped through me. I managed to speak over it. "I was here."

"All night?"

I nodded.

"And your husband can verify this?"

I felt the sheen of cold sweat on my forehead. My voice sounded far away but reasonably calm considering the whirlwind of fear churning my insides. "No, actually. He was in Miami. I was here with the kids and our nanny, Aurora."

She scratched in her notebook and then met my eye again. "And you didn't leave this residence at any point in the evening?" I could hear the expectation in her voice. She thought I did leave, but she also expected me to lie about it. *Why?*

"Not that I know of." This seemed safe enough. It wasn't a lie.

When her brow lifted, I knew it was a mistake. Her brown eyes had a new light behind them. Almost excitement. "Not that you know of? Do you often do things that you don't know of?"

I could hear Jake's voice rising in the dining room. Then Aurora's. They'd woken her. *Please don't wake the kids.* Also, some scraping and moving of things came from the bedroom. *What were they looking for? Oh God, what if they found the notebook? I needed to end this.*

"My ... my husband said I shouldn't say anything without a lawyer present."

She smiled grimly. "That's probably wise. Considering we have a security video of your vehicle on Mr. Brooks's street at 3:55 the morning he died."

"My white Range Rover?" I pushed out on a breath. I was going to hyperventilate. "But it couldn't be. It's a popular car, there must be a mistake."

"There was a partial plate match. We also took the security video from your condo parking garage. It shows you getting in your vehicle and driving away at 3:40 a.m. Are you sure there's nothing you want to tell me? I can help you, if you talk to me now. Later..." She shrugged, letting the threat hang in the air.

I lurched, separated. I was suddenly in the dark, but I could hear my voice from far away. "I have nothing to say without a lawyer present, Detective." I was so calm, I knew it was Kali speaking.

And then I was back. But not fully, I still felt detached and a bit confused.

"You have my card. Please have your lawyer accompany you to the station tomorrow for an interview then."

She was looking at me strangely, then she was getting up. I followed her back out to the dining room to the buzz of activity. Officers had piled a grouping of plastic bags full of items by the elevator. Another one was carrying a plastic bag toward the pile. I glanced down. Inside were my pink running shoes.

Jake came over and blocked my view. His eyes were brimming with worry. "You okay?" He was keeping his voice low. Still not touching me, I noted with some irritation. *Is he afraid of me? Afraid I'll infect him with my crazy?*

I had a sudden urge to scream, to watch the glass around us shatter and rain down into the sea. "I'm fine."

After they left, we entered the room they'd searched ... our bedroom. It was a mess. Our clothes were hanging out of drawers, the laundry basket in the bathroom had been tipped over and gone through. I checked to make sure the notebook was there while Jake collapsed on the bed. Mercifully, it was right where I'd left it under the books. I went into the closet next. My box from Garden of Hope had been pillaged, files opened. I couldn't tell if they'd taken anything. They could've taken photos of everything. *Were they allowed to do that?*

I fell to my knees. Rested my face in my hands. This feeling of being violated brought a memory floating to the surface. It had to be a memory.

I'm suddenly a child in the bedroom at Garden of Hope that I share with four other girls. I'm tearing up my bed, pulling off the mattress. My doll, Annie, is gone. I'm so frantic I can't breathe. Why? Oh yes. She was the only thing I got to keep from my adoptive parents. She had red yarn hair and one of her button eyes was missing, but she was my only friend. I must be around seven years old because this is shortly after I lost them.

I keep looking in the place Annie should be, tucked safely between the wall and mattress. One of the girls walks in ... Christina. She's older by two years and she always pinches me viciously when there are no adults around.

"Looking for something?"

I whirl on her and see the smirk and know. "Give me back my doll," I say to her.

"What doll?" She is smiling like a crocodile. I can see her one missing eye tooth. The urge to smash the rest of them in becomes a screaming command. I feel myself flying through the air and then feel the air rush from my lungs, the sharp crack of my skull as I tackle her, and we both hit the floor hard.

It was the first memory of my life before thirteen that had come unbidden, even though I felt no emotion around it. It felt like a story that had happened to someone else. The walls in my mind were crumbling.

TWENTY-TWO

Jake and I sat in front of Mark Phang's desk. He was the criminal defense lawyer Rolf had recommended to us. He was a slight man in his fifties, dark hair, calm demeanor. His office was full of bookshelves, mahogany furniture and neat stacks of files. It smelled like expensive new leather. Rolf had said he was the best. His name, Phang, made me think of a vampire. We'd been here for an hour and my back was starting to ache. He was looking over the copy of the search warrant the police had left last night.

"Seems like they were looking for a specific set of clothing." He looked up. His eyes met mine over silver-rimmed glasses. "Probably related to the video they claim to have of you getting in your vehicle that night."

The pink running shoes.

He removed his glasses and twined his fingers together. "What I'm going to suggest is that you do not voluntarily go in for an interview at this time."

"Won't that make me look guilty?"

"Guilt or innocence depends on only one thing— the evidence they come up with. If they come up with enough evidence to convince a prosecutor to charge you, then they will arrest you at that point. Until then, you have the right to silence.

"In fact, they may come back to you ... say with some hard copies from your parking garage video and ask you to confirm that it's you getting into your vehicle. Don't. You simple do not give them any information, no matter how harmless you think it is." He leaned back and surveyed the paperwork we'd filled out, which was now spread out on his desk. He handed me a yellow notepad across the desk. "What I need from you, is for you to write down everything you did that night." He paused. "And also everything you can remember about your encounters with the deceased, the conversations you had about him with your friends, times, dates. I need to know the prosecution won't have any surprises for me.

"And, Alice, if you are arrested, you immediately invoke your right to an attorney. No answering questions even then without me present. Understand?"

"Yes." I took the notepad and glanced at Jake. His jaw was clenched tight, his knuckles bloodless as he clutched the edges of his black binder. He had asked me not to mention the dissociative disorder yet, which was fine with me. I didn't need the man who would be possibly defending me to think I was crazy. I wondered if Jake was rethinking keeping that from Mr. Phang, but no. He dropped his head and unzipped the binder, slowly removed the pen from its tiny leather halter and wrote the first check.

⬤⬤⬤

Jake finally left me alone Wednesday morning and went to work. At first I was grateful. His constant vigilance and protection made me feel like an incompetent child. I was no longer his partner, his equal. Now I was a problem that he had to fix. But, as I stood out in the morning sun with my coffee, loneliness settled over me. The great expanse of water spreading to the horizon suddenly made me aware of how insignificant I was. Tiny. Just a speck of compressed energy for one brief moment in time. I didn't matter at all. What would it matter if I spent the rest of my life in prison? Despair stole the air from my lungs. My legs threatened to collapse. But then I heard *her*...

We are eternal. We are the narrators of our own stories. This is what life is ... a collection of stories. Don't make ours insignificant.

And then I saw her, larger than life floating in front of me. Her eyes were black as night, her legs folded in lotus position, her expression serene. But her dark hair was blowing around her like she was in the middle of a storm. I watched her like I used to watch my children as infants, with a mixture of wonder and fear. I suddenly understood that *she* was the inferno I'd always felt within me. But I also understood that it wasn't destruction she wanted. It was justice for the wounded.

—◆◆◆—

They came for me while I sat at the dining room table, sculpting clay monsters with Aurora and the kids.

Jake entered the room, his face drained, the phone clutched in his hand. He nodded.

My hand went to my throat. Tears sprang to my eyes, but I tried to keep them at bay for the sake of the kids. Reaching over, I squeezed Aurora's hand across the table. We'd explained everything to her and told her to prepare for this. She was so understanding, so non-judgmental that I'd broken down in her arms and then realized she wasn't just a mother-figure to the kids.

"Take care of my babies." I stood on shaking legs to gather them up. "Mom has to go someplace for a little while." I felt their small, warm hands on my back. I pressed my lips onto both their cheeks.

"Why, Mom?" Charlie asked, eyes wide, lip trembling. He sensed the seriousness of the moment, of course he would.

"It's complicated, Charlie. Just know that I love you both to infinity. And," my voice cracked. I hugged them to my chest so they didn't see the tears that had escaped. "And know that I'll see you as soon as I can."

"Mommy, I'm scared. I don't want you to go," Addie said into my neck.

"Don't be scared. Be good for Aurora and Daddy, okay?"

"What about the monsters?" Charlie whispered in my ear.

I slipped my hairband from my hair and pressed it into Charlie's small palm wordlessly. If I opened my mouth, the despair would be a roar. I gave them one more squeeze as I heard the elevator doors open. One more deep breath, filling my lungs with their scent. Then I nodded to Aurora to take them, feeling a profound emptiness as they left my arms.

Her eyes were filled with tears, also. "Come on, kids. Let's get our hands washed up for dinner." She gave me a quick, tight hug then rested her palms on my cheeks. "Everything will be okay. I pray for you."

I watched them disappear down the hall and then turned to face the two detectives behind me.

"Alice Brown-Leininger, you're under arrest for the murder of Oliver Brooks." Detective Mendoza stepped forward with handcuffs. "Turn around, please."

"Wait," Jake said. In a few steps, he was in front of me. He took my hand, stared at my wedding ring. "You should leave your jewelry here."

"Right." I slipped my hand from his and removed my wedding rings, placing them in his open palm. This felt like another small death. Reaching up with shaking hands, I removed my necklace and earrings and handed those over, too. My eyes meet his and I saw the deep sadness. "I'm sorry."

His shoulders dropped in surrender as he reached out a hand to cup my damp face. He kissed me lightly. "I'll call Mr. Phang. Hang tight."

"You have the right to remain silent." The cold metal cuffs tightened around my wrists as Detective Mendoza recited my Miranda rights, and then her iron grip was clamped onto my arm. "Let's go."

—◆◆◆◆—

At the station they seated me on a stool in front of a plastic window, one wrist handcuffed to a bar beneath the counter. *Where did they think I'd go?* I was "checked in" to the system and dutifully gave them all my information, then I was uncuffed and told to stand with my legs and arms spread. Humiliation warmed my face as a female officer, with blue latex gloves, patted down each part of my body. She made me open my mouth and show her under my tongue. I'd managed not to cry again until then. I wasn't a person to her, but a job. She ran a wand over my body, ignoring my tears.

"Step over here, please."

I stood against the wall, on a painted yellow square, wiped my face with both my palms.

"Look here." She held her finger up in the air and snapped my mug shot.

There were other officers milling about as all this was going on. This was the thing that made me feel like I'd been stripped of personhood. All these things done to me were in public. My shame and fear were not worthy of privacy, though they were worthy of a few contemptuous glances.

I felt the darkness closing around my vision, the separation pulling at me.

It's September 7th and I'm an adult. It's September 7th and I'm an adult.

After I'd changed into a red jumpsuit, I was led down a concrete corridor, buzzed through a metal door, and then a second door the guard used a key to open. We turned a corner and walked down another corridor. "Those are the showers," she nodded to a door on my left, "and this is you." She motioned me inside the tiny concrete box. I stepped in and another memory lit up my mind like a flare.

Christina and Mycah have locked me in the closet. It's dark and the boxes stacked in here are full of roaches. I stay standing and move my toes around to keep them from crawling on my bare feet. My own breath is hot on my face against the door. My eyes are squeezed shut. I won't let them see me cry.

A sliding sound came from behind me and I whirled around. *Click.* I was locked in, like an animal. It was a solid door with a window. I guessed I should've been grateful it wasn't bars.

Stiffly, I moved to sit on the bed. It was a concrete rectangle with two thin pads. No pillow. The only other thing in that beige concrete box was a stainless-steel sink with a toilet attached like a growth. I glanced up. Oh, and a black plastic dome in the corner that must've been a camera. So, no privacy in here, either. I scooted back on the bed and leaned my head against the wall.

What now?

After thirty minutes of staring at the wall, I began to think it was entirely possible that if I wasn't already crazy, it would happen in here. Then, my door slid open and the large, uniformed woman was back, minus her latex gloves. I found that a bit comforting.

"Turn around please," she said, cuffs in hand.

I was led back through the corridor, then another and then into a room that was smaller than my cell. It held one folding table, four folding chairs and a mirror on one wall. My heart began to hammer. They were going to ask me more questions.

"I'm not answering any questions without my lawyer present." The words came out breathless, scared.

She removed my handcuffs and motioned for me to have a seat. "The detectives will be with you shortly."

Only my eyes moved as I took in my new cramped space. I avoided the mirror. Someone was probably watching me from behind it. Same black dome in the corner, one of those old-fashioned large white clocks on the wall, a switch by the door with a sign taped beneath it: Turn on Recording Device. The walls were concrete with a sickly layer of shiny gray paint like sludge. It smelled like stale, sour sweat.

My stomach churned, contracted. I stared at the door. I rested my head in my hands and tried to practice the calm inhale and exhale I'd learned in Angeline's yoga class. At the thought of my friend, my lungs seized. *Had Jake called them and let them know I'd been arrested?* They would feel as helpless as I did, and I desperately wanted to apologize for putting them through this.

I was observing myself, trying to make sure I was behaving as an innocent person would. *Because I am an innocent person.* A sliver of doubt poked a hole in my confidence. *I am. Even if Kali did this, it wasn't me, Alice. Right?* I glanced at my hands. My hands and *her* hands, one and the same. I shoved them back under the table.

I'd watched each second tick by on the wall clock so I knew forty-three minutes had passed by the time Detectives Mendoza and Burrows finally came in.

Detective Burrows was dressed more casually this time in gray slacks and a blue polo shirt. He smiled as he sat a water bottle in front of me. "How are you holding up?"

"Fine." I glanced at Detective Mendoza, who was still in black slacks and a suit jacket. Her dark hair was pulled back into a severe bun, her mouth set in a hard line.

She made no effort at small talk. "It's now 7:35 p.m. on September seventh, and we're here in a room that is being video and audio recorded. Before we ask you any questions, you have the right to understand what your rights are." She removed a sheet of paper from a folder and read my Miranda rights again. Then she turned the sheet around on the table and placed a pen beside it. "I need you to initial each statement to confirm you understand these rights and then sign at the bottom."

I couldn't see any harm in this so I signed, but then as I handed it back I said, "I'm not answering any questions tonight."

Detective Burrows folded a sheet over in his notebook. "Alice, you have to understand, we wouldn't have arrested you if we didn't have enough evidence to convict you. What we're after is to hear your side of what happened. Fill in some blanks for us."

"I can't fill in any blanks for you," I said out of frustration. Then I squeezed my fingers and reminded myself to stay quiet.

"Can't or won't?" Detective Mendoza asked with a bite to her tone.

I let my gaze fall to my lap. "I should probably talk to my lawyer."

"Okay, you don't have to talk to us, but I'm not sure that's going to be in your best interest. Remember that evidence we told you about? You should know we pulled your fingerprint from the door handle to Oliver Brooks's bedroom."

I glanced up quickly at Detective Mendoza. A slight smirk was tugging at the corner of her mouth. She had to be lying. *Surely the fire would've destroyed any fingerprints?* Besides, I'd never been in Oliver's bedroom. *But ... Kali...*

"So, either you were a guest of his bedroom previously or you were there the night he died. Which is it? If you were having an affair with Mr. Brooks now would be the time to tell us. It would explain the fingerprint."

I stared at her in horror. *An affair?*

"Here's your situation," Detective Burrows said slowly. "You remember this interview is being recorded, right?" He waited for me to nod. "That means at some point, it will be shown to the jury in your trial. If you refuse to talk to us tonight but then suddenly come up with an explanation for this later, the jury won't buy it. They'll think you're lying since you could've very easily explained yourself now."

The pressure and panic were building up inside me. I squeezed the water bottle to try and relieve it. I wished they would stop staring at me for a moment so I could gather my thoughts.

We were interrupted by a knock on the door. The policewoman popped her head in and gave it a little jerk. Detective Mendoza left with her.

"We really are trying to help you out here, Alice. But you've got to talk to us."

I took a sip of water to have something to do. It stuck in my throat, and I had a coughing spell.

Detective Mendoza came back in looking even less happy. She glanced at the clock. "Detective Mendoza suspending interview at seven forty-eight p.m." Then she glanced at me with undisguised contempt. "Your lawyer's here."

TWENTY-THREE

I was cuffed with my hands in front of me and taken to a different room. This one had a long, wooden table and many chairs with worn burgundy padding. Mr. Phang was seated at the end of the table, reading something in front of him. I was so happy to see him, the tears welled up.

He gave me a distracted smile as I took a seat across from him. They didn't remove my handcuffs this time.

"Thank you for coming so quickly."

He nodded and then removed his glasses. "How did the interview go? Did you say anything to them? I know it's hard not to."

I eyed the corners of the room.

"Don't worry. This is an attorney-client interview and legally not allowed to be monitored."

I relayed the whole conversation to him and then asked, "Do you think they lied about the fingerprint on the door knob?"

"They can and will use that tactic to get you to confess." He kept his voice neutral as he handed me the blow. "But in this case, no. They really did pull your print from the doorknob of Mr. Brooks's bedroom." Then he slipped on his glasses, shuffled the papers in front of him, giving me time to digest this news. "They've given me a partial list of the evidence against you. The video of you getting in your car that night, the security video of your car on his street, the fingerprint on the doorknob and ..." he stopped and took a breath, blew it out before continuing. "There was gasoline residue on the running shoes they removed from your home in the search. Gasoline was the accelerant used in the fire."

I felt myself collapse. My shoulders, my posture, my belief in my own innocence. "There's something I have to tell you."

Mr. Phang glanced up sharply. "Go on."

"It's possible I did go to Oliver's house that night. I mean, not me but ... an alter personality. I've been diagnosed with dissociative identity disorder. So, I may have gone there but don't remember." A tear of frustration slipped down my face. "I'm sorry I didn't tell you before."

Mr. Phang sat back in his seat and stared at me and then down at his paperwork. He seemed stunned at first, but recovered quickly. He began to nod. "All right. I'll have to do some research and rethink our strategy. You can prove this?"

"Yes. My therapist has taped sessions where the other personalities have come out."

He tapped his pen on the table edge. "Good. That's good."

"There's something else you should know." I told him about the other incident where I was accused of starting the fire in Bill's bedroom and institutionalized for it. I didn't mention Drac's car burning, since I couldn't be one hundred percent sure

Kali was responsible. He listened quietly. I watched him for a moment and then asked, "So, what now?"

"Well." He sat upright and laid his hands flat on the table. "Tomorrow will be your arraignment before a judge. In light of what you just told me, I suggest you come clean tonight about your dissociative disorder diagnosis, so we can use it in your defense."

Jake was going to hate that. Everyone would know his wife was crazy.

"It's true, what the detective told you. The jury will think it's suspicious if you don't have an explanation for things until later, so we'll need to talk to them now. The flip side of this is they want to tie you to a particular story that they can later dismantle with evidence or testimony, so we have to be careful what we give them. I'll be right there beside you and let you know whether to answer a question or not, or to stop the interview if necessary. Are you ready?"

I nodded, though inside I was screaming *no*.

"Then let's go."

The room was even more cramped now, with an extra person, as Detective Mendoza reminded me of my Miranda rights once again and that the room was recorded.

Mr. Phang was leaning back in his chair beside me, a yellow notebook in his lap. He'd told me he would write out any instructions to me during the interview to keep them private. "My client is ready to share some information with you." He nodded at me.

I addressed my words to Detective Burrows, the less hostile of the two. "The reason I don't know if I left the condo the evening Oliver died is because I have dissociative identity disorder and sometimes suffer blackouts and lose time. The last thing I remember that evening is taking an Ambien and going to bed. I woke up in bed the next morning when my alarm went off at 6:45 as usual, so there was no reason for me to believe I'd gone anywhere."

"Except the video evidence that you did," Detective Mendoza said slowly. She leaned forward on the table, directing my attention to her. "So, you're saying you don't remember driving to Oliver Brooks's house that night?"

"My client is not saying she drove there and doesn't remember. She's simply saying she doesn't remember doing anything except going to bed that evening."

"Let's go back to this dissociative..." Detective Burrows looked down at his notebook, "... identity disorder. Have you been officially diagnosed with this?"

"Yes."

He ripped a piece of paper from his notebook and handed it to me with his pen. "Do you mind writing down the doctor's name and information who's diagnosed you."

I glanced at Mr. Phang. He nodded so I wrote down Dr. Evelyn's information and handed it over.

"So with this *disorder*," Detective Mendoza said the word with thinly veiled disbelief, "you do things you don't remember? That's pretty convenient."

A tiny burst of anger popped in my gut like a firecracker. It gave me the courage to meet Detective

Mendoza's gaze. "Convenient? No, actually it's complicated my life greatly."

"How long have you had problems with these blackouts?" Detective Burrows asked with a more understanding tone.

"My client will not be answering questions about her past at this time."

I knew he was trying to keep the other fire incident under wraps for as long as possible. He'd explained to me how damaging it would be.

"Let's talk about your relationship with Mr. Brooks then," Detective Mendoza said. "Were you having an affair?"

"No."

"You were never in Mr. Brooks's bedroom then?"

"No."

"But your fingerprint says otherwise. So, you were there, you just don't remember?"

I didn't say anything. *Is she trying to trap me?* She nodded like I'd answered her anyway and wrote something down in her notebook.

The fatigue was starting to weigh on me like a heavy, wet blanket, though I found some comfort in the fact that their theory about my relationship with Oliver was so far off. I wondered how long that would be the case. Not long if I told them about the notebook. That would be the motive they were looking for.

"Help me understand these blackouts," Detective Burrows said. "Are you conscious at all during them?"

"A part of me is. It's not like I'm sleepwalking or anything. Most of the time, no one even notices when I'm gone."

"When you're gone?" His eyebrows rose.

"It's complicated. Apparently consciousness is like a spotlight and mine is shared with ... other personalities. When they take the spotlight, my consciousness is in the dark. Sometimes I'm aware of what's happening but sometimes I'm not."

"So we're talking about multiple personality disorder?" he asked, trying and failing not to sound skeptical.

"Well, they don't call it that anymore."

"You're saying one of these *other* personalities got in the car and burned Mr. Brooks's house down that night?" Detective Mendoza's voice had an edge of biting humor to it.

"My client is not stating that she got in the car at all."

Detective Mendoza shot Mr. Phang an amused but dangerous glare and then turned back to me. "You seem like a smart girl, Alice. What's your IQ?"

"That's not relevant," Mr. Phang said. "I would ask you keep to the related line of questioning."

The detectives shared a glance. Then Detective Mendoza nodded. "All right. Then let's discuss how gasoline residue got on your running shoes." She slid a photo of my pink runners across the table. "The shoes you were wearing on the security footage when you got into your vehicle that evening."

I stared at the photo. Mr. Phang was scratching something in his notebook. I glanced over and recited what he'd written, "I've worn those shoes when pumping gas in the past."

Detective Mendoza smiled at Mr. Phang, then folded her hands and glared at me. "What about the phone call you received from Mr. Brooks at 3:34 that morning? According to his phone records, he called you at that time. Then you returned his call and spoke with him for approximately a minute. This was right before you were caught on your building's security camera leaving the premises."

I glanced at Mr. Phang's notebook and said, "I don't recall speaking to Oliver that evening."

"Because maybe one of your other personalities talked to him? Is that what you'd like us to believe?" she scoffed.

"I'm going to have to insist this interview be suspended at this time. My client is too tired to proceed."

"Fine," Detective Burrows said. "But, Alice you do realize this is an open-and-shut case. We don't need you to talk to us, but it will help you. Think about your kids."

I glanced at Mr. Phang, my heart aching at the mention of my kids. His jaw muscle twitched, and he shook his head so I stayed quiet.

"And I have to say." Detective Mendoza smirked as she gathered up the photos and papers in front of her. "You've been a model prisoner so far. We've seen no evidence of other personalities, violent or otherwise so," she shrugged, "good luck with that defense."

Mr. Phang reached out and squeezed my shoulder with a nod. "Just try and get some rest. I'll see you in court tomorrow."

TWENTY-FOUR

Sleep had not come last night. My body felt like lead, my skin was on fire from the anti-lice shower I'd been given and my stomach was cramping around the stale, sugary pastry I'd choked down at breakfast. As I was led into the courtroom, the first person my gaze found was Jake.

His eyes were light blue orbs in a sunken face, and though he'd put on a suit, his tie was crooked, which told me all I needed to know about his state of mind. He did attempt a smile as he held up a hand. I returned a small smile and then noticed Angeline and Rhys beside him. Ang held up both palms and then pressed them to her heart. Rhys had his fingers steepled in front of his mouth. He blew me a surreptitious kiss. Gratitude sprang to my eyes in the form of tears.

And then, as I turned to sit beside Mr. Phang at the table, I saw *them* behind the prosecution's table, Graham and Joy Brooks. It took my brain a few seconds to figure out why they were glaring at me. Of course. It was because they hated me now. They thought I'd burned their son alive. Joy was pasty and stiff, like she was sitting on broken glass. Graham's face was a mask of rage.

They don't like us anymore. We're bad.

I froze as I untangled that thought from the others racing through my head. It hadn't been mine. *Lyssie Grace's maybe?*

An officer put a heavy hand on my shoulder. I dropped into the chair.

Mr. Phang was leaning toward me. The morning salt air clung to his suit and made me ache for the outdoors. "You'll only have to answer basic questions from the judge today, otherwise I'll be doing the talking."

The officer behind me removed my handcuffs. I rubbed the raw spots on my wrists.

"Everyone, please stand for the judge," the bailiff announced.

A slight, graying woman in a black robe entered from a side door and climbed behind the judge's desk. "Please be seated."

My breath grew ragged as I watched her shuffle through some papers. I tried to force myself to breathe normally so I didn't hyperventilate.

"I'm ready to call the people vs. Alice Brown-Leininger, case number 406673Y," she said.

As the prosecutor from the D.A.'s office introduced himself, I stole a glance at Jake. He was whispering something to Angeline as she nodded. I'd give anything to be sitting there with them. *How did I get here?*

"Your Honor, Mark Phang appearing on behalf of Mrs. Brown-Leininger."

He sat back down and the judge was looking at me. "Please state your name and address for the court record."

My voice seemed inadequate for the space, like a lost child's. But she nodded and continued when I was done so she must've heard me. "I want to advise you that you're being charged for crimes committed on or about September second in Sarasota County, Florida. Count one is homicide murder in the first degree, which is with premeditation, of Oliver Brooks. That is a felony punishable by life in prison without possibility of parole. Count two, arson, is a first-degree felony punishable by up to thirty years in prison and or up to fifteen-thousand dollars in fines. Do you understand the charges against you?"

I glanced at Mr. Phang and he nodded.

"Yes."

"You have the absolute right to be represented," she began and read me my Miranda rights, which I could've probably recited in my sleep by then. She ended with, "Do you understand these rights?"

"Yes."

As the prosecutor made his statement, I stared at my hands, at the tiny half-moon scars in my palms. *Are these hands really capable of murder?*

"How does the defendant plead?"

Mr. Phang stood back up. "Your Honor, she pleads not guilty by reason of insanity. My client suffers from dissociative identity disorder, formerly known as multiple personality disorder, and so she doesn't have reasonable access to the memories she needs to assist me in reconstructing what happened during the morning in question. That being said, I request that Mrs. Brown-Leininger be examined as to both criminal responsibility and competency to proceed."

I wished Jake wasn't present to hear that.

"Mr. Cline, do you have any opposition to this competency evaluation request?"

"I do not, Your Honor."

"Very well, then. Because of the unusual claim of dissociative disorder, I'm reprimanding Mrs. Leininger to the state mental hospital for forensic psychological evaluation to assess her mental state in regard to her competency to stand trial. We will schedule the preliminary hearing for the week after the competency hearing to have it on the calendar." She glanced over at Mr. Phang. "Unless your client is waiving her right to a preliminary hearing?"

"No, Your Honor."

Being in court and hearing the charges out loud made this whole situation suddenly too real. I felt trapped in my own body. *Am I even strong enough to survive this?*

TWENTY-FIVE

Present Day, September 30ᵗʰ

Mr. Phang is sitting across from me at the tiny wooden table in the dayroom at Bayside. I like this particular table because it's beside a window, and I can see snippets of green grass and palm fronds dancing in the wind through the metal mesh cover. I always sit at this table when Jake makes the two-hour drive once a week to visit me. Most of our time is spent with him telling me about the kids. I haven't seen them in three weeks now. He says they're holding up well, but I can't imagine having their mother carted away in handcuffs and disappearing won't warrant some kind of future therapy. The aching for them takes my breath away.

We ignore the other patients wandering around in robes and slippers. The man they call Tuttle is particularly hard to ignore this morning as he's jumping from one large brown square tile to a tan one and back, and singing out loud. The orderlies are leaving him to his game.

Mr. Phang moves his attention away from the spectacle. "I've been going over the evidence and one of the most damaging pieces is that phone call." His dark eyes are shiny, like he has a fever. He's found something that has excited him. I sit up straighter.

"Here's the thing. The police have Mr. Brooks's phone records but not the phone. His phone wasn't found anywhere in the remains of that house."

The anti-anxiety drugs they're giving me make my brain feel like it's processing in slow motion. "What does that mean?"

"If his phone wasn't there physically, maybe someone else had possession of it. Maybe it was that other person you talked to. And if you did go meet someone, we can reasonably argue it's possible it wasn't Oliver Brooks."

I blink slowly, feeling skeptical. "That seems like a long shot."

"It's enough to cast doubt. Remember, it's up to the state to prove their case beyond reasonable doubt." He seems disappointed by my lack of a positive reaction. "I'm also working on your D.I.D. defense. I spoke to your doctor, Dr. Evelyn?" He's sliding out papers from a folder.

At the mention of her name, I sink a little more inside. I miss her.

"She's agreed to provide me with copies of the videos where your alters emerged during therapy, as long as you consent." He pushes a paper and pen in front of me. "Just sign there."

I glance up at him. "Who will see them?"

"Well, if we go to trial, the idea would be to show them to the jury to prove you're not faking the disorder, which is what the prosecution will try to say."

They won't understand us. They'll laugh.

Nausea grips me, the room tilts. An image of me naked, bound to a stake and set on fire is so real in my mind, I actually push my chair back with a start.

"Alice?" Mr. Phang's voice clears the image.

"I'm fine," I say, though my whole scalp and back has broken out in a sweat. "Fine." I pick up the pen and sign the consent with a shaky hand. When I look up, his normally serious expression has softened. "Are you sleeping okay?"

His kindness hurts. "Enough." What I don't say is what's keeping me awake. The thought that if I did this, if I actually murdered Oliver—as awful a person as he was—that would make me just like him. If that's the case, I don't deserve to be saved. I'd never be able to look my children in the eye again, and then what would be the point of living?

"Okay." He blows out a loud breath and rubs the shiny, flat spot on his forehead. "Okay." Straightening his back, he goes through the papers once again. "This is going to get tricky, but I have found a few cases that set precedence. One case in particular, the *Denny-Shafer* case says a D.I.D patient can be considered insane if the host personality, which would be you—Alice—wasn't aware of and didn't participate in the crime."

"Jesus," I whisper. It slips out along with a tear. "I'm not insane." *Am I?*

"No, don't worry. The 'not guilty by reason of insanity' plea that we're going for, it's just a legal definition, not a medical one. But it may not even come to that, if we can prove incompetence to stand trial in the first place. You have to meet the *Dusky* standard, which means you have to understand the proceedings and being able to assist with your case. So a competent alter—you—has to be present. Can you control when you switch alters?"

"No."

"Good. Because we can then argue that if your child-alter comes out during trial, she wouldn't understand the proceedings or be able to assist in your defense. And since *when* you switch is unpredictable, so is your competency."

I'm nodding, but his words have melted into the fog hanging over my ability to process complicated ideas. He seems to be confident in what he's saying, though, so I force my mouth to move into what I hope is an encouraging smile.

"Your hearing is scheduled for next Thursday. The sole purpose of that hearing will be for the judge to decide if you're competent to stand trial. I've looked over Dr. Meekum's initial notes, and he's concurred with Dr. Evelyn's diagnosis of D.I.D. so ... hopefully the judge will understand the scope of the disorder."

"What happens then?"

"If it's determined that you're not competent to stand trial and your competency cannot be restored you'll either be released or civilly committed ... indefinitely."

Indefinitely? That's a big gamble with my life.

—◦◦◦◦—

The days are sliding together into one long river of wasted time. I slip away more often now, and I no longer try to hold on. The darkness, the nothingness is a relief, especially now that Jake's told them to stop giving me the drugs. He didn't like how they clouded my mind and apparently they can't force me to take them.

One moment I'm sitting out in the exercise yard, face tilted to the sun, trying to remember the feel of Charlie's arms around my neck or the sound of Addie's giggling, and the next moment I'm sitting in front of Big Vera playing checkers, the scent of the peppermint candies she perpetually sucks on thick in the air.

I am shattered. Dr. Meekum has met both Kali and Lyssie Grace and also a new alter, who came out once, but who refuses to speak. But not Gia Rossi. *Maybe she's a real person after all?*

❈

"Hey, sweets." Angeline whispers in my ear. I can feel her wet cheek against mine and hear the words clog her throat. "It's so good to see you."

"Thanks for making the drive." My eyes are squeezed shut against the flood of emotion. "And you." I pull Rhys into our embrace. I can't believe they're really here.

"Vivi sends her love. She wanted to come but couldn't rearrange her schedule. Are you eating? You don't feel like you're eating." He squeezes me tighter. I feel safe for the first time in a long time. They smell like home. The orderly is gesturing to me behind their back; they don't like physical contact in here. I reluctantly release them and motion for them to sit at the little wooden table.

Angeline leans across the table and folds my hand up in hers like a broken bird. "I have some bad news so I'm just going to get it out of the way." The afternoon light through the window makes her tear-filled eyes transparent, like warmed honey. It's killing me to see her so upset. "The police talked to Veora yesterday. They asked her if she knew Oliver had been implicated in Reyna's death and if anyone else knew. She had to tell them about me knowing his identity and of course, that lead to our group discussions about getting him to admit it on tape."

"So they have motive now." I should feel more scared but I'm just numb.

"I'm sorry." She squeezes my hand tighter. "I couldn't lie."

"No, of course, you couldn't. It's okay." This news feels like a sign. I'd been struggling with turning over the notebook and changing the course of my children's lives ... this news makes the decision easier. An aching fear still grips me. We won't be able to afford their Montessori school so they'll have to leave their teachers and friends behind. Jake will blame me for losing the business he spent his entire career building. He'll probably want a divorce. We won't be able to afford Aurora's salary so the kids and I will lose her, too. I tune back in as Angeline continues.

"Here's the worst part. They've served me with a subpoena to testify at your preliminary hearing. They're going to make me testify for the prosecution. How can I do that? It seems so wrong. I can't imagine sitting up there and ... being a part of the side trying to put you away."

I glance over at Rhys. He looks like he's in physical pain, his face is blanched, his forehead wrinkled with concern.

I make my mouth smile. "Hey, guys, it'll be fine. My lawyer, Mr. Phang—who Rolf says is a magician, by the way—already knows about those conversations we had about Oliver. He's already prepared for them, so don't worry. Nothing you can say will be news."

"Yeah," Rhys says, straightening his shoulders. "Besides, it should be a good thing that we were only plotting to get him to confess, not murder him, for Christ sake. That should look good for you."

"It should."

A loud bang interrupts us. We all glance over at the commotion as two orderlies chase a patient down who has thrown a chair at another patient. His crazed yell cuts through the room as they tackle him and another orderly rushes in to sedate him.

"Just another day at the office," I quip in embarrassment as everyone goes back to what they were doing.

"Jesus. You don't belong here," Rhys says, a deep, sharp edge to his voice.

I appreciate the support, but I'm not so sure I agree anymore. "Two more days and the judge will decide just that."

TWENTY-SIX

When I open my eyes, I know immediately something is different. It's the ceiling and the hardness beneath my body. The confusion is making me dizzy. I try to sit up and can't.

Deep breaths.

The red jumpsuit I'm wearing is clouding my mind like a poisonous fog. I can't see past it. My chest is heaving beneath it. I'm going to pass out, and I haven't even moved yet.

A sliding sound distracts me. I turn my head and see a familiar guard. Then it hits me. I'm back in prison.

I bolt upright as she shuffles in. "Your lawyer's here." She holds up cuffs. "Come on."

She cuffs my hands in front of me. They are shaking so badly that she glances up and asks me if I'm okay. I nod as I fight the tears threatening to spill down my face.

She leads me back into the room with the long table and chairs with worn burgundy seats. Mr. Phang is there, chin perched on his fists, glasses lying on a folder in front of him.

"Hello," he says, watching me intently as I take a seat across from him. "Alice?"

I nod and the tears do fall then. I'm so confused, so fatigued. I want someone to stop the world so I can get a grip on one single moment. "I don't understand. Why am I back in jail? What happened?"

Mr. Phang shakes his head slightly and his usually bright, hard eyes have melted, softened with something like compassion or sadness. "What's the last thing you remember?"

My gaze drops to the table and I elbow my way through the fog, trying to find the moment before I woke up back in jail. "Sitting on a bench in a van. There were no windows, so it was stuffy and I was starting to feel carsick and claustrophobic and ... the bumpy ride, the rain pounding on the roof."

He nods. "That was two days ago, Thursday, the day of your competency hearing."

I glance up at him sharply. "You mean that's already passed?"

"I'm afraid so. I didn't realize you weren't there until after it was over. You refused to talk to anyone. I just thought you were nervous. But then when the judge said she was declaring you competent to stand trial, I looked over at you and saw the change. You were smiling and looking around the courthouse like you owned it. Even your eyes were different. Honestly, I've never seen anything like it. It was—" He looks baffled. "Anyway, you can guess who I met that day."

"Kali," I whisper. She must've been protecting me. And I've stopped fighting. There's a well-worn groove now, a river I let carry me into the darkness. "Dr. Meekum said he met a new alter who refused to speak. She must've come out first, in the van."

I can almost feel these others within me now, like their presence has substance and weight. They are watching from the shadows. My body feels denser and not entirely belonging to me. "So, what happened at the hearing?"

"Honestly, I don't know. I thought it went well. Dr. Meekum took the stand and confirmed your diagnosis and agreed that it wasn't possible for you to control when your alters took over. Said he believed you have no knowledge of the alleged crime.

"But the judge ... she dismissed all that. She said basing incompetence on your inability to assist in your defense, because you have no knowledge of the alleged crime, wasn't enough, and that someone having no memory of committing a crime should still be held responsible for their behavior. Also that children testify all the time so ..." He rubs his hands together roughly. "What we have to do now is concentrate on the preliminary hearing, which is scheduled for Monday. There's still a chance this thing doesn't go to trial."

I try to dig through the wreckage my hope has become; try to find some tiny corner not ravaged. I'm having a hard time. "What happens at a preliminary hearing?"

"Well, the prosecution will have to prove they have probable cause to go to trial. On the plus side, we'll get to see most of their evidence. They'll present that evidence, they can call witnesses—"

"Oh," I interrupt, "my friend, Angeline DeLaVoye, she said they've subpoenaed her to testify at the hearing about our conversations about Oliver."

"Yes, don't worry about that. I'll cross-examine her and reiterate the fact that not once did you entertain the idea of actually killing Mr. Brooks. What's most damaging right now is that phone conversation. I'll bring up the fact his phone wasn't found in the house so they can't say with certainty it was Mr. Brooks you had a conversation with. As for the security video of you on the street of his residence ... they only have a partial plate and no visual on the driver, so we can argue that."

"So, worst case scenario is the judge says we have to go to trial, which means I have to sit in prison for what ... months? Years?"

"No, I'll request bond be set on Monday. It'll be high, probably around three to five million but you only have to come up with ten percent of that. Is that feasible?" I nod. *For now it is.* "Good. And you're an upstanding member of the community and not a flight risk, so I don't think the prosecution will object."

The realization of what he's saying feels like an electric jolt through my body. "I'd be able to go home?"

He smiles. "Yes. There'll be restrictions of course. Probably a GPS tether, and you may not be able to leave your home at all ... but yes."

The hope is tender, almost too painful to hold. I poke it gently. Like squinting with one eye in my mind, I imagine being in the presence of my children again, hearing their voices, tucking them in. The tears are hot on my cheeks. "That would be ... amazing."

He nods. "Okay, let's go over some more details of what's going to happen."

I try to listen, but I'm floating on the idea of being with Addie and Charlie again, drifting back into my shattered fairytale.

Sunday I try to will one of the others to take over. Sitting in a monitored cell is driving me mad. I don't know what to do with myself. I try to do some stretching, some yoga but the fact someone is watching me makes my muscles seize up. I want to curl up into an invisible ball.

Jake visits in the afternoon. We have to talk through a phone, looking at each other on a video screen. It's not our only barrier. I feel miles away from him and the cold, professional demeanor he takes with me now. He doesn't know if I'm going to destroy our family and everything he's built by turning over the notebook; I get it. It'll be a betrayal since the notebook will take down all of his business partners. Also, bankruptcy and failure are not things a man like him can easily swallow. It still hurts.

A thought crosses my mind. *Would he have looked for the notebook already? Destroyed it to take away my choice?* I'm not sure. A sudden need to get home overpowers me.

"Mr. Phang says he's going to ask for the judge to set bond on Monday. It'll be high, but we just have to pay ten percent, then I'll be able to come home."

Even through the low-resolution screen, I see the hesitation in his eyes. He's not sure he wants me home. "Great. The kids miss you. Charlie's been sleeping in our bed because I don't know how to get rid of the monsters, apparently."

"They are tricky," I say, trying for lightness but my tone is too weighted down with all the things not being said between us. *Monsters sure are tricky.*

—◆◆◆—

When I'm led into the courtroom in my jumpsuit and cuffs on Monday, it's packed and everyone turns to stare at me. I see this from the corner of my eye as I try to keep my head down. I understand. I'm the splash of red in a brown-paneled room, the blood they want spilled in the name of justice. The officer leads me to the defense table.

"Good morning ... Alice?" Mr. Phang says with a touch of apprehension.

"Yes," I reassure him. "Good morning." I look up. The judge is already seated and reading something in front of her. A low murmuring is coming from the crowd in the wooden benches behind me. I know Jake is there somewhere, but I'm not sure that comforts me so I don't look for him.

The judge clears her throat. Everyone grows quiet. "Okay, we're back on the record, the state of Florida vs. Alice Brown-Leininger, case number 406673Y on charges of first-degree murder and arson. Mr. Cline, please call your first witness."

"Thank you, Your Honor. We call Detective Mendoza to the stand."

Detective Mendoza strolls to the witness box, looking every bit as polished and professional as she had while interrogating me. And hard, like a walking hammer. My heart is pounding beneath my jumpsuit.

"Please raise your right hand, Detective," says the bailiff. She does. "Do you solemnly swear the testimony you're about to give is the truth, the whole truth and nothing but the truth?"

"I do."

"Please have a seat. State and spell your name for the record."

She adjusts her tailored jacket and leans into the microphone to state her name.

"Good morning, Detective," Mr. Cline begins. "Can you please tell us your job title and department."

"I'm a homicide detective with the Criminal Investigations Unit of the Sarasota PD."

"And you are in charge of gathering evidence in the investigation of Oliver Brooks's death?"

"Correct."

"Okay. I'd like to start with people's exhibit number 12." He picks up a folder and glances at our table. "I believe defense has a copy?" Mr. Phang nods so the prosecutor opens the folder and walks it over to the witness stand. Sliding out a white sheet of paper, he places it in front of the detective.

The judge says, "For the record, people's exhibit number 12 is hereby entered into evidence."

"Let the record reflect I'm showing Detective Mendoza a copy of Mr. Brooks's phone records from the night in question. Detective Mendoza, do you recognize this item?"

"Yes. These are the records we requested from Mr. Brooks's cell phone carrier. They were faxed to us on September sixth."

"Can you read the last two log entries please."

"At 3:34 a.m. on September second there is an outgoing call to 942-517-5434. Then at 3:35 a.m. that same number is an incoming call. The call duration is approximately one minute."

"And did you find the owner of 942-517-5434?"

"Yes, we did. It's the defendant, Alice Brown-Leininger's cell phone number."

"And this was the last call made on Mr. Brooks's cell phone?"

"Correct."

"Thank you." He retrieves the paper from Detective Mendoza. "We'll come back to that later. Right now, I'd like to offer into evidence people's exhibit number 22, surveillance video from the parking garage at Golden Gate Towers where Mrs. Leininger parks her white Range Rover."

The judge nods. "Let the record reflect people's exhibit number 22 has been hereby entered into evidence."

The pace of the proceedings has a rhythm that's lulling me into some kind of trance. I watch from a distance as Mr. Cline goes through the motions of rolling forward a large flat screen and playing the surveillance video. It's an amazingly clear video in color. Nothing like the fuzzy black and white video I expected it to be. There's no doubt it's me.

My eyes go to my pink running shoes as I walk with a confident, liquid stride to the car. *Definitely*

Kali. She's holding the car fob, as she lifts a hand and points it at the car. The lights blink to life. She doesn't have anything else with her that I can see, no purse or cell phone. I can't imagine leaving the house without either. I'd feel lost.

As Mr. Cline talks about the timing of my early morning trip and how long it would've taken me to make the drive to Oliver's house, I find myself searching for Jake in the seats. I only get to scan one side of the courtroom, however, because there—perched on the end of the back row—I catch a glimpse of a face that stops me cold.

It's a face that has grown thin, the curve of cheekbone sharper. It's hiding behind dark glasses and a shoulder-length wig. But it's a face I know and it's staring back at me.

"Carmen!" I gasp with constricted lungs. I lean back in my chair as a tall man shifts and blocks my view of her for a moment.

Mr. Phang has put his hand over mine and is squeezing, trying to get my attention.

Then I see the door swing open and the back of her head slipping out.

No. No. No.

My breathing is ragged. I'm glancing around wildly at all the things holding me in this seat when I should be running after her ... the uniformed police officers stationed around the room, for one.

Mr. Phang is tapping on the notebook in front of me.

I'm staring at the notebook, but my mind is still in shock. *That was Carmen. She's alive!*

Finally, I blink and let the scrawled words come into focus. They say, *What's wrong?*

I pick up the pen. The adrenaline rushing through me is making it hard to steady my hand, but I get the job done. *Carmen Castiel was just in here. The girl who's been missing.* I push the notebook back to him.

He reads it, glances around and then nods.

I wonder if he believes me or even understands the significance of this. I crane my neck to search the seats behind me. I find Jake, Angeline, Rhys and Vivi seated together. They're all watching Mr. Cline with dark expressions. If only I could slip them a note or something, tell them to go after her. Frustration prickles my skin and makes me squirm. It's warring with the relief loosening my chest, letting me breathe easier. *She's alive. Thank the stars, she's alive.*

As the hearing rolls on and it's Mr. Phang's turn to cross-examine Detective Mendoza, I'm trying to pay attention, but I'm starting to doubt myself. The harder I try to hold the image of the wigged-woman in my mind and trace the curves of her face, the more she's dissolving. I close my eyes and see the dark glasses facing me, the full lips, the stillness in her shoulders. It has to be her. But...

What if that's just wishful thinking? Do I even trust myself anymore?

I sink into a gray funk as I realize the answer is a definitive *no*.

TWENTY-SEVEN

Day one of the hearing is over, and I'm lying on the concrete block trying to digest the chicken and mushroom pie full of gray sauce we were fed for dinner. Also I'm trying to stay positive. The judge has agreed to set bail tomorrow so I'll be going home. *Home*. The word is like a balm on my sore heart, but it also knocks my heart out of rhythm. *How much has this damaged the kids? My relationship with Jake? How much damage will still be done?* Going home will mean facing the fallout. But it will also mean I will know the fate of the notebook.

That night I dream of fire again. But this time I'm in the middle of the flames, Addie and Charlie held close to my body. There's a warm, dry breeze around us and the fire's orange and yellow tongues are licking us gently. It is the first time I'm not afraid.

—◆◆◆◆—

Something is wrong. I was supposed to be taken to the courthouse for the hearing at nine a.m. That's what Mr. Phang had said. But it feels later than that. I pace the small concrete box. Maybe it only feels like a lot of time has passed since I'd choked down packaged, peach oatmeal for breakfast. Maybe it's an illusion of prison time. But, I know I'm right when the guard swings by for the ten o'clock cell check.

I rush to the window and motion to her. She slides it open.

"I was supposed to be taken to court at nine for my hearing," I say breathlessly.

She gives me that half-lidded, bored look I've gotten used to. "I don't know nothin' about that. I'm sure they'll let you know what's going on soon." She writes something on her clip board and slides the window back without a second glance.

I stand there numb. What does this mean? Does it mean I'm not going home?

Home is not going to be the same.

"I know that," I say aloud, then wince as I glance up at the shiny black, bulbous eye watching me.

—◆◆◆—

I'm a nervous wreck. I just sit, staring at my tray of breaded fish stacked on three pieces of white bread, shriveled green beans and a watery puddle of mac & cheese. The voices are loud around me in the cafeteria but my anxiety is louder.

"You gonna eat that?"

I glance up at the woman with a shaved head pointing at my tray. I slide it over to her wordlessly.

After lunch I sit on the edge of the concrete pad, staring at my cell door so hard that by the time it opens after God-knows-how-much time passes, for a moment I believe I've willed it to happen.

The guard shuffles in and this time she's looking me in the eye. "Got some good news. You've made bail."

I stand, ignoring the numbness in my feet, the pain in my tailbone. I don't know what's happening, but right now I'm not questioning it. I'm going home.

I keep waiting for someone to snatch this away from me as they lead me to the front lobby an hour later in the clothes I was arrested in and a tracking device strapped to my right ankle. But they never do, and Jake is waiting there for me.

We share a forced smile. He squeezes my shoulders. "Let's get out of here."

I've asked him to put the top down on the Jaguar. It's the middle of October now, but temperatures are in the low eighties. To feel the sun on my face, the salty-air on my lips, it's almost euphoric. I'll never take this ... this freedom for granted again, even if it is temporary.

I sigh and rest my head on the back of the leather seat. Close my eyes. "So, what happened? Why didn't I go to court this morning?"

"Well, the judge was kind enough to grant bail even though Mr. Phang has asked for a forty-eight-hour continuance. Basically postponing the hearing for two days."

I roll my head toward him. "Why?"

"I don't know. Something about new evidence and needing time to verify it. He called this morning to tell me about bail but was in a big hurry, and said to tell you to be at the courthouse at ten Thursday morning."

"Huh." I roll my head the other way and take in the scenery, the lines of swaying palm trees, the baby blue sky, the familiar shops and restaurants. I let out a breath I didn't know I was holding. The kids will be in school right now, but that's okay. It'll give me time to shower off the jail residue and readjust to being home.

••••

Jake has to go back to the office for a while so after an awkward goodbye, he leaves me alone. The first thing I do is look for the notebook. Fortunately, it's right where I left it under the books on my nightstand. I fall on the bed in relief, clutching it to my chest. The relief only lasts a moment though, because now I have a decision to make that will affect my kids' futures. With a sigh, I place it in the nightstand drawer then head to their bedrooms.

I lie down in their beds, hold their pillows to my face and breathe them in. Charlie's bedspread is blue with quilted sharks and other fish. A puzzle sits half-finished on his dark wood floor, evidence his life has continued in my absence. Addie's pink walls have two new pieces of artwork. I let my fingers run over the raised, painted figures on one of them ... five stick people standing on brown lines in front of blue waves, which I assume is our family on the beach, including Aurora. My heart cracks a little more. Something for the "don't turn in the notebook" column. They would miss Aurora terribly. We all would. I can only stay for a few moments though because their absence in these spaces is too reminiscent of the emptiness that's been my constant companion this past month. Funny how pain has signatures, patterns.

Next I stand under the hottest spray my body will tolerate and watch my skin turn red beneath the steam, suds my hair and body with more soap and shampoo then is necessary and use a bristled brush to scrub away anything I might have brought home with me. Slipping into my softest, worn-thin sundress I step out onto the balcony and lift my face to the sun. The brightness of it seeps through my eyelids, soaks into my bones, and the comfort I felt standing in the middle of the flames during my dream last night returns.

Kali materializes in front of me, her eyes black and shiny. Her voice is heartbreakingly real and compassionate, "*Things burned in the fire are not always lost, Alice. Sometimes they are transformed. Burning away ignorance, self-doubt, melting suffering until it is only recognized as love, this is my gift to you. And you will find happiness in the ashes.*"

Her words lift the hairs on my arms, but I'm afraid to think about the future she's laying out for me, a future where I'll have to sift through ashes to find happiness.

"Mrs. Alice?" A tentative voice calls from the opened sliding door behind me.

Kali steps back into the darkness as I turn and smile at Aurora.

"Mrs. Alice!" She rushes out and wraps her short arms around me. Her skin is cool from the car air-conditioning, and she smells like fresh baked bread. "You are home?"

"For now," I say. I release her and motion to my ankle. "House arrest during the hearing."

Her smile is consuming her small, round face, pushing her cheeks up to hide her eyes. "But you are home. Oh, the children! They will be so happy. Do you want me to get them early from school?"

I squeeze her hands, which she's slipped into mine. "I do, but we should probably keep their routine as normal as possible."

She's nodding and crying and gives me another hug. "I'm so happy you are home. My prayers are answered. Okay, I make the best dinner."

It hits me again and the guilt almost knocks me over. If I turn over the notebook, Aurora will lose not only her income but a family, children she's grown to love. I choke down the pain. "You know, hold off on that. We may have company." I need to see my friends.

I'm just about to call Angeline to invite her over when another call comes in. It's the concierge desk.

"Yes?"

"Mrs. Leininger, there's a Ms. Amber Acosta here to see you. She's a reporter for the *Gulf Coast Times*. Should I send her away?"

I freeze. I've been avoiding the reporters at the courthouse, getting in and out of the transport van, and in front of the condo gate at home, throwing out no comment like a seasoned pro. I've even avoided reading any newspapers or online articles about Oliver or my case. So why am I hesitating now? Mr. Phang has specifically warned me not to talk to reporters.

I close my eyes. "No, Guthrie. Send her up."

TWENTY-EIGHT

"Thank you for talking to me. I won't print anything we discuss without your approval. You have my word." Ms. Acosta has a genuine smile. She's younger than I thought she'd be, maybe early thirties with large, fawn-like eyes and a calm demeanor. "This is a lovely place."

We're sitting side by side on the sofa. When Aurora brings us tea, she shoots me a questioning look before leaving us alone.

"Thank you." I glance around, trying to view the condo through her eyes. It's an almost embarrassingly lavish space. Jake had wanted me to enjoy myself decorating and furnishing it. I had tried, but eventually I'd just hired a decorator. Honestly, I'd been afraid he'd judge me for my taste or lack of. *Could I give this up? The only home our children have ever known?* It won't be half as hard for them as having to split their time between parents and losing Aurora forever, but it will still be a loss.

I shift my attention back to Ms. Acosta. Uneasiness ripples through me as I watch her pull out a black notebook and pen. I have no idea why I let her in. No, that's not true. I'm following some thread in my mind, which I have a growing suspicion leads back to Kali and her motives. I shift my weight onto my right hip and angle myself toward her. "Honestly, I'm not sure I want anything in print. I'm not even sure why I'm talking to you."

Ms. Acosta shoves her notebook back into her bag, then leans forward and picks up her tea cup. "Then we'll just talk woman to woman and I won't take notes. I bet your kids are so relieved to have you home. I've got a two-year-old daughter, Samantha. I can't imagine being separated from her."

"It was hard. I actually haven't seen them yet. They'll be home from school in a few hours." I pick up my cup to have something to do with my hands, which are surprisingly steady.

"Which school do they go to?"

I glance at her. "I'm sorry. I'm not comfortable giving out information about my kids." Even though I know she could probably find out on her own anyway.

Her smile doesn't falter. "I understand. I was actually only asking because I'm starting to look at preschools. I didn't mean to pry. Let's try a different subject. Did you start that fire in Oliver Brooks's home?"

I blink and then laugh. I can't help it. She's bold, I'll give her that. I put my tea down and wipe my eyes on the napkin. I should be angry, but I'm actually feeling grateful for the emotional release. I lean back into the leather sofa and study her. There's a slight smile, no judgement, mostly curiosity as she waits patiently for my response. I like her.

"I don't know," I answer honestly.

Her eyes register concern but her expression is soft, open. She leans forward, studying my face. "Because of the dissociative disorder?"

"Yes." I know I should feel uncomfortable talking to a stranger about this, but I don't. I scan my mind for Kali. *Is she making me feel brave?* No, I can't find her. I shrug. "You probably know as much as I do about what happened that night."

She chews on the inside of her cheek. "What about other nights then? I've heard some rumors about Oliver Brooks throwing parties with prostitutes and underage girls. Would you be able to confirm those?"

And there it is. My stomach jolts like I've just fallen off a cliff. This is why I've let her in. This is what Kali wants. *But is this what I want?* Yes. Yes, it's the right thing. This is what Angeline would call serendipity. My insides are trembling as I stand up, not with fear but with certainty. "I'll be right back."

When I return with the notebook in my hand, there's an alert expression on her face. I sit down and without giving myself time to think about it, I hand it to her.

"What's this?" She begins flipping through the pages.

I clear my throat. "Stories collected from some of the girls at those parties you mentioned."

Her hand covers her mouth as she reads a page. Then another. By the time she looks up at me, her eyes are glassy and registering shock. "Where did you get this?"

"Apparently I contacted these women ... well, not me, but one of my alters did, and convinced them to tell their stories. They're willing to come forward if they're not alone. They name names in there. I want you to find these women. Give the original notebook to the police but tell their stories in your paper. I don't know how many friends Graham and Oliver have in the department, and I don't want this covered up."

She reaches out and squeezes my hand. Her hand is cold and trembling. "Alice, thank you. Thank you for trusting me with this. Do you want to be kept as an anonymous source?"

I think about that only for a second. "No. The police may need more information from me and I'm done being scared."

Nodding slowly, she is clutching the notebook to her chest. "My God," is all she can say. Then she reaches into her bag and hands me a business card. "This has my cell number on it. Call me anytime." She also jots down my number. "I'll keep you informed as things move forward." Her expression softens to one of sympathy as she adds, "I'm going to move quickly on this. You understand?"

I do. A weight has lifted off me, even though I've just set in motion the dismantling of my own life.

—◆◆◆◆—

I'm pacing in front of the elevator. I've changed into a longer dress that hides the ankle monitor. Aurora should be back with the kids any minute. And then I freeze as I hear the elevator motor. My hands go to my mouth. The door slides open.

There is a shocked silence and then, "Mom!" as two beautiful creatures rush at me in a flurry of red hair, wide green eyes, arms outstretched and tossed aside backpacks.

I'm on my knees, drowning in so much joy, I squeeze them until they squeal with laughter. "Look at you." I swipe at my tears and grin at them both. "You've gotten so big. So big." I pull them to me again, and we fall back onto the floor in a tangle of bodies, laughter and the kind of relief that wipes the mind clean like a giant eraser. Nothing matters in that moment except the fact that we are together.

"Guess what?" Addie says.

I stroke a piece of baby-fine hair curling against her cheek. "What, what, chicken butt?"

She grins at our familiar word game, and I spot an empty space where her bottom front tooth used to be. "You lost a tooth!" I squish her face between my palms and kiss her on the nose. My heart is also being squeezed by the fact I missed this monumental childhood first. I concentrate on pushing the sadness aside. "You know, that was the very first tooth that came in when you were a baby." *God, that seems like yesterday.* "Did the tooth fairy come?"

She nods. "She left me a dollar." She crosses her arms, giving me a glimpse of her teenage years. "Jessica says she got five dollars."

"She did, huh?"

Charlie rolls his eyes. "Jessica lies all the time."

"Does not!" Addie's cheeks are red.

"Does too."

"Okay. Do we want to argue or ..." I hold out a hand to each of them to help me up off the floor. "Do we want to make cookies?"

"Cookies!" They are back to grinning as they use all their might to pull me up to standing.

We make chocolate chip cookies while singing in the kitchen with Aurora. I help them with their homework, try to explain where I've been without mentioning *jail* or *mental hospital* and finally convince them we should just enjoy being together now. I also can't stop staring at them or touching them, a stroked cheek, a quick ruffle of hair, a stolen kiss. My hands belong only to my heart right now.

Eventually Jake comes home and the dynamics change, the atmosphere becomes weighted with heavy emotion. He's tense and distracted. He's also obviously angry with me, even before he knows what I've done.

"Hey." I find Jake in his office after I've bathed the kids and tucked them in. "I hope you don't mind, the gang's coming over in a bit."

He's reading something on his laptop but pulls his attention away for a moment. "Yeah. No, that's fine. I've got some work to do tonight anyway."

I move deeper into his office and stand in front of him. "Are we okay?"

He leans back in his leather chair and intertwines his fingers. His eyes meet mine for the first time since I've been home, and I see the chasm between us in the way he's looking at me. "I don't even know who we are anymore, Alice." He softens his mouth a little, tries to smile to take away the sting of his words.

I tilt my head. "You mean you don't know who *I* am anymore."

A small movement of his shoulder is all I get at first. And then, "I don't know much anymore except you believe those girls' accounts of what happened at

Oliver's house without question. But I'm going to need proof before I condemn a friend and allow his reputation to be ruined, especially now that he's not here to defend himself. I owe him at least that much." His face is darkening, his breath shortening as his anger bubbles. "And I'm afraid you'll turn over that damn notebook, despite the fact it will ruin us financially."

I stare at him and decide not to tell him I've already turned it over to a reporter. He'll find out soon enough, and I can't deal with his reaction on top of everything else right now. Instead, out of curiosity I ask, "What would you have me do?"

He throws down his pen and holds my gaze, his voice full of barely disguised rage. "Not choose some strangers over your goddamned family, Alice."

—◆◆◆—

They propel themselves from the elevator, bags of food and wine in hand, and surround me like a stirred-up beehive. "This is a win, yeah?" Angeline's eyes are smiling into mine as she squeezes my arm. "Home with your babies for the hearing."

"Of course it's a win. God knows the wheels of justice turn slowly," Vivi says, kissing my cheek. "Here." She hands me a bag from Macy's.

"What's this?" I smile, despite the sadness lingering from my earlier conversation with Jake.

"Shoes, of course." Rhys threads his arm through mine and leads me to kitchen. "To take the focus off that God-awful thing on your ankle."

I throw my head back and laugh ... really laugh for the first time in so long, I'm startled by my own voice. I lift myself up on the counter to sit and watch while Vivi finds the wine glasses in the cupboard, and Angeline rustles through the dishwasher for clean plates. Rhys is lifting a shoe from the box. He holds up a bright red heel in buttery leather and whistles his approval. "Yeah, that'll do it." Turning, he lifts my bare foot and slips the shoe on. "Definitely steals the spotlight."

I admire the shoe as he slips the other one on my left foot and think about Dr. Evelyn. She'd appreciate these. I wish I could see her again but house arrest doesn't allow for a visit to my psychologist. "These are great, Vivi, thank you. I feel like Cinderella."

Vivi parks a glass of chilled white wine in my hand. "You're no sad sack waiting to be rescued, honey. You're a goddess and don't you forget it." She clinks my glass with her own. "Cheers."

"Speaking of," Angeline says, arranging spring rolls on a plate. "When do we get to meet her?" She glances up. "You know ... Kali?"

Curiosity is like a magnet that pulls all their attention to me.

I smile sadly. "You already have. Remember at the end of our conversation with Josette in the diner? After we learned the businessman was Oliver? The shock of that sent me away. I can only assume it was Kali who took over at that point. I woke up hours later at home with no memory of what'd happened between those two moments."

Angeline is nodding. "You know that makes sense now. You did change. You turned and smiled confidently at Josette and told her not to worry and thanked her for her time. You were so calm and in control, but I just thought you were trying to make sure Josette didn't notice we were freaking out."

I nod. "There were other times, too. Like at Reyna's funeral. And she's growing stronger. I can hear her and see her now, and sometimes I'm still conscious and watching when she takes over. Dr. Evelyn says this is supposed to happen, my dissociative walls are crumbling." It feels so freeing sharing this with them that I keep going. "I've heard Lyssie Grace a few times now and actually saw her once. She likes to hide in the corner and chew on her hair. And there's apparently another personality who's been coming out but refusing to speak. I don't know anything about her yet."

"You're really taking this well," Angeline says, shaking her head. "I can't imagine what you've been through these last few months."

"You guys are really taking this well, too. You have no idea how much I appreciate that."

Rhys grabs my hand and hauls me off the counter. "Come on, let's go sit under the stars and you can tell us jail horror stories."

I laugh and hold up my wine to keep it from spilling on him.

"Rhys Ellis," Vivi chides him. "I'm sure that's the last thing she wants to think about."

"I don't want to think at all," I say with a sigh. "So, I want to hear everything I've missed in your lives this past month."

"Rhys is still dating Ben, if you can believe that." Angeline throws him a teasing look.

"Wow, what is that? Six whole weeks?" I grin up at him.

He acts indignant. "Seven." Then he kisses the top of my head and adds, "I'm seeing a therapist about Lenny. She's really great. So, not running this time."

"How very brave of you." I squeeze his arm. "Let's go find us some stars to thank."

We all grab a plate, a bottle, napkins and silverware and head out to the balcony amidst a cloud of soft laughter. I feel us moving as one unit, knitted together with a familiarity that only comes from shared time and hearts cracked wide open together. It crackles like electricity between us. I look around at my friends as they seat themselves on the balcony and wonder if they feel it too, or if I'm noticing it because it's such a contrast to the way I've lived in isolation this past month.

"Oh, before I forget." I set my glass down on a clear resin coaster with tiny embedded seashells. "You guys will never guess who I thought I saw in the courtroom yesterday."

"Who's that?" Angeline asks, licking her finger and getting situated with her plate of food.

"Carmen." I let her name hang in the salty night air.

"What? Where?" Their words burst in unison.

"In the back row. She was wearing a wig and dark glasses, but I'm sure it was her." Well, I was pretty sure. There was that whole issue of me trusting that the people I'm seeing are actually there.

"She's alive then. She's all right," Angeline says, excitement sending her voice high.

"Where has she been?" Vivi asks.

"In hiding I imagine, which was smart," Rhys says. "I guess she feels safe now that Oliver's dead and probably came to support Alice."

"Then why the disguise?" Vivi asks.

"And why did she slip out when I noticed her?" I ask.

No one has an answer. "Guess we'll have to wait and see if she shows up again."

I squeeze my hands together to keep them from shaking. "So there's something else I have to tell you guys." I moved my attention to Vivi. This was going to devastate her the most.

They all watch me expectantly. A boat motor starts up and idles in the water below us. I take a deep breath and then just begin, "Kali apparently has been going out on nightly excursions."

They are all silent as I explain how I found the notebook and recount some of the details that I can remember. "I've turned the notebook over to a reporter named Amber Acosta with the *Gulf Coast Times*, and asked her to tell the girls' stories and give the original notebook to the police. The girls are willing to come forward together. They named the men that went to the parties. The thing is it doesn't just implicate Oliver but also Graham and the whole inner circle ... Jim Masters, Mick Burns, Seth, Cliff and Rodney from Low Key Construction, Kelly White from White Realty and ..." I force myself to face Vivi, my eyes filling with tears, "I'm sorry but Rolf's name was in there. Rolf, he ... he took part."

Vivi is still but I can see her mind reviewing their life together. Then she collapses inward. I rush to kneel in front of her, grab her hands. "I'm so sorry." Rhys and Angeline squeeze into the wicker loveseat, pressing into her on both sides. We hold her while she falls apart.

TWENTY-NINE

This time upon entering the courtroom on Thursday morning, I immediately scan it for any sign of Carmen. Disappointment settles over me. She isn't there. Graham and Joy are there, though, sitting like grief has hardened their bones, turned their faces to stone. Jake and Rhys are seated together right behind me. Vivi and Angeline are absent, which seems odd. *Is Vivi okay?* I push away dark thoughts of her breaking down, of Ang trying to comfort her. Instead I nod at the guys and then take my seat at the table.

"Good morning." Mr. Phang has an odd look on his face, like he's suppressing a grin.

"Morning," I say, raising my eyebrows. "What's going on?"

He lets part of his mouth curve into a smile and reaches over and squeezes my forearm. "I have some very good news."

Before I can get more information, the judge enters the courtroom.

"All rise," says the bailiff.

We go through all the motions. In the background I hear her reading my charges once again, but I can't focus because of the hope coming in waves off Mr. Phang. It's like heat radiating from blacktop on a sunny day. *What is going on?* This must have something to do with the new evidence he told Jake about. He must've verified it. I feel the hope rising in me, too, the weight moving from my gut into my chest. *Dare I hope? What can possibly refute all the evidence the prosecution has against me?*

"Okay Mr. Phang. Please call your witness."

Mr. Phang stands and moves in front of our table, buttons up his suit jacket and folds his hands. "Your Honor, I'd like to call Carmen Castiel to the stand."

There is an audible gasp behind me. The doors open and she is there, minus the wig and dark glasses, hesitating in the doorway. I can't believe it. Her eyes find mine and she takes a deep breath, her shoulders straighten and she pushes herself forward.

"Your Honor, I object." Mr. Cline is standing now, too. "This is highly irregular."

"Yes, Mr. Cline but I've been informed that this witness can bring a swift close to the case, so I'm allowing it."

Mr. Cline has his hands out in front of him helplessly. "But, Your Honor, with all due respect, we weren't given enough notice about this new witness to prepare for questioning."

"Objection noted," the judge said. "I want to hear what this young lady has to say." She motions for him to sit.

My body is shaking uncontrollably. I'm leaning my forearms on the table to try and steady myself but it's not working. Carmen is wearing a too-big red dress that looks borrowed. She is thin and fragile as she raises her right hand and promises to tell the truth, the whole truth and nothing but the truth.

I steal a glance behind me. Everyone looks confused or in shock.

Mr. Phang approaches her slowly, his head bowed. "Thank you for coming today, Miss Castiel. I understand you've been in hiding, afraid for your life, is that correct?"

"Yes," she says. It's too soft so she clears her throat and leans into the microphone. "Yes."

"Will you tell us why, please."

"I saw a crime go down. It happened at a party when my friend, Reyna Flores, was raped and beaten. I was gonna testify, but I got spooked 'cause I knew the man who did it had Reyna killed after she went to the cops. After her funeral, it hit me, ya know? This was real. He could kill me, too and no one could do a thing about it. So, I panicked and took off."

"Objection, your honor. Heresay," Mr. Cline cries as he stands.

"I'm allowing it," the judge says. "Go on, Miss Castiel."

I glance over at Mr. Cline. He's exchanging a concerned glance with Detective Mendoza behind him. I still don't understand what this has to do with me.

"At first I didn't know what to do. I thought about leavin' Florida, seein' if I could stay with my cousin in Atlanta but then I got mad. I mean, why should this man get away with murder? And nobody's gonna stop him? No," she shakes her head, "I couldn't do that to my sister, Reyna. I couldn't abandon her."

"And to be clear, who is this man you're speaking of?"

She leans into the microphone again. "Oliver Brooks."

An angry rumble rises from the pews. The judge knocks her gavel a few times until silence is restored.

Mr. Phang is obviously leading Carmen somewhere important, but he's got his hand in his pocket, his posture as casual as a Sunday stroll in the park. "So, you decided you weren't going to let Mr. Brooks get away with murdering your friend and intimidating you into leaving the state. Did you have a plan?"

"Yes, sir." She presses her lips together and glances up at the ceiling. "But it didn't go right."

"Why don't you start from the beginning."

She takes in a deep breath and then blows it out. "Well, I was hidin' out with one of my girls who's still in the life."

"You're speaking of a life of prostitution?"

"Yeah. She's one of Mr. Brooks's favorite girls, 'cause she was willing to trade sex for Roxy. Roxycodone—"

"This is outrageous!" Graham Brooks bellows from the pews. "It's slander!"

The judge knocks her gavel and points it at him. "Another outburst like that and you will be removed from this courtroom. Do you understand, sir?"

He puffs a concession and falls back into the seat. He glares at me.

I feel Kali smile.

"Go on." Mr. Phang nods.

Carmen glances at Graham nervously. Mr. Phang casually moves to block her view of him.

"Yeah, so, this girl, we got to talkin' one night and came up with a plan. If she could get him handcuffed to the bed, I'd come in and make him confess to killing Reyna. So, that's what we did. She called Oliver Brooks and got a date. I hid in the backyard 'til he'd had enough to drink that he let her handcuff him, and then she let me in the house."

My hands go to my mouth. I'm starting to understand what this has to do with me.

"What night was this?" Mr. Phang asks gently.

"It was early Friday morning, September 2nd."

"And why have you come forward now?"

"Because I couldn't let Alice go to prison for somethin' she didn't do."

The courtroom erupts. I can't tell if the cries are angry or relieved. Probably a mixture of both.

Bang. Bang. Bang. "I will have order in my courtroom!"

Carmen lets her gaze meet mine as everyone settles back down. Her eyes are dark and sad. A small smile appears beneath her hollowed cheekbones. I nod in gratitude.

"Please continue, Mr. Phang," the judge says, throwing a warning look at the courtroom.

"Thank you, Your Honor." Mr. Phang straightens his tie. "So, we've established you were there with another female the night Mr. Brooks died."

"I'm not namin' her," Carmen says defiantly. "She had nothin' to do with what happened next. She bolted after she let me in."

"Her identity isn't my concern. So, she leaves the house? Then what happened?"

"I go into the bedroom and see Oliver Brooks handcuffed to the bed like we'd planned. He wasn't too happy to see me. He starts screamin' at me to get the handcuffs off him, that he's gonna kill me when he gets a hold of me. Only he didn't say it so nice." She squirms at the memory. "Then I realized I forgot the most important part of our plan. I forgot to get my friend's cell before she took off, so I could record his confession, ya know? So then, I see Oliver's cell on the nightstand so I used that."

"What was Mr. Brooks doing at this point?"

She glances down, her shoulders tense. "He was goin' crazy. Shakin' the bed like an animal, kickin' out at me with his feet, screamin' he was gonna kill me. I hadn't really thought it through, ya know? But I knew I was gonna have to make *him* feel like the one in danger. Make him believe I'd kill him if he didn't confess. So, I went back through the house tryin' to find somethin' to threaten him with." She turns to the judge. "I wasn't really plannin' on hurting him. You gotta know that." She takes a deep breath. "I checked out the knives, which gave me the creeps. I couldn't bring myself to threaten him with a knife. But then, in the garage, I see this gas can, right? I kick it and hear the sloshing. It seemed perfect. Scary enough, he'd have to take me seriously, but all he'd end up with was a big cleaning bill.

"So, I drag it into the bedroom and start pourin' it around the room, all the while he's screamin' at me like a crazy person. I didn't think about the fumes, they were pretty bad. By the time I splashed the last of it over him and the bed, I was gettin' lightheaded and started to panic." She rubs her forehead. "So, I take his cell and step out of the bedroom. I try to call my girl back and ask her to come make sure I don't pass out while tryin' to get him to confess. But she wasn't answering. Then I see Alice's number in his cell so I call her. She didn't answer at first, either. But then she calls back, and I tell her what I'm tryin' to do, and ask her if she could please make sure I make it out of the house alive."

"And did she? Come to Mr. Brooks's house that night?"

She glances over at me. "Yeah. Yes. It took her about fifteen minutes to get there. I'd been trying to get Oliver to confess and record it, but, he wasn't sayin' nothing. Until Alice showed up. Then he just lost it. I've never seen a person so piss—so angry before." A visible chill shakes her body.

"And you used Mr. Brooks's cell phone to record the events of the night in question?"

"Yes, sir."

"And what did you do with his cell phone afterwards?"

"I kept it with me. I wasn't sure what to do with it, ya know? I mean, I didn't want to get in trouble for what I'd done. But then I couldn't keep it to myself anymore after watching what Alice was going through. She has kids," she chokes and then recomposes herself. "I couldn't let them take her away from her kids."

"And then what did you do with Mr. Brooks's cellphone?"

"I brought it to you two days ago, and you took me to the cops to have them verify it was Oliver's phone. I don't know what happened to it after that."

"Thank you." He retrieves a plastic bag from his black leather case beneath the table, carries it over and hands it to Carmen. "Miss Castiel, do you recognize this item?"

She nods. "Yeah, yes, this is Oliver Brooks's cell."

"The cell phone containing the recorded video of the evening in question?"

"Yes, sir."

He turns to the judge. "Your Honor, at this time, I'd like to introduce into evidence Mr. Brooks's cell phone."

The judge nods. "Let the record show Oliver Brooks's cell phone is being entered into evidence."

Mr. Phang rolls a cart to the front of the courtroom with a large flat screen and laptop beneath it. "For the rest of the story about what took place that evening, I'd like the evidence to speak for itself." He removes the phone from the plastic bag and plugs it into the laptop.

The courtroom is now eerily silent, like everyone's holding their breath. I steal a glance back at Oliver's parents as Mr. Phang finishes setting up. Joy has a bony hand poised over her mouth, her large diamond wedding ring glittering in the harsh courtroom lighting. Graham's chin is set high, defiant, his eyes are half-closed. Contempt is seeping from his every pore.

"Miss Castiel, there are a few moments where I'll be pausing the video to have you explain what's going on, okay?"

She nods, darting a nervous glance my way.

Mr. Phang uses a remote to start the video. He's got the volume cranked up, so Oliver's vicious yelling is like a bomb going off, echoing off the courtroom walls. He's crazed, kicking out and screaming at Carmen. "I'm going to squeeze the fucking life out of you with my bare hands!"

Reflexively, I lean back in my seat, away from him. There's a cry from the seats, and I glance back in time to see Joy stumbling down the aisle and out through the wooden doors. I don't blame her. I wouldn't want to remember my son this way either.

We hear Carmen's voice behind the camera telling him repeatedly that she isn't going to hurt him if he just confesses to what he did to Reyna. But if he doesn't, she's going to light a match and let him burn. Mr. Phang fast forwards through some of it to get to part where I show up.

When I appear in the bedroom doorway, he freezes the video.

My heart is racing. In the frame, I look like I'm coolly assessing the room. It's the strangest feeling, looking at myself being somewhere that I don't remember being. Definitely Kali.

Mr. Phang has a laser pointer aimed at the screen. "I'd like to point out that this is where my client touches the bedroom doorknob and leaves the fingerprint Detective Mendoza has so enthusiastically claimed as evidence of her guilt. And," he turns to

Carmen, "Miss Castiel, you've already splashed the gasoline around the bedroom at this point, correct?"

Carmen had sunk back in her chair but leans forward into the microphone to answer, "Yes, sir."

"So, this is also the point where my client picked up the gasoline on her running shoes." He presses play and Oliver's yelling once again fills the courtroom.

"What the hell are you doing here?"

Carmen sweeps the phone camera from me back to Oliver. He's trying to push himself up onto his elbows. "This crazy bitch has doused me in gasoline! Get these handcuffs the fuck off me, Alice! And call the police!"

"She's not gonna help you, Oliver." Carmen's voice is calm. "She's here to make sure I leave this house with your confession. Or to bear witness to your death. Your choice."

"What!" Oliver's face is flushed a deep red. He is staring behind the camera, presumably at me, with a hatred so hot it could ignite the room. "God damn it, Alice! You bitch, you want a confession fine. I confess to having your little tryst in the mental hospital sent to Jake. So fuck you! You little piece of crazy trailer-trash garbage!" He spits at the camera.

And the monster reveals himself.

I hear the gasps from Jake and Rhys behind me amid a small burst of activity from the rest of the courtroom. The judge taps her gavel in warning.

The camera jerks back to Kali. She's casually leaning against the door now, arms crossed, head cocked. "You've been harassing Alice for years trying to get her in bed, so I know you are speaking out of anger and frustration right now, as the rejected do."

Mr. Phang pauses the video. "Your Honor, I'd like to note here that in the video my client refers to herself as 'Alice' supporting her claim of having dissociative identities and not remembering these events."

She nods. "Noted."

He pushes play.

Kali is speaking. "You disgust her, you know. All that privilege and power, used only for your own perversions. No one ever challenged your belief that all that money made you desirable. But, I'll tell you the truth. Every time you cornered her or touched her or used your words to try and get your way, that wasn't seduction. That was a declaration of war."

"What are you talking about? Her who?" A roar and a clanging metal sound fill the courtroom. With a jerk, the camera moves back to Oliver, who is shaking the metal bedframe, trying to tear it down. It doesn't work. After all, it's the best money can buy.

"Just admit that you beat and raped Reyna," Carmen repeats, a quiet desperation in her plea. "Then had her killed when you found out she went to the cops. Admit it and this will all be over. We'll leave and call the cops to come get you out of those."

Oliver laughs then. It's the manic, crazed laughter of a man pushed over the edge. His voice is a low growl. He enunciates his words clearly and slowly, leaving no room for doubt that he means what he says. "I will kill you both for this."

The camera shakes, recording the wood floor for a few moments as Carmen coughs. Then it changes position as she steps out of the bedroom and resumes recording from the doorway. "You know who's going to die, Oliver? You, from those fumes!" She coughs again. "You need to get out of there soon. So what's it going to be?"

"Fuck you!" Oliver yells and then has his own coughing fit.

Kali suddenly turns and looks right into the camera. Her face is serene, her eyes gold and calm, like she's falling through the sky with the decision to jump already behind her, and there's nothing left to do but enjoy the ride. She turns her head away, and Mr. Phang pauses the video.

"Please pay attention to where my client is standing at this moment." He pushes play, there's a whooshing sound and suddenly it's Carmen who's screaming, "Oh God! Oh my God!" The video is shaky and darting around wildly like Carmen's forgotten about it but the flames are unmistakable. They have engulfed the bed, silencing Oliver's screams and reaching the ceiling in seconds. Thick, gray smoke is already filling the air. Carmen's arm reaches out and yanks me from the bedroom doorway.

We're both coughing and from there, there's only audio because Carmen's still holding the phone, but she's not aware of videotaping anymore. It's pointed at the floor.

Carmen's crying, "We have to put it out!" There's a loud pop and we both fall back.

"We have to get out of here. It's too late for Oliver. He's gone," Kali says.

Mr. Phang stops the video and walks over to Carmen.

Tears are streaming down her face. She wipes them with her palms and stares at my attorney expectantly.

"Miss Castiel, can you tell us where Alice Leininger was when the fire that killed Oliver Brooks started?"

"She was standin' in the bedroom doorway."

"Is there any way she could have started that fire?"

"No, sir. She didn't move from the spot and she didn't have nothin' in her hands."

"Do you know how the fire did start?"

She's shaking her head. "No sir, I don't. Maybe static electricity or a spark from the handcuffs rubbing against the metal? No idea. I only know there were no candles lit, no open flames, nothin' like that. It just happened. Neither of us started the fire. It was shocking, ya know? Like I said, I didn't plan on really hurtin' him and Alice knew that. I told her I just wanted to scare him, to make him fess up to what he did to Reyna."

"It just happened. That's what the witness says and that's what the video shows." Mr. Phang turns to the judge. "Your Honor, in light of the evidence exonerating my client of starting the fire that killed Oliver Brooks, I make a motion to dismiss."

The courtroom explodes.

I watch in stunned silence as the judge pounds on her desk, stands and orders officers to start escorting people out, including Graham Brooks, who's made a beeline for me, his face bloated with rage. Mr. Phang has jumped up and put himself between us. Two officers are dragging Graham by the arms out the door as he's yelling something I can't understand. I twist to find Jake. He's sitting still in the sea of chaos, hands resting on his knees, head bent like he's about to be sick. I catch Rhys's eye and he holds up his palms in a questioning gesture, hope trying to bloom but unsure of its safety.

I shrug, having no idea what's going to happen next.

As the court settles back into silence the judge calls for both attorneys to approach the bench. I try to gauge their conversation by her expression and their posture. After a few minutes of back and forth, both attorneys return to their tables.

The judge folds her hands. Her gaze finds mine for a moment and then moves to the courtroom. "In light of the video evidence and witness testimony, the court declares all charges against Alice Brown-Leininger dropped, and the defense's motion to dismiss is granted. Mrs. Leininger, you're free to go." She turns to Carmen, who is still in the witness box. "Miss Castiel, I'm sure Detective Mendoza would like a word with you." She removes her reading glasses and drops them on her desk. "Court is adjourned."

"All rise," comes from the court clerk but we are all already on our feet.

Rhys is the first to reach me. He hugs me tight with breathy, gleeful cries of, "I can't believe it!" and "It's over!" His relief spills over into hugs of appreciation for an obviously pleased Mr. Phang.

"I don't know how to thank you," I say to him, still in shock. *Can it really be over? Just like that?* Then Jake is there, squeezing my attorney's hand and shoulder, expressing his gratitude. I rest a hand on Jake's stubbled cheek as he steps to stand in front of me. Slowly, he takes me in his arms and I feel a deep tremor run through his body. It will be the final affectionate touch between us. The last time we are on the same team. He doesn't say a word, but then again, he doesn't get a chance to as an officer approaches to remove the tracking device on my ankle. As I sit for this, I scan the courtroom for Carmen. She's in front of the prosecution's table. Her back is to me, and another officer is putting her in handcuffs while Detective Mendoza talks to her. *What will they charge her with?* I keep my eye on her hoping she'll turn my way so I can signal my support, but her head is down as they lead her up the aisle and out the door. I will find some way to repay her for coming forward, and allowing me to go home at the expense of her own freedom. I silently promise her this.

We burst out of the courtroom's inner doors, Jake in front of me, Rhys with his arm protectively around me. In the hallway, we're immediately swarmed with hulking video cameras and reporters shouting questions over one other.

"Can you talk to us now, Alice?" "Were you surprised at the dismissal?"

Jake holds up his hand. "Not answering questions, folks. Please give us room." He leads us forward, pushing back the crowd and then stops as he comes to Joy and Graham being interviewed by a window directly in front of us. Graham spots me at the same time. His chin drops and he charges at us like a bull, arms stiff, fists by his side, Joy rushing in behind him like she's being pulled in his wake.

Jake stands his ground in front of me and holds a hand in front of Graham's chest. "It's over. I know you're grieving but Alice didn't kill Oliver."

"She could have stopped it. She's just as guilty in my book."

The reporters with their cameras and microphones are surrounding us. Something is happening inside me. The fire is licking my insides, burning away the last residue of fear. Kali suddenly appears next to me. We make eye contact as she takes my hand.

I step sideways, out from Jake's shadow and Rhys's protective arm. I feel myself straightening, pulsing with Kali's confidence but the words are mine as I stare down Graham Brooks. "The only reason your son is dead is because of the kind of person he was. His type of sickness wasn't just allowed to exist, but was rewarded, nurtured, given immunity along with the power your money granted him. He treated women like objects, to be his entertainment and then discarded. Which he learned from you, as the world will soon know." I move my glare to Joy. "And where were you? Shame on you for not teaching your son to respect women. That is our job as mothers of boys."

Joy has the decency to look ashamed.

I can see the heat rising beneath Graham's skin. His bloodshot eyes move to Jake. "Are you going to let her talk to us like that?"

Jake glances at me and he regards me silently for a moment. I see the questions there, the hurt, but also something new ... respect. He turns back to his friend. "Yes, I am, Graham. Because frankly, your son was an asshole."

This is the clip that will be played over and over on every news station and every internet outlet. This thirty-second exchange becomes the distilled version of my hearing ending that goes viral.

We step out into the sunshine and everyone stops in their tracks.

THIRTY

Angeline and Vivi break from the crowd of women who are gathered on the sidewalk and rush up the stairs to meet us. They are holding fluorescent signs with large black letters.

"What's going on?" I ask in confusion as they hug me.

"We just heard! I can't believe it's over." Angeline's tears are meeting the corners of her smile. With her arm around me, she points down at the crowd pushing in closer to the stairs. "They are here for you. To support you." I'm trying to read their signs as Vivi grabs my hand and lifts my arm into the air.

Shouts of victory, whoops and clapping explode from the crowd.

I look at the grin on Vivi's lips and know that she will be okay. Rhys slips in and says something in her ear. Then I hear my name being chanted. "Alice! Alice!" I squint into the sun and make out my name on their signs.

"But why?" I shout into Angeline's ear. The reporters and cameras have followed us out and are now either trying to push in closer to me or make their way into the crowd of women.

She directs my attention to the reporter hurrying up the stairs, a camera crew behind her. It's Amber Acosta. She waves as she approaches. Then my attention catches on the bleached blonde hair behind her, in the front of the crowd. *Gillian*. Around her, also holding signs are a dozen or so other women I've seen working at Oliver's parties. And around them are women I recognize from Project Freedom, both the ones who work there and the women they are helping get out of the life. I notice Sparkle standing there with Danna and Jo-Jo. She is actually smiling. I never thought I'd see the day. Then I spot Veora, the director. She gives me a thumb's up, and my own mouth turns up at the corners.

"Amber's first article about Oliver's sex parties was published in the *Gulf Coast Times* this morning." Angeline squeezes my shoulder. "Though she didn't name anyone beyond Oliver yet, it's all coming out soon. The girls are so relieved and grateful."

Wow. Amber wasn't kidding when she said she'd move fast. I glance over at Jake, who's standing off to the side with Mr. Phang. I suddenly wonder how much he really knew. How was he not aware his best friend, Rolf, was involved? Well, I'll never know now. The days of us confiding in each other are over.

Endings make space for new beginnings. Remember there will be love in the ashes.

"Alice, how does it feel to be heading home?" Amber asks when she reaches me.

I pull my attention away from Kali's voice and lean in to speak into the fuzzy microphone. "Good. It feels good for this whole thing to be over."

"Is there anything you'd like to say to all these women who've come out to support you today?"

I shade my eyes with a hand and look out at all the expectant faces. And what I see is Kali. In each one of the women I see the same fire that burns inside of me. They may not have a name for it. They may not even know it's there yet ... but I do. An emotion that I can only describe as fierce love crashes over me. I see this side of Kali—this fierce love—in each of them, also, and I understand. Kali isn't just the fire, she's the love that flows out from every woman to nurture the world. She is the fire and the love.

I gasp as Kali suddenly fills my mind with a vision. A vision of the fire and love I see inside these women merging into an inferno that grows and sweeps over the world. It is breathtaking and I can't tear my attention away. I know she is showing me our destiny. We will help these women see the power they possess and unify them to change the world, make it a safer place for all women.

I finally shake my head to clear the vision and focus on what's in front of me.

Vivi and Angeline must've caught my reaction, because they're on either side of me, holding my hand. I squeeze their hands in gratitude.

There are many microphones vying for my voice, but I make sure to speak into Amber's. "First, thank you to all my sisters who've showed up today to support me. You are all so brave and such a great example of how we can have each other's backs, and I promise I will spend the rest of my life returning the favor. I see you all. And just because this trial is over and one dangerous group of men has been exposed and stopped, doesn't mean our job is done. We still have important work to do, and we will do it together."

I wait for the applause to die down and then shift my attention, stare into the camera behind Amber's shoulder. "And if you didn't read Amber Acosta's article this morning I will warn you, there's going to be a scandal breaking in the next few weeks. You will recognize the names of prominent members of our community. Some of you will be shocked, some of you won't. This scandal involves not only sex workers being abused, drugged and even murdered, but young women not in the life who were lured into situations where they were drugged, raped and blackmailed. This cannot continue. This cannot be 'just the way men are.' We will not allow it any longer. So, open your eyes. See us. See that these experiences you force on us affect us deeply."

Angeline leans forward and glares into the same camera. "Alice is right. Stop supporting the sex trade and trafficking business where women's bodies are used like bloody disposable toys."

Vivi's voice trembles with emotion as she, too, leans forward and adds, "And teach your sons that an unconscious woman cannot consent to sex, that a woman who says no doesn't mean 'convince me.'"

Angeline waits for another round of applause from the women below the stairs and then continues. "Understand that it's not up to us to cover up our bodies. It's up to you to look at a woman and not see a few minutes of entertainment, but instead to recognize what she's really got to offer. Look at her and see a mother, a sister, a creator, a partner, a goddess with the ability to heal your world."

I feel the pulse of energy flowing through our clasped hands. The physical boundaries between us have been swept away. I've never felt such power and lightness before. I'm sure I'm smiling like a lunatic as I add one more thing, but I don't care. "And teach your daughters to be the heroine of their own lives. Teach both your daughters and sons that the world can change and they can be the ones to change it." I hold up my hands. "That's it. Not so hard, right?"

Shouting and whistling and applause explode from the crowd. The other reporters are pushing in, shouting questions at me. I am drained. Angeline and Vivi release my hands and thread their arms around my waist. They try to lead me down the stairs but the crowd is too thick. Rhys is suddenly in front of us, elbowing through the press of bodies to give us a path. People are reaching out to touch me, shake my hand, shout things at me through smiles and tears that I can't hear because it's all too overwhelming.

The car doors shut and I breathe in the silence as Angeline squeezes my hand. "You all right?"

I nod. "I am now, thanks."

"We can wait here for Jake, or I can drive you home," she says.

I notice her head is cocked and she, Vivi and Rhys are exchanging looks. "What?" I ask. "What's wrong?"

"Nothing is wrong. Is it? I mean," she bites her lip. "Are you ... Alice?"

It takes me a second to understand what she's asking and then a deep laugh escapes me. "Yes, I'm Alice."

Her shoulders collapse with relief and she grins. "Oh, brilliant. It's just that speech ... I mean, wow, I thought for sure that was Kali back there, and I had no clue what to say to her. Right?" She glances into the back for confirmation.

"Sure sounded like a goddess talking to me," Rhys laughs.

Vivi squeezes my shoulder from the backseat. "You inspired me for sure."

I feel Kali radiating inside me. She is pleased. "Kali has taught me a lot," I say. "And made me braver." My perspective on having D.I.D. shifts as it hits me how true that is.

Angeline starts the car. "Anyway, did you want to wait for Jake?"

"Can you text him and let him know you're driving me home. I don't have my phone."

"Sure thing."

As we drive away, Rhys leans forward. "The men that are going down ... Jake's business is pretty tied up with them. You guys going to be okay?"

I turn and stare into my friend's concerned gaze, then check Vivi's reaction. She smiles sadly. "Don't worry about me. I'll be fine."

I nod, accepting her answer. "There will be hard changes for us ... for me. But I'm not afraid anymore." I rest my elbow on the back of the seat and focus on Angeline. "Do you think Veora would give me a job?"

She shoots me an amused look as she coasts up to a red light. "Are you kidding? After what you and Kali have done getting those girls' stories out and what just happened on those courthouse steps? We're going to do great things together. All of us ... I can feel it."

I grin. "We are." But first, I have to deal with the dismantling of my current life.

THIRTY-ONE

Six Weeks Later

Even though I'm on the other side this time, the anxiety of being back in this space is almost crushing. The sharp tang of body odor, the feel of the heavy phone receiver in my hand smelling of disinfectant, and the round hard stool beneath me, it's all triggering a deep desire to flee.

You survived this fire already, you've tasted the ashes, you've lived in them. Now it's time to rise up from them and bring your sister with you.

Kali's voice has become that mother voice I've always felt I missed out on. Since I've accepted her being around, she no longer feels the need to take over so my blackout periods have all but stopped.

"Hey," Carmen says into the receiver. She looks unsure as we meet each other's gaze on the screen.

I feel the tears thick in my throat as I take her in. She's no longer a ghost. She's solid, alive. "How're you holding up?"

She waves a hand in front of the video camera. "Fine. Three meals a day yada, yada. It's all good. How're the kids?" I see the genuine peace soften the lines around her eyes as she asks.

I smile and hope that my pain is hidden. The kids are confused and sad. They don't understand why

Mommy and Daddy won't be living together anymore, why Aurora had to go away, why they have to change schools. I hate that it's the hardest on them. "Very happy to have their mother back, thank you. And in order to properly thank you, we've hired Mr. Phang to take your case. He should be coming in to talk to you soon."

Jake had balked at this request when I'd insisted on it during our divorce negotiations. But he'd eventually given in. He knows our children are better off with me out of prison and Carmen is the reason I'm free.

Relief collapses her shoulders. "Oh thank the Lord Jesus. The public attorney they set me up with looks about twelve. I swear he's got pimples." She smiles for the first time. "Seriously, thanks, Alice."

"It's the least we could do. What are they charging you with anyway?"

"Detective Mendoza says false imprisonment and involuntary manslaughter." A mixture of fear and resolve passes over her face. "I can get up to twenty years."

"That won't happen. Mr. Phang is really good."

She nods and shrugs in a 'we'll see' gesture. Then she leans closer to the screen. "It's a cryin' shame we'll never know what really happened to Reyna, ya know? Who actually killed her. But ... I'm glad Oliver's dead. Does that make me a shitty person?"

I shake my head. This young woman, she has so much guilt to carry now. "I think that makes you human."

She stares into my eyes, seems to hesitate but then asks, "Do you know how that fire started?"

I blink in confusion and shake my head. "I don't remember anything about that night, I'm sorry. You heard the testimony about my dissociative identity disorder?"

She nods slowly, studying my face. "I heard about Drac's car burnin', too. Just so you know, I didn't do that."

Why is she telling me this? I stare at her. Whatever her reasons are, I believe her. She didn't do it. "Do you know how the fire at Oliver's started?" I ask, my pulse quickening.

She runs her teeth across her bottom lip, then glances around and shakes her head. "Nope. Thought you might have some idea is all."

She's lying. But, I don't press it. The phone conversations are probably recorded. Instead I change the subject, try to lighten the mood. "A little advice? Don't eat the gray stuff they try to pass off as gravy."

—◆◆◆—

It's Friday morning when my eyes flutter open. I wait for the first seconds of awareness to pass. They are still painful, the sight of the empty pillow next to me, the realization that I'll be drinking my coffee alone, my naked ring finger that I still stroke with my thumb out of habit. It's these little things, and the normal daily moments with Jake that I miss the most. Not being part of a couple anymore feels like a strange form of emptiness, and there are so many more decisions to make on my own. Things like what to feed the kids for dinner or which internet company to use, which is probably a sign I'd grown too dependent on the people in my life, anyway. The big things—the small apartment I've moved into, the used sedan with chipped paint that I now drive, the budget I had forgotten how to live on—these things surprisingly aren't as hard.

I walk to the small rooms with generic white paint and boxes piled along the walls and wake up the kids for school. They will spend every other weekend with Jake in his new, smaller condo. I cook breakfast and then watch them carefully as they push around their scrambled eggs, searching for any signs of trauma or depression in their behavior.

"These aren't as good as Aurora's," Addie says almost too softly to hear.

Charlie glances up at me and I know he's watching for my reaction.

I sit down with my coffee cup at the small, wooden table and wait until they are both looking at me. "I miss Aurora, too," I say. "Which is why I've invited her over for dinner tonight."

Their faces light up. "Is she coming?" Charlie asks.

"Yep. So, you can ask her how she makes such good eggs."

Addie jumps out of her seat and wraps her arms around my neck wordlessly.

"Mom?" Charlie is tearing off bits of his toast. He doesn't look up. "I don't want to go to a new school."

I stroke Addie's hair and swallow the lump in my throat. "I know. But you don't have to start the new school until after summer so we have plenty of time to make some new friends before the year starts." I kiss Addie's crown. "And guess what? You don't have to wear uniforms so you can dress however you want."

Addie pulls away and tilts her chin up. She's about to say something, but there's a knock on the door.

I squeeze Addie one more time and then push away from the table. "Finish your breakfast. We're leaving in twenty minutes."

"Hey," Angeline says as she gives me a quick hug and hands me this morning's *Gulf Coast Times* with a meaningful look. "Front page. I'm going to go say hi to the kids."

I stand there and unfold the paper. Addie's and Charlie's chatter becomes background noise as I find Amber's article: *Sex Scandal Hits Sarasota Community*

"Sarasota police have filed a probable cause affidavit stating that seventeen prominent Sarasota businessmen and politicians should be charged with various counts of unlawful sex and molestation of minors and various felony charges of sexual battery against a helpless victim." I take in each of the names, including Graham's and Rolf's. I've had conversations with all of the men, met their wives, their children.

I close my eyes and fold the paper back up. There are so many things I'm feeling. A deep, aching sadness. Satisfaction for the victims. Anger. A new peacefulness. Gratitude, even for my dissociative disorder. But not fear. For the first time, not fear and uncertainty.

Angeline is riding with me to drop off the kids so we can go to the morning staff meeting at Project Freedom after that. Aurora not only gave me a job, but created a position for me—Director of Education—and Angeline and Vivi will be working with me part-time. Graham had immediately donated ten million dollars to Project Freedom in some desperate effort to show himself in a good light. But also, seven of the women have each filed a $50 million civil lawsuit against the men. They plan on eventually using the money to get involved with our efforts, too, so we are excited about the new programs and expanded reach this windfall will bring.

—◆◆◆—

"So, I have some news," Angeline says. She's been quiet during most of the ride, which is unlike her.

"What's up?" I say, distracted as I inch forward in the car line. When she doesn't answer, I glance over and see her grinning at me, her eyes glittering with unshed tears and I know. "Oh my God! You're pregnant!"

She wipes at her nose and nods. "I'm going to be a mum."

I hit the brakes hard as I've almost run into the car in front of me. Then I lean over and hug her. "That's just ... just ... congratulations!"

We're both half-laughing, half-crying when Charlie asks, "What's happened, Mom?"

I turn my head and smile at my own two little people. "Miss Angeline has a baby in her belly!"

"Is it a boy?" Charlie asks, wide-eyed. "Can I be its cousin?"

"How'd a baby get in her stomach?" Addie asks.

We both bark out a laugh then. "Yes, you can be his or her cousins," I say. "And Addie, we'll discuss that tonight at bedtime." I reach the drop-off gate and twist behind me with my arm out. "Hugs." They both unbuckle their seatbelts and fall forward into my arms.

"I love you, Mom," Charlie whispers in my ear.

A wave of relief and joy and a feeling of barely escaping the sharp jaws of disaster washes over me, gratitude riding on its crest. I squeeze them harder. "I love you both, too."

<hr>

I don't know why I'm nervous as I sit in Dr. Evelyn's waiting room. Maybe it's the sticky memory of the last time I was here, trying to wrap its suction-cupped tentacles around my mind. Maybe it's excitement. Whatever it is, it morphs into joy as Dr. Evelyn motors out into the waiting room with a wide smile and stretches out her arms. "Alice!"

I stand and fall into her hug, tears blurring my vision. "It's so good to see you."

She pats my back and then grasps my hands as I straighten, her eyes damp and the same smile on her face that I feel on my own. "I am so glad you're here. Well, come on. I'm not sure fifty minutes is going to be enough time today."

I sink happily into the gray sofa, an overwhelming feeling of coming home warming my chest and face, like I've just taken a seat in front of a fireplace. "Oh." I suddenly remember the bag I'm carrying. I lean up and offer it to her. "For you. A small thank you."

"I appreciate the thought," she smiles to lighten the blow, "but I'm not allowed to take gifts from clients."

I feel my own smile dissolve. "Oh, I hadn't thought of that. Well, at least open it."

"All right. No harm in that." With a curious expression, she pulls out the box and then opens it. Her eyes light up and she throws her head back in laughter. "Oh, these are exquisite!" She holds the six-inch, sapphire-beaded heel up to the sunlight.

I'm smiling again, enjoying her surprise and joy. "They're from Jimmy Choo's fairytale collection. They're called the Fairy Godmother. Seemed appropriate." It was a splurge I could no longer afford. But, Kali and I agreed it was the perfect gift to show our gratitude.

She laughs out loud again, then her face sobers. "But really I can't, especially something this expensive."

I feel Kali stirring and find myself sitting back, throwing an arm nonchalantly across the back of the sofa. "You either have to take them or spend the rest of today's session explaining to Kali why you won't."

She shakes her head slightly then smiles and nestles the shoe delicately back in its box. "Okay, you win. Thank you both. That was very thoughtful." She lowers the bag to rest beside the table and folds her hands in her lap.

"So, how are things with Jake? I assume since you're here, he's accepted your dissociative disorder? Is he supporting you now?"

I shrug a shoulder and rub the empty space on my finger where my wedding rings used to be. "No, we're getting a divorce. He can't forgive me. The way he sees it, I chose to put the welfare of strangers over that of our family, but I'm sure it wasn't just that. He doesn't know what to do with the D.I.D. diagnosis. I'm okay though. I realized that not only would he never be able to have a relationship with my alters, he wouldn't even acknowledge their existence. We don't need that kind of rejection."

She nods. "Understandable, considering your background of rejection. And how are *you* dealing with the D.I.D?"

"Adjusting. Some things have shifted within me. For one, Kali is now present a good portion of the time so my blackouts have mostly stopped. Dr. Meekum, the psychiatrist I saw at Bayside met another personality, Alyssa, but she refused to speak when she came out. When I do have the rare blackout, I think it's her."

"Really?" Dr. Evelyn jots that down and then looks up at me thoughtfully. "Alyssa was your given name at birth, wasn't it?"

"Yes."

"So, she would've been there before Lyssie Grace." She takes a deep breath and then studies her pen as she turns it in her slim fingers. Then she grows still and meets my gaze. "Alice, I don't want you to panic, but I have a theory I'd like to discuss with you. Do you feel strong enough to hear something you may not like?"

"I think so."

"All right. Typically in Dissociative Identity Disorder there's a host or original personality who identifies with the person's given name. Usually, this personality is not aware of the other alters. This personality who calls herself by your real name, Alyssa ... she may very well be the original host in your system. She might be fragile, guarded by the other alters and protected from their memories."

"What does that mean? Why would that upset me?"

"Well, usually they're the ones who manage daily life ... though there can be more than one Apparently Normal Parts, or ANPs as they're now called, during a lifetime and more than one at any given time. Anyway, if Alyssa is the original personality, she could choose to come out whenever she wants to. She's apparently afraid for now, but that may change as you heal. Also—and this is the part that may be tough for you to hear—you, Alice, have no memory before your thirteenth birthday, which means that day may've been the day you were created in the system. The day you were born, so to speak."

I sit stunned, trying to piece together what this means. Kali is beside me, calmly watching. Lyssie Grace is in the corner, knees pulled up under her chin. I don't feel or see Alyssa. "I did start remembering some things from before thirteen, but they do seem to be more like someone else's memories that are being shared with me, instead of something that happened to me. I ... I'm not sure how to feel about this."

"It's okay. Take your time processing it. And don't worry, just because you weren't the first doesn't mean you're not valuable to the system. You being in control most of the time is obviously working for everyone, so I suspect that won't change."

I check in with the others. No, I don't feel like they want me around less. Though, I have no idea what Alyssa is thinking. I suddenly remember Gia Rossi. "You know, there's this strange woman I've met at the park a few times. She seemed real at the time, but she was too close to my thoughts. Like mentioning a drawing I did back in school. And telling me there are things that I'm not going to believe because they'll be too strange, or something like that. And she said she helps people remember who they are. I know this is a crazy question because I sat there and had a conversation with her, but is it possible she's an alter?"

Dr. Evelyn cocks her head and then shrugs. "Sure. If she's saying she's there to help you remember who you are, she could be what we call an Internal Self Helper. I guess time will tell."

Time. The thing that I used to misplace like my keys or my hope. No longer is it my enemy. No longer is forgetting the bad days something I hope for. Now I embrace both time and memories as precious.

THIRTY-TWO

Six Months Later...

I don't have nightmares very often anymore. Though there was one specific night a few weeks ago that made me question the nature of truth.

It had been storming all evening. The kind of vicious storm that rattles the walls with its thunder, lights up the room with bright, crackling strobes and sends periodic tornado watch alerts to your phone. But the rain pounding against the small window in my bedroom was soothing, so I lay there quite content listening to it. My eyes had closed. My guard was down. I suddenly saw Oliver thrashing around in a rage on the bed. At this point, I'd usually turn away from Kali's memory. In a way, I felt like an intruder. That night, whatever happened, it wasn't my story to rehash.

But then I was suddenly next to Kali in his bedroom, and I heard her whisper, "Goodbye, Oliver." I felt a heat building in our skull, a heat from a dry, hot wind. Kali's hair was blowing wildly in this wind and an eerie howl rose up from her. It shook me to my core. Just when I thought I'd go mad from the sound, it suddenly stopped, the heat fled and at that moment the fire flared up around Oliver. A high-pitched scream sliced through the silence... then there was only the crackling, whooshing sound of an impossible fire.